CW00494168

THE BORDEAUX BOOK CLUB

GILLIAN HARVEY

Boldwood

First published in Great Britain in 2024 by Boldwood Books Ltd.

Copyright © Gillian Harvey, 2024

Cover Design by Alice Moore Design

Cover Photography: Shutterstock and Alamy

A CIP catalogue record for this book is available from the British Library.

Paperback ISBN 978-1-80549-949-7

Large Print ISBN 978-1-80549-948-0

Hardback ISBN 978-1-80549-947-3

Ebook ISBN 978-1-80549-950-3

Kindle ISBN 978-1-80549-951-0

Audio CD ISBN 978-1-80549-942-8

MP3 CD ISBN 978-1-80549-943-5

Digital audio download ISBN 978-1-80549-944-2

Boldwood Books Ltd
23 Bowerdean Street
London SW6 3TN
www.boldwoodbooks.com

For Matthew.

'I think books are like people, in the sense that they'll turn up in your life when you most need them.'

— EMMA THOMPSON

PROLOGUE

George was just stepping out of the café, takeaway coffee in hand, when he saw Grace appear in the window of the *tabac* opposite. He recognised her instantly, despite his throbbing temples, and felt his neck prickle as he remembered trying to talk to her at the gardening club meet and finding his tongue had tied itself in knots. It had shocked him, this sudden mutism; he'd always been able to talk for England, so everyone told him. But then again, he wasn't in England in any more. And he'd felt a bit out of place amongst all those posh retirees.

The cold, silvery, winter light crept softly around the edges of the white, February clouds, and fell on Grace's skin as she searched for an empty place in the window. Reaching up, her tongue protruding slightly at the edge of her mouth, she pressed the corners of the A4 sheet against the glass alongside the adverts for a local artisan market, a babysitting service and a poster advertising a music night, the date of which had already passed. He could just make out the word 'club' in bold on the paper.

Another club. He tried not to laugh. He barely knew the woman, but he'd gathered that if there was an event or club or fête or pretty much anything going on in the local community, she'd be involved somehow. He wondered what she was up to this time.

He busied himself, looking at the property adverts in the estate agent window while he waited for her to leave then, when she had, strolled nonchalantly across the street and had a quick gander.

Sure enough, it was an advert for a new organisation – with Grace at its helm. This time, it seemed, she was starting a book club for 'Anglophones' – the advert written in English, with French translation underneath in the hope of attracting a wider clientele.

He wasn't sure why he took a picture of the number with his phone. Just in case, he told himself. He hadn't read a book for years, not a fiction one at least. But maybe it was time. Another night in with the boys at the house would probably finish him off – he was getting too old for so much alcohol. And he couldn't just sit around in his tiny flat – he'd go mad.

At least it would be something to do.

* * *

The noise of Monica's phone made her jump – she hated the way its shrill sound pierced the silence, bouncing from the high ceilings and wooden floors which magnified the noise horribly. Bella's limbs stiffened in her arms and Monica shushed her baby gently, annoyed that her hard-won sleep had been disturbed. Moving Bella onto her other shoulder she picked up the mobile, expertly navigating its screen one-handedly with dextrous use of her thumb.

It was from Peter. It said simply,

Saw this

She clicked on the attached photo to enlarge it and saw an ad for *The Bordeaux Book Club*. For English speakers. She looked instinctively at the book, spine-cracked, that she'd placed face-down on the table when Bella had cried, but found herself shaking her head, although there was nobody there to witness it.

Could she manage it? It was hard work simply changing nappies and preparing bottles – anything for herself seemed to have taken a back seat since Bella's arrival. And she could only imagine the sort of people who'd be there – probably a bunch of retirees desperate to read war stories or drink red wine while discussing the latest John Grisham.

Still, she had promised herself she'd make more connections locally. And this was a chance to at least do something different – to keep her busy while Peter was away.

What do you think?

Peter messaged. She replied,

Maybe

* * *

Alfie placed his rucksack at his feet, then lifted his phone and took a quick snap of the advert. It could be just the thing he'd been looking for. Something that could prove uplifting, a distraction from the worst parts of life. He slipped the phone back in the pocket of his jeans and shouldered his backpack with a sigh of effort.

Camille left the shop, slipping a pack of cigarettes into her bag. 'You have found something?' she asked him, in French.

'Maybe,' he said, shrugging. 'A book club. For English speakers.'

She raised an eyebrow. 'For...'

He nodded. 'It just... well, it might work. You know.'

'Perhaps I should come too?' she suggested. 'To improve my English.'

He nodded. 'Yeah, if you want.'

They turned and walked slowly down the road, disappearing into the melange of pedestrians making their way to work or university, or strolling more slowly, with no particular destination in mind.

A little further along the road, she slipped her hand in his and he squeezed it gratefully.

'You will find a way,' she told him softly.

He wanted to thank her, but the word stuck in his throat. Instead, he looked forward intently until the moment passed, then murmured a short, 'Hope so.'

Then they turned the corner and were swallowed into the heart of Bordeaux – just a couple of students on their way to class.

* * *

Grace sounded almost breathless on the phone. 'Four enquiries already!' she told Leah.

As usual, Grace's enthusiasm made Leah feel slightly drained. She resolved to rummage in Grace's medical cabinet next time she was around to see if she was taking some high-strength vitamins, or something. Whatever it was, Leah needed a healthy dose of it herself. Despite being almost fifteen years Grace's junior, she often found herself ready for bed by nine o'clock, whereas Grace's restless energy often kept her up and active into the wee small hours.

'So, you'll come?' Grace said.

'Um, well, do you need me to?' Leah asked, hesitantly. 'I mean, it sounds as if it might be a... well, a nice size already.' She longed to say no, rehearsing the word in her head. But somehow it wouldn't come. What was it about Grace? Something about her manner, her confidence, made Leah feel she ought to agree with everything she said.

'Of course you must come!' Grace responded, missing Leah's reluctant tone entirely. 'Won't be the same without you.'

Leah doubted this very much, seeing as she would probably end up sitting in the corner and watching others talk about books she might not find the time to read. But she found herself agreeing anyway.

'How does she do it?' she asked Nathan as he walked into the hallway a few minutes later, banging his gloved hands together in an attempt to warm them up.

'Who? Scarlett?' he said, glancing at the stairs as if their teenage daughter might suddenly make a rare appearance from her room.

'No – Grace. I always tell myself I'm going to say no to things, and I end up agreeing.' She slipped her phone into her pocket and walked through with him into the kitchen.

He laughed. 'You have to admit, she does get people involved.'

'Which is great, if they want to be,' she said. 'Only she can't seem to take the hint.'

'Did you actually tell her you didn't want to do it?' he asked, sitting in the chair opposite and beginning to worry at a knot in his shoelaces.

'Well, not in so many words...'

He fixed his eyes on her. 'Well then,' he said.

'I know. But she's... Well – you know Grace!' she said weakly.

'That I do. Whether I want to or not.' He smiled and she found herself grinning back.

'Exactly.'

'So what are you going to do?' he asked, picking an apple from the fruit bowl and biting into it hungrily.

'I guess I'm going. I mean, I think she probably just wants the moral support of a friend. And I do always say I ought to read more,' she said.

He nodded. 'Well then, sounds like it's problem solved.'

1

FEBRUARY

'As you can see, it's quite the spread,' Grace said proudly, gesturing towards the coffee table on which she'd laid out an array of different biscuits, all home-made of course, stacked on an elaborate, three-tier stand.

She'd asked Leah to arrive a little earlier than the others, to be there to chat to newcomers if Grace got tied up answering the door or making tea. It seemed a little excessive to Leah, for an event that promised four or five guests at most. But she'd agreed. Because when it came to Grace, for some reason, she always did.

She'd pulled up outside Grace's house at six. As she'd exited the car, she'd seen her friend, standing in her warmly lit living room, hand to mouth, looking uncertain, almost fragile for a moment. Then she'd turned and noticed Leah's car, smiled and given a small wave.

'It's lovely, Grace,' Leah said now, glancing at her watch and hoping beyond hope that she wouldn't be the only one to turn up. Grace seemed supremely confident – supremely *Grace* – that there'd be several attendees, but somehow her confidence only seemed to inflate Leah's own worry and doubt that the evening might not be the success Grace hoped for – as if Leah had absorbed any negativity into herself and held it on behalf of her friend.

Grace's sitting room was spotless as always – wooden furniture, painstakingly chalk-painted in pastel colours, parquet floor shining from a recent polish. Grace had an eye for furniture and a penchant for upcycling, and had even reupholstered the vintage sofa herself a few years ago. The only part of the room that wasn't gleaming was the area by the bay window, where Grace's bookshelves stood stuffed with texts, ramshackle and disorganised and somehow at odds with everything else in the house. But then Grace was an avid reader; she probably enjoyed rifling through and pulling out books and simply didn't have time to rearrange them every week. Once when Leah had mentioned them, she'd given a dismissive wave towards the disorderly shelves and simply said, 'Oh I'll get to it. I just never seem to have the time.'

When the doorbell finally chimed, Leah's hand jerked, sending coffee whirling in her mug, but thankfully not sufficiently to make a spill. She felt a flood of relief that it wouldn't just be the pair of them. 'That'll be our first member!' she said, in a voice that barely sounded like her own.

She wondered, sometimes, why she felt such a loyalty to Grace. While they'd known each other a few years, they weren't particularly close. Perhaps it was because Grace had helped her and Nathan at the start – pointing them in the right direction for getting the permissions they needed for their home improvements, and introducing them to several growers via the gardening group. Leah enjoyed her company, for the most part, but they'd never quite clicked in the way she had with friends back home.

Before she could speculate further, the living room door opened and Grace appeared with a tall man at her side. He was dressed in paint-splashed jeans and enormous work boots and stood, hands-in-pockets, looking slightly awkward as she gestured to one of the chairs. 'Make yourself comfortable, George!' she said. 'Have a madeleine!'

'Are you sure it's...' he said, indicating his far from pristine attire. 'I can always...'

'Don't be ridiculous!' Grace smiled. 'We don't stand on cere-mony here, I can tell you!'

Leah took a sip of coffee to hide the incredulous look that no doubt appeared on her face at that moment. Because Grace's home was very much her palace, and Leah knew better than to turn up in anything that might wreck the upholstery. But perhaps there were different rules for new recruits, she mused. Or maybe it was George's smile... He had one of those smiles – a kind of twinkling, relaxed grin that might have made even the inflexible Grace soften a little.

George was just easing himself into one of the high-backed, vintage armchairs when the bell rang again.

'Ooh!' said Grace. 'That'll be another one!' She disappeared, leaving the two of them in sudden silence.

Leah smiled awkwardly at George, balancing her coffee cup on her knees. 'So,' she began, 'where did you...'

But before Leah could finish her sentence, Grace appeared again, a young man standing awkwardly by her side. He looked at Leah and George and the immaculate room and the three-tier cake stand and the piles and piles of books and his cheeks flushed. 'This is Alfie,' said Grace, giving him a gentle pat on the back – with perhaps a little too much force, as the poor boy then stumbled forwards – encouraging him to join them. She smiled reassuringly, then turned to exit the room again.

'Hi,' he said, blushing to his roots. He looked to be about twenty – only a few years older than Scarlett.

Leah smiled, feeling her motherly instincts rise up. 'Take a seat, Alfie,' she said, patting the sofa next to her.

'Thanks,' he said, sinking into it, his hands clasped together as if he was perhaps praying for an escape route.

Grace reappeared before they could settle into any sort of conversation, this time brandishing a tray with cups and a coffee pot, a jug of cream and a vintage sugar bowl complete with tongs. She was truly going all-out for this gathering.

'So do you think that might be it for tonight?' Leah asked her.

'Oh, I think there might be a couple more. But perhaps we ought to get going just in case,' Grace said, smiling. There was a certain stiffness in her smile – something Leah noticed from time-to-time with her friend. As if her veneer had slipped slightly and someone altogether more vulnerable and unsure had appeared for a moment. Leah wondered whether Grace was disappointed at the turnout.

Whatever it was, her friend seemed to shake it off pretty quickly, and stood, once everyone was catered for, clapping her hands together like a schoolteacher commanding attention. 'So!' she said. 'Welcome one and all!'

The three of them looked at her, not quite sure how to respond.

'So, a book club. A chance to meet up, share our favourite books, expose ourselves to new authors, discuss and really get into literature,' she beamed. 'I'm so glad I've finally got around to arranging this – and thank you all so much for being here.'

The speech had, perhaps, been planned for a far bigger audience, but Grace soldiered on, nonetheless.

'Let's start by introducing ourselves,' she continued. 'I'm—'

But the doorbell interrupted them.

Grace's face flooded with excitement at the prospect of another recruit and she turned and whisked from the room, her pleated skirt billowing behind her.

In the silence that followed, the three of them shifted uncomfortably. George reached forward and grabbed a ginger snap, biting into it and filling the room with the sound of crunching. 'Lovely biscuits,' he said, between chomps.

'Yes, Grace is quite the...' began Leah, before stopping as Grace returned with a woman, who had such glowing skin and glossy hair that she could have literally stepped out of one of the magazines Grace kept tidily in a sofa-side rack. She was dressed casually, in an enormous hoodie that perhaps belonged to her husband, with leggings protruding from beneath, but this didn't detract from her almost breathtaking beauty.

'This is Monica,' Grace said, beaming. 'Come to join our little tribe!'

'Hi Monica,' they said in unison like children in a school assembly.

'Sorry I'm late,' Monica said. Her voice was quiet, barely audible in comparison with Grace's booming tones.

'Not at all. Not at all,' Grace – who hated tardiness – said, still beaming. 'We're just glad you made it – aren't we?'

They all nodded and shuffled and quietly agreed. Leah wondered – not for the first time – whether Grace was wasted tucked away in a corner of rural France. She seemed to have an ability to take charge of any situation, to assume leadership and have it granted. A natural teacher perhaps – and she knew Grace had spent years at the chalkface – but maybe she'd be even better placed as a councillor or an army officer or... or President of the world. She'd soon whip everyone into shape and sort out those pesky little scraps the male leaders seemed intent on having.

'So,' Grace went on, and Leah experienced the little frisson of anxiety that came with realising you hadn't been paying attention. 'I vote we all choose one book, then come back together and discuss it each month. Perhaps each of us hosts one of the

evenings. It could be the ideal way to ward off this winter and transition to sunnier days!' She ended so triumphantly that Leah
wondered whether they ought to clap.

In the end, only Alfie gave in to the urge, banging his palms
together twice into the silence before realising that none of the rest
was going to join in.

It was 7 p.m. Outside, the February darkness was just beginning to fall and the solar lights that peppered Grace's perfectly
organised garden began to glow as if in appreciation of Grace's
efforts.

Leah was the first to speak. 'Well, it sounds great,' she said,
smiling at her friend. 'Really positive.'

She meant it too, she realised. While she hadn't been over-
joyed at the prospect, now she was here and there were enough of
them to make a decent go of it, she started to wonder whether the
group might be just what she needed to get out of her reading
slump. Or, well, her slump in general. She'd thought, before
moving to France, that she'd have enough time to read as much as
she wanted here – something she'd had to squeeze into her
commutes or the brief moments of free time she'd had before bed
in the past. But there was always something else to do. Always
work, or the garden, or something to sort out for Scarlett's school.
At least this would force her to prioritise something more
pleasant.

'I thought the first meeting could be at mine,' Grace rose to her
feet with a barely perceptible grimace of pain and walked over to
the dresser that she'd rescued and repurposed with chalk paint last
summer. Opening one of the drawers, she pulled out a stack of
books. 'And – we agreed, didn't we, that we'd each choose a book.
Mine's *Great Expectations*. Now we don't have to start with this, and
I'm open to suggestions. But I just so happen to have accumulated
a few copies of this one over the years. Such a favourite! I even

managed to pick up a couple this week at the Anglophone book sale. So it might be easy to...'

She handed out the slightly worn copies like a teacher at the start of a lesson, smiling indulgently as each of her new recruits took one from her outstretched hand. Leah looked at the fellow members of what Grace had already named 'The Bordeaux Book Club' and caught the eye of Alfie, who seemed to be regarding the brick of a book Grace had gifted him with a slight grimace on his face.

Clearly no one else was going to say anything. But Leah felt suddenly that the wrong choice at this stage might mean nobody turning up to the first real meeting.

'I wondered,' she said, feeling nervous as if she was approaching a predator, 'whether we might start with something lighter.' She nodded at Alfie as if to say *I've got your back* – because, really, it was important to encourage young people to read and Dickens was quite an ambitious start for what was meant to be a casual, pleasant club experience.

Grace wheeled around. 'Lighter?' she said, her eyebrows raised. 'But this is *Great Expectations!*'

'But... perhaps something... modern?' Leah's mouth felt dry.

Grace laughed. 'I think we can tell someone hasn't read the book yet,' she said. 'There's incredible humour in *Great Expectations*, and honestly, Dickens is timeless. What better than to read about the human experience?' she said. 'All manner of life is here.' She smiled at the rest of them, assuming their agreement.

'Of course,' Leah said, sitting back. The springs of the vintage sofa creaked underneath her. 'It was just an idea. I *have* actually read...'

'No, I think it sounds great,' said George, beaming at Grace before turning the book over in his hands and reading the back. 'Pip,' he said, to no one in particular, as he scanned the blurb. He looked at Leah and gave an apologetic wink at having sided with Grace and she smiled.

'Thanks Grace,' Monica said, as she received her own copy. She set it in her lap of and drummed at it lightly with her long, slender fingers. Leah noticed that all but one of her nails were chewed almost down to the skin.

'It's fine,' Alfie said, turning the book over and over in his hands. 'My mum loves Dickens.'

George cleared his throat. 'And the Bordeaux?' he enquired.

'Sorry?' Grace turned, her blonde hair staying fixedly in position.

'Well,' he said, running a nervous hand through his salt-and-pepper hair, 'I thought... I assumed when I saw the name that this was going to be a...'

'A...?' Grace prompted, back in teacher mode.

'Well,' he said. 'A wine club too.'

'Whatever gave you that impression?' her voice sounded slightly sharp, as if she was insulted by the idea that her book group in itself, wasn't enough to have tempted the four of them into her living room.

'The...' George coloured slightly and shifted in his seat, still clutching his copy of the Dickens classic, 'well, the Bordeaux bit.'

'Oh,' Grace seemed momentarily flummoxed. 'I suppose that was more of a location thing. And... well, a bit of alliteration.'

'Oh. It's just... aren't we in Cenac?'

Grace turned herself fully to face him. 'Cenac, Bordeaux,' she said firmly.

Grace was fond of describing herself as living 'in Bordeaux' and it wasn't the first time this had caused confusion. The first time Leah had 'popped round', she'd found that instead of the five-minute drive she'd imagined, she'd had to clock up thirty minutes to get to Grace's stone cottage, tucked away in a little commune, rather than in the heart of the city as she'd imagined.

'Right,' George nodded, clearly embarrassed at his faux pas.

'A bit of wine could be fun?' Leah ventured, in an attempt to rescue him. She felt all eyes – Alfie, Monica, George and Grace – fix on her. 'Well, it could be nice if we all chose, um, local wine to sample when we discussed the books?' she suggested.

'Well, I suppose I'd already thought we'd sort out some nibbles while we talk, that kind of thing...' Grace said after a moment's silence.

The others – already in awe of Grace, it seemed – quickly agreed that yes, it did sound like a good idea.

'Bordeaux in Bordeaux,' Leah quipped, hoping to appease herself in Grace's eyes.

Yes, Grace could be a lot, sometimes. Bordering on interfering. But her heart seemed to be in the right place. It had taken Leah a little while to realise this – and in fact, she'd spent some of their initial weeks avoiding spending too much time with the woman. 'I don't want to encourage her,' she'd told Nathan at the time.

She'd sometimes heard people comment or gossip about Grace – once or twice heard her referred to as a 'busybody' or a 'do-gooder' – and she understood what they meant. A little of Grace went a long way at times. But there was good there – a desire to help, underneath it all.

'Grace is always right', a mutual acquaintance had once said when they'd met up at a craft sale. 'And as long as she's always right, she's great company'.

'Yes,' said Grace at last, sinking into her chair, clutching three further copies of *Great Expectations*. Clearly, she'd been hoping for a larger showing. 'Yes, Bordeaux in Bordeaux. I like it. In fact, did I tell you I went on a wine tour recently to *Saint-Émilion*?' she said, turning to Leah. 'I learned an awful lot about local grapes.'

Leah smiled, relieved that Grace had found she was still the voice of authority on all the matters relating to the group. Order was restored.

A surreptitious look at her watch revealed it was quarter past seven. Outside, thick, black darkness had absorbed everything except the dotted light of the solar lamps, and the comforting glow that surrounded the one streetlamp on Grace's road. Cloud cover had obliterated the stars, and a light rain had begun to fall, pattering gently against the window as if not wanting to interrupt. Leah didn't blame it. Who was brave enough to cut off Grace in full flow?

'Of course, each grape is different,' she was saying. 'You have your Cabernet Sauvignon, Merlot, that kind of thing. But it's the blend that really makes the wine. You've probably all heard of Malbec – but...'

Leah looked across the room and caught Monica's eye. Both women glanced away quickly and Leah had to fight the urge to giggle, the kind of bubbling laughter that she remembered from school – the type you'd get in the class of a strict teacher – deliciously forbidden and highly dangerous. She tried to concentrate on Grace's words.

'Perhaps I meant that all along,' she was saying of the 'Bordeaux' idea. 'Yes, I did wonder about wine, I must admit.'

'I'm more of a beer drinker myself,' Alfie piped up – unwisely – into the silence. 'Would it be OK if I brought a bit of...'

'Ah, then young man, you can consider this your education!' Grace said, enthusiastically. 'We'll convert you by the end, I'm sure of it.'

Alfie nodded, sitting back on his chair and pushing his glasses back up his nose.

He was a bit of an anomaly in this group of forty and fifty-somethings, with his band T-shirt and black-rimmed glasses, enormous, white trainers and the small spray of acne at his jawline. Leah wondered whether he'd meant to come to the group at all. Perhaps he'd written down the wrong address. He looked more suited to a chess club, or some sort of gaming type organisation. He looked up and caught her eye and she quickly looked away, embarrassed to have been caught staring. She somehow doubted he'd be there next week.

'We read *Oliver* at school,' he said, cutting Grace off during an anecdote about wine-tasting: *I just couldn't spit it out! So uncouth! And what a waste! But then I ended up making quite a fool of myself in the vineyard...*

Grace looked at him, 'Well, don't let that put you off,' she said. 'I find that school...'

'Oh no. It didn't,' he added hurriedly. 'Actually I... well, I loved it.' His finger went to the bridge of his glasses, already firmly fixed on his nose, and gave it a nudge. 'It was... I found it quite moving actually. So... I think this'll be good.'

The statement seemed so out of place with their assumptions of him that they all fell silent.

George cleared his throat. 'Don't remember doing much at school myself,' he said. 'Mostly just pissed about. Wish I'd read more, really.'

Grace shuddered slightly at the language but let it pass. 'Plenty of time to catch up,' she said. 'I've got a virtual library here, and you're welcome to borrow.' Her cheeks looked pink.

'I can hardly remember anything I read at school,' admitted Leah. 'Then again, it's a lot longer ago for us than you.' She looked at Alfie, trying as always to knit everything back together. 'You'll have to be patient with us oldies.' It was one of those things that you say, then sit for the next ten minutes wondering why you let yourself say it. It made them seem, she thought later, completely past it.

'Not that long ago for all of us,' Grace said, her brow furrowed, despite the fact that she was older than Leah by over a decade.

'Right then,' George said, slapping his thighs and groaning to his feet. 'Sorry to love you and leave you, but I'd better get on.'

They all gratefully rose with him. 'Yes,' said Monica. 'I told the babysitter eight at the latest so...' She looked at her watch, a neat strip of weaved gold on her nut-brown wrist.

'Oh, you have a child?' Grace asked, looking at Monica's slim frame incredulously.

They hadn't actually asked many questions of each other at all during the short meet-up, Leah realised. They'd dutifully given their names and occupations during the introductions – shared a few basic facts. But nothing deeper. Still, it was a surprise that Monica hadn't mentioned she was a mum, especially after Leah had told them all about Scarlett.

'Oh, she's just a baby,' Monica said. 'Three months old. Bella.'

'But you don't look...' Grace began, before falling silent.

'Here she is,' Monica pulled a white phone from her pocket and expertly scrolled with her thumb. She passed Grace a picture of a baby wearing a hat with teddy ears and looking at the camera with enormous, brown eyes.

'Lovely,' Grace said, decisively, barely glancing at the screen before passing the phone quickly to Leah.

The others made the appropriate noises as they inspected Bella, en route to the front door.

'Well, thanks again,' George began, his hand on the catch, brandishing his book as if to remind Grace that she'd given it to him. 'This has been...'

'Oh! I almost forgot!' Grace interrupted, picking up a digital camera that had clearly been placed on the hall table for the purpose. 'We ought to capture this first meeting, don't you think? For posterity?'

Without waiting for a response, she set a timer on the camera and placed it down, then rushed to the wall opposite. 'That's it! All together. And you'll need to bend slightly George. And hold the books up!'

The camera flashed. Leah, leaning against the wall with the rest of them, wondered if they'd look more like a police line-up than a book club; most of their expressions were startled and unprepared.

'Thanks so much for coming,' Grace said. 'So, shall we say first Friday in March to start? Here? Say about seven-ish? I'll lay on a bit of a spread. And of course, some wine...'

With various mumbles in the affirmative, Monica, Alfie and George stepped onto the wooden porch with its hanging baskets and enormous, terracotta pots before being swallowed up into the early February night.

'Do you want me to...?' Leah asked, hanging back, aware that their mugs and plates were still scattered in Grace's immaculate living room.

'No, not a problem,' Grace said firmly. 'You get back to that husband of yours.' She said the word 'husband' with a slight inflection of distaste. 'Up early tomorrow – getting the rotavator out, didn't you say?'

'Yes,' Leah said, smiling, pleased that Grace had remembered.

She wrapped her coat around her as she stepped from the warmth of Grace's home to the bitter cold of the winter air. Her breath clouded in front of her as she made it quickly to her Renault Scenic and wrenched open the door. Inside, she rubbed her hands together vigorously before sliding in the key card and pressing start.

She felt the flood of relief she did after most social gatherings – for her, they were a bit like exercise. She knew that they were good for her, and that the more she did, the better she'd get at them, but it was nice to disappear back into her head for a bit and not have to worry about what other people were thinking.

As she pulled away, she wondered whether Nathan had managed to knock together any semblance of dinner.

Grace remained on the freezing porch, dressed only in the blouse and pleated skirt she'd worn inside, waving until they all disappeared into the night.

2

Half an hour later, Leah bumped the Scenic along her driveway, almost running over one of the neighbour's cats, which skittered in her wake. She switched off the car and listened for the automatic handbrake to click into place. Then opened the door and stepped into the cold.

Inside, she could hear Nathan clattering around in the kitchen. At least she assumed it was Nathan rather than Scarlett who, at fourteen, wouldn't be seen dead listening to Nathan's 'noughties playlist' – all the tunes that had entertained them both during their younger years. As she listened, a new intro began, and she recognised the strains of the Pussycat Dolls. Yep. Definitely Nathan.

'Hello,' she said automatically as she stepped into the tiled hallway and hung her coat on the peg above the radiator. But of course nobody replied. Nathan was getting his groove on whilst (hopefully) putting something together for their dinner, and Scarlett... Well, getting a nicety out of Scarlett would be startling these days. Her daughter spent most of her time in her bedroom, chatting to her friends on WhatsApp or TikTok, or begging for a lift and disappearing to her best friend Mathilde's house.

'Hi,' Leah said again pushing open the door of the kitchen, her nostrils flaring as she tried to ascertain the source of the smell. Soup of some kind?

Her husband stood at the Aga with his back to her. He was wearing his habitual muddy jeans and wellies, with a washed-out, chequered shirt and apron, whilst moving his hips and jiggling to the words 'hot like me' as he stirred an enormous, stainless-steel saucepan on the hob. Smiling, she moved up behind him and wrapped her hands around his waist, only to have him jump a mile and turn, wooden spoon brandished like a weapon.

'Oh, God! It's only you,' he said, thankfully lowering the spoon once he realised. Leah wondered briefly what death by wooden spoon might feel like. How many days would it take? Would it make a difference if he was cooking something hot or stirring a dessert? Her musing was cut off when she saw his features turn from surprise to what looked like annoyance.

'Sorry,' she said. 'Didn't mean to startle you.'

'Well, a hello might have been nice,' he turned around and put the wooden spoon back in the saucepan, turning down the heat a little. The steam had warmed and reset his usually well-gelled hair and it flopped forward over his forehead boyishly.

'Are you OK?' Leah checked her watch. It wasn't yet 8 p.m., so about the time she said she'd be. Not that Nathan was a stickler for timing or anything. But he seemed disgruntled.

'What do *you* think?' he said, looking at her pointedly, one eyebrow raised.

Leah resisted the urge to smooth the tousled brow back into place. 'I'm sorry,' she said, 'you've lost me'.

'Oh, come on.' He was serious, she realised. She tried to think of anything she might have done to upset him.

'Nathan, stop being weird. If I've done something wrong, just tell me,' she said, trying to keep her tone light. What with Scarlett's constant moods, she could do without another smouldering grump in the house.

He turned, his features unreadable. 'Let's just say, I'm making *carrot* soup,' he said, the eyebrow travelling back up his forehead again.

'Well, that's lovely,' she said, still confused. 'I mean, yum. Yay soup! Um...' she trailed off.

'*Carrot* soup,' he said again.

She wondered, briefly, how far an incredulous eyebrow could travel. If the incredulity level was high enough, could it begin to travel to the top of the head? Where would it stop? She focused on the hairy caterpillar interestedly. 'I like carrot soup,' she said.

'I bet you do,' he said, shaking his head. 'I bet you do.'

She put her bag down and sat on one of their bar stools – sourced from the local *dechetterie*, after they'd fashioned the breakfast bar using an enormous piece of oak that they'd found in the stone barn attached to the property. She leaned her elbows on the worn wood, waxed by them both for days last year and still gratifyingly smooth.

'Love,' she said. 'No offense, but I'm completely knackered. I seriously don't know what you're talking about.'

He looked at her, his eyes searching her face. Then slumped, the angry energy seeping out of him. 'The carrots,' he said.

'Yes?'

'You *bought* them.' Once again, he was tense.

'Yes, from the supermarket.'

Then she realised what he was getting at. 'Oh, look,' she said hurriedly, 'I'm sure your carrots are going to be lovely when they finally, um... kick in. But there just weren't enough.'

She felt his eyes on her. His eyebrows were now so high, she wondered if it was possible to pull a muscle in the forehead. She smiled apologetically.

Meeting her gaze, something in him changed. As if someone had let a little air out and deflated all his features. He switched the heat from under the steel saucepan and sat down on the stool opposite her. 'I'm being stupid,' he said.

She didn't reply. It was hard to know whether to agree.

'I just...' he reached for her hand and took it in both of his. She felt the roughness of his skin against hers, saw the stubborn mud embedded under some of his nails that simply didn't seem to want to shift. 'I thought we'd do better this year.'

Carrots had been the first thing they'd tried when they'd finally rotavated their garden and started their growing project three years ago. 'They're meant to be easy,' Nathan had said. 'Start off simple.'

Since, they'd grown several other vegetables with varying degrees of success. Potatoes, a glut of cucumbers – which surged into life each June and seemed to disappear soon afterwards, leaving them giving cucumbers to pretty much everyone they knew and having to buy from the shop the rest of the year – green beans and radishes, which did really well, but which admittedly neither of them liked very much. But the carrots had never really taken off.

Nathan, who seemed to be relentlessly optimistic about his prowess as a grower, had hoped this season would be the one where they finally produced enough to feed them each week.

'Oh Nathan,' she said. 'It's only February.'

'I know.'

'We don't know what we'll find when we dig those others up. Those enormous shoots!' she said.

'I know.'

'So what if I had to top up, um, this week's crop?' she said.

'It's just...' He looked at her, his brown eyes serious and searching. 'It feels like a criticism, somehow. You buying carrots, those pathetic four we were going to use... then that enormous bag...' He trailed off.

'You're being daft.'

'I know.' He sighed, leaning against the counter. 'It shouldn't matter really, should it? God's sake they're only eighty cents a kilo anyway.'

'I know,' she said. 'But I get it. I really do.' She'd felt a similar attachment to the strawberries she'd tried to nurture over the past three summers with varying success. The day she'd woken to find that slugs had dispatched the crop she'd earmarked for an Eton mess had been a dark day indeed.

She felt her insides sink a little as she wondered yet again whether they'd ever achieve anything close to self-sufficiency. The remote copywriting job she'd managed to land to provide an interim income was part-time, but it pinned her to set hours: a routine. Something she'd hoped to stay away from after their move. And while she enjoyed writing, she'd hoped she might be able to do something creative once they'd moved to France rather than being paid a paltry sum to write catchy descriptions for 'Brian's Brogues' – a shoe company that specialised in footwear for those with bunions and other nuisance foot complaints.

But it wouldn't be fair to raise this, not now. Especially when Nathan was already so upset.

She leaned forward and cuddled him, and he sank into her embrace. 'I bet your carrots are much better than those store-bought ones anyway,' she said into his ear.

'Thanks,' he said, meaning it. She remembered the dynamic editor she'd met when they'd worked together on the *Cambridge News*. He'd have laughed at this. But she shook the image away.

They were building their dream; it was nice that he was so invested.

It hadn't been the work so much as the relentlessness of it that had made them look for another sort of life. Nathan had thrived on editing, doling out assignments to junior reporters, sorting the wheat from the chaff when it came to local events; and she'd enjoyed her time as a local reporter. But arriving home each evening and disappearing first thing in the morning had left them little time to spend together. With their enormous mortgage, dialling back on the hours was out of the question. Instead, they'd quit, sold up and taken a leap. And it was wonderful in so many ways.

Just once in a while, she'd look at him, covered in mud and sweat, or see herself in the mirror, hair in disarray, or check their dwindling bank balance and feel a surge of fear, and wonder whether they'd simply swapped one difficult situation for another.

'Chickens are laying lots this week,' he said, getting to his feet, his voice returning to its habitual positive tone. 'Thought I might make frittatas.'

'Lovely.'

'I've shut them up – put in some extra hay. It's going to be two degrees later.'

'Brrr. Poor things.'

'Ah, they've got feathers. They'll be fine,' he grinned, as he turned towards her, his mood seemingly lifted. 'Unless you want to let them in – have them all by the fire.'

'Not likely.' She shuddered. She'd loved the idea of chickens from a distance. When they'd discussed their plans a few years ago, she'd talked of collecting eggs, even eating their own chickens sometimes. When confronted with the scrawny, feathered reality of them – their sharp beaks, beady eyes and strange, jerking movements, she'd felt less enthusiastic. These days, the chickens were solely Nathan's domain.

He laughed. 'I didn't think so.'

'Oh, you know me. I love them really.'

'Just from a distance?'

'Definitely from a distance,' she grinned.

'How was book group?' he said, decanting some of the soup into Tupperware and setting it aside to cool.

She shrugged. 'OK. There were a few of us there.'

He nodded. 'Grace on form?'

'Grace is always on form.' She smiled and saw him grin in return.

'Good point,' he said.

The door to the kitchen opened suddenly, hitting the wall behind, and Scarlett appeared in the room, somehow flooding it with an emotional charge. She was wearing her pyjama bottoms and an enormous, black T-shirt with a picture of Kurt Cobain sketched onto it. This was a recent obsession, and Leah wondered at times whether she'd chosen this particular 'role model' simply to worry her. Topping the ensemble off was one of Nathan's enormous wool cardigans, acquired from a local Christmas craft market, which hung heavily on her daughter's permanently cold shoulders.

'When's food?' she asked, her face unsmiling.

'Hello, Mum. How's your day?' Leah found herself saying. It was the type of thing her mum had used to say to her as a teen, and she'd vowed never to adopt the same verbal clichés, yet here they were.

Scarlett gave her the kind of look the sarcastic comment deserved, then moved across the kitchen to look into the saucepan. 'I hate soup,' she said. 'Why can't we eat any normal food in this house?'

Leah thought of the eleven-year-old who'd skipped into the house when they'd first brought her over, had squealed when they'd told her they were getting chickens. The girl who'd helped peel vegetables from the allotment and look up recipes for cucumbers (there were few) online during the glut. The girl who had seemed to pick up French with rapidity and ease, and was able to chatter away with her friends from school within a term.

Until recently, Leah had been certain that the whole 'teenage phase' – and she remembered her own struggles at that age – couldn't possibly be as horrible as depicted on TV or on internet forums. Sure, she'd had her own difficulties back in the day, but that was then. These days, parents were so much more clued up on the psychology of it all. She'd convinced herself she and Scarlett, with their closeness and shared humour and the amount of time they were able to spend together, would buck the trend and remain close despite the hormones.

Yet, a year ago, it was as if someone had spirited away her little, happy, cuddly daughter in the night, and replaced her with a snarly, prickly version. The type of person who had you treading on eggshells, who moved away from cuddles. Who found things to criticise in almost everything Leah did.

Leah had read the books and she knew the part that hormones played. She knew that children needed to separate from their parents in order to become fully fledged adults. And she'd thought she'd be OK with it, until it began to happen.

To her own surprise, she'd been so bereft since Scarlett had pulled away that she'd become like a needy ex – craving her daughter's attention and approval, despite realising this made her seem pathetic. It wasn't much fun viewing herself through a teenage girl's eyes.

'Scarlett! Dad's worked hard on that soup.'

Scarlett's lip curled a little. 'So?'

'Well, the least you could do is try a bit. It smells delicious.' She said loyally.

'I'm not hungry.' The door to the kitchen closed behind her retreating daughter.

Nathan and Leah exchanged eye contact.

'Just ignore her,' he said. 'She doesn't mean it.'

'I know, but...'

'I know,' he said, ladling soup into small bowls and breaking off some of the loaf they'd painstakingly baked this morning – it was a simple, white *pain*. They'd dialled back on anything adventurous since the case of the 'wholemeal sourdough' with its unyielding crust that even the chickens had refused to peck. He brought it to her without a plate, but she managed not to say anything (although, really, why not just grab a plate? Just because they were living 'the good life' didn't mean they had to live in a complete mess too).

After they'd finished the soup and stacked the dishes in the dishwasher together, Leah wandered through to the living room and sank into their leather sofa, feeling the worn material creak beneath her. She tried to ignore the sound of Nathan removing and restacking the dishes in the way he called 'doing it properly.'

Instead, she pulled a tartan rug over her knees and felt herself begin to relax as warmth flooded through her. Nathan had lit the wood burner earlier and it radiated a comforting heat. The shutters were still open and, despite the slight bite of draught she could feel from the single-paned windows, it was lovely to look out into the darkness. The rain had stopped now, the clouds cleared and the sky was sprinkled with jewel-like stars. The moon – almost a full-one, she noticed – glowed coldly in the blackness, giving just enough light to make out the fields that dropped away from their house into a small valley, then rose again, their tops decorated with dark fir trees.

She pulled *Great Expectations* out of her bag, noting that it was an old library book from the UK. The last borrower – if the piece of stamped paper in the front cover was to be believed – had been in 1993. She turned the pages, inhaling the scent of well-read book – that comforting, papery smell – and began to read.

3

To: Bordeaux Book Club
From: Grace
Subject: Confirmation

Dear all,

Lovely to meet you all yesterday!

Just wanted to confirm that the first meeting of the 'Bordeaux Book Club' will be on Friday 7th March. That gives us three weeks to enjoy Great Expectations! I'll provide the wine for this one – I have a cheeky blend from the independent vineyard I was telling you about that will go wonderfully with my cheese straws.

Happy reading!

Grace

Grace pressed *send* on her email and sat back in her chair, satisfied. Drawing her A4, leather-bound diary towards her, she wrote the meeting into its appropriate space, then allowed herself to smile a little at the fact there wasn't a single day in the displayed week when she wasn't doing something. No – more than that – when she wasn't an *integral part* of something.

Her hand hovered over her mouse and she paused for a second. The sharp, white winter sun shone through the window, making a patch of light on her vintage rug. Hector, her beloved white cat, had stretched himself out so as to maximise the resultant warmth magnified by the window. He was gloriously asleep, his little chest moving and – if she wasn't mistaken – emitting a tiny snore now and then.

She really ought to go to the market. There was hardly anything in the fridge and she had her Canasta group this evening. She'd promised to bake some of her fabulous brownies for them all – 'they are to die for' she'd told them. They'd be ever so disappointed if she didn't make them. So really, she hadn't got time to scroll through social media.

But her hand crept, as if independent to her, it felt, to the mouse and clicked on her browser. She carefully typed 'Facebook' into the search bar and clicked on the social media site. She wasn't going to go on his profile anyway, she told herself. But it was important to keep abreast of things in the groups. There'd been a lot of spam in the 'Expats Survival Group' recently and she didn't want anyone falling for a scam on her watch.

Whenever an opportunity to be an admin came up in one of the online groups she favoured, she always volunteered. It was nice to support these little online collectives, after all – they were a lifeline for some people. Nice to feel part of things.

She quickly approved posts and rejected one advertising a water butt for sale. She messaged the sender:

Please move to the selling group.

But then, almost before she was aware of it, she was on his page. They weren't friends, but really his security settings were so terrible. Nearly every one of his photos was set to 'public' – he ought to be more careful. Anyone could be trolling his page.

There were a few new shots and she studied them, her heart leaping in recognition at his smile. His face was older now, but it was still recognisably him. The girl his arm was around looked all of thirty-five. Grace shook her head; he really had become a cliché.

There was a new picture, this time of him relaxing in a deckchair in a garden surrounded by a stone wall. Was he in France? She peered at the snap, but it was one from last summer – only recently uploaded – of a trip to Bath.

She knew she shouldn't scroll back too far, yet she found her finger pressed on the left-hand side of her mouse, sending time shooting backwards one year, two, six, ten, more. And there it was. The picture of this house – in need of a paint and a jolly good tidy up, but recognisably this house. Her: younger, slimmer, innocent of what was to come, standing triumphantly on the doorstep with an enormous set of keys. At one time she'd wondered whether his keeping that picture in his online albums meant something, but she'd concluded long ago that all it symbolised was the fact that Stephen didn't move with the times – and was still as internet incompetent as he'd always been. Probably, his PA handled that sort of thing at work.

She didn't envy him, his new life, in the slightest. If anything, she felt sorry for him.

She'd always been the one to keep up with things, she thought, clicking on the photo to enlarge it. A scroll of emojis appeared in a floating box and she moved her mouse away quickly. The last thing she wanted to do was 'like' anything on his page. She didn't want to give him the wrong impression.

Instead, she forced herself to click on the x in the corner and the photo, the Facebook page and her email inbox disappeared in one fell swoop. She clicked her tongue against the roof of her mouth. She'd meant to upload the picture she'd taken of the book group – all triumphantly holding their *Great Expectations* books.

She'd do it later.

She stretched her legs out and pushed back on her chair until her thighs emerged from under the desk, then stood up and took a breath. Hector opened a lazy eye and looked at her. 'You've had your food, mister,' she told him, crouching down and giving him a stroke. He rolled and revealed his tummy – a tangle of white hair – for her to rub. 'You really do take the biscuit,' she said, rubbing it nonetheless. He purred triumphantly.

Then, out of nowhere, that sudden feeling she sometimes got when the house was silent flooded over her. The feeling that she ought to open the door, step into that room again. But no. She just needed air. Decisively, she got to her feet and went to remove the shopping list from the pad she kept in the kitchen. She grabbed her keys from the bowl on the powder-blue dresser she'd painstakingly restored last year, and slipped them into her handbag.

'Market,' she said to the indifferent Hector as she passed the open door to the office. She grabbed her white, woollen coat from the hook and buttoned it up, checking her hair in the mirror before slipping on a red beret and grabbing her organic tote bag.

'Right,' she said to no one, as she opened the front door and felt the chill of the morning air, sharp on her face. 'Right, no time to waste.'

She made her way as swiftly as she dared across the iced front drive and slipped into her Peugeot, starting the engine and letting the warmth blow vigorously against the windscreen. She had time; she didn't have to stand in the cold and scrape the ice. Eventually, the windscreen wipers broke through, sending shards of icy water dripping wetly from her screen.

She put the car in gear and steered it slowly to the end of the drive, stopping to look for non-existent traffic before disappearing around the corner, on her way to the market.

4

'You're looking smart,' Leah said, as Nathan appeared in the doorway wearing a fresh pair of jeans and – for the first time in an age – an unsullied jumper in place of his usual mud-stained hoodie.

He walked into the kitchen and poured himself a coffee, leaning against the counter to drink it. 'Thanks,' he said, looking down at his outfit as if realising what he was wearing for the first time.

Leah shut her laptop. She'd reply to Grace later. 'I thought we were rotavating?' she said. 'You said we'd be at it all day.' In truth, she hadn't been looking forward to it, but it wasn't the point. She was there, duly dressed and now feeling incredibly scruffy in her tracksuit bottoms and one of Nathan's old jumpers, and he was looking – comparatively at least – as if he was about to attend a wedding.

'We are,' he said. 'I just... I thought I'd pop out first. You know, we were saying we ought to keep an eye on prices at the market. So when we're ready to sell...' the words trailed off. They were months, probably years, from having surplus to sell at market. It sounded 100 per cent the lame excuse it was.

She didn't blame him, though, for wanting a break. 'OK,' she said. 'Why don't you wait a few minutes and I'll slip into...'

'Do you mind if I get on?' he said, draining the last of his coffee and clinking the mug down on the kitchen worktop. 'I just thought I'd shoot off on my own, if that's OK. I'll be back soon.'

'Oh, OK.'

'And Scarlett's here, so...'

'Scarlett's fourteen. She hardly needs a babysitter.'

'I know.'

'And she won't be awake for a couple of hours probably.'

'I know.'

Leah scrutinised her husband. It was fine, of course, for him to take a bit of time for himself. It was no different to what she was doing, joining the reading group. And she had a few different clubs and associations she attended from time to time by herself. Even so, the fact that he clearly didn't want her to come made her feel a childish sense of rejection. She couldn't put her finger on it, but it felt as if something was up. 'Is this about the carrots?' she said at last clutching the only straw – or vegetable – she could think of.

'What?'

'Are you still upset about the carrots?'

A smile spread across his face. 'Don't be ridiculous! I'm petty but I'm not that petty.'

She grinned in response. 'Sorry,' she said, feeling embarrassed. 'Look of course, it's fine. The ground's probably frozen solid anyway. I just wish you'd given me a heads-up, is all.'

'I'll be back by lunchtime, and we can get that patch done this afternoon if you want?' he said, picking up his wallet and keys.

'Sure,' she said, getting up to give him a kiss, noticing the fresh smell of aftershave and suspecting it clashed a little with the musty smell she was giving off in her work clothes with her unwashed hair. 'You smell nice,' she said. 'Who's the lucky lady?'

He laughed, briskly. 'Wouldn't you like to know?' he quipped. 'So, see you twelve-ish?'

'Sure you don't want me to...?' she trailed off. 'Sorry. You go. Have fun. Scope out the competition.' She smiled, as he turned at the door and blew her a kiss.

'Oh, and I haven't brought the eggs in this morning,' he said. 'Get Scarlett to do it?'

'Chance would be a fine...' she said, but the door shut before she could finish.

Once the car had pulled away, she poured herself another coffee, wrapped herself in Nathan's work coat – which was enormous and sheepskin-lined and smelled of mud and chickens and cats – and took it out to the little bench in their front garden. From here, she could watch the ice-cold sun play on the barren fields and imagine how life was hiding, just under the surface, ready to burst forth in a few weeks' time.

March was her favourite month. Not in terms of the work it involved with planting and watering and harvesting and planning, but the way in which the world came back to life after the winter. Living on the land the way they were trying to do made you more aware than ever of the weather – how it affected your daily life, how it made you change plans, how it made a crop thrive or falter. Back home in the UK, working in the glass-fronted offices of the *Cambridge News*, they'd been under the illusion that they – the humans – ruled the world. Here, she was in no doubt that it was actually nature in charge.

Although their lives seemed to revolve around their growing – or at least trying to – when they'd decided to make the move three years ago, it hadn't really been born from a desire to live off the land, but simply the desire to *live*...

At first, they'd thought about buying a B&B, or maybe even a café. But as Nathan had put it, they'd only end up being slaves to their customers instead of their boss at the newspaper. 'Why not try to be self-sufficient? Answering to no-one,' he'd suggested.

Only it wasn't no-one, she'd realised in the years that followed. Now their boss was bloody Mother Nature. And she could be unpredictable at best, and downright mean on a particularly bad day.

Leah had loved it at first. This idea of living more naturally. Of bending with the seasons and becoming more attuned to things. Now, sometimes, she felt completely at the mercy of nature. Hated the sudden ice-snaps that would come in May just when you felt things had improved. And the way a packet of seeds rarely produced what was pictured on the front. Hated the fact that until they actually became not only self-sufficient, but able to generate some income (something that now seemed impossible), she was stuck with one foot in the UK, working shifts remotely and not fully immersing herself in her chosen country.

As she heard the car purr out of the drive, Leah blew the steam from the top of her coffee and sipped, feeling the warm liquid move down her throat into her grateful stomach. Maybe it would be nice to have the morning to herself, she thought. Spend a bit of time with Scarlett.

She looked over at the chicken house, its inhabitants already out in the wire-fenced run, stalking and looking and clucking together. She really ought to collect the eggs. She was nervous of the chickens and always relied on Nathan to deal with them. If anything, his willingness to always be official egg collector had exacerbated her fear – it had been a long time since she'd ventured into the coop. She knew it was irrational – for goodness' sake, they were only chickens! But something about the way they looked at her just freaked her out.

'I honestly don't think they like me,' she'd told Nathan once.

'Don't be silly,' he'd laughed. 'Think of all those lovely peelings you keep feeding them.'

She'd smiled and tried to shake the feeling, but it had remained.

Then again, if she was absolutely honest, the thought of getting Scarlett up and trying to convince her to reach into the chickens' poo-sprinkled straw nest and retrieve warm, dirty, feather-stuck eggs was even more terrifying. She sighed as she remembered a smaller version of her daughter slipping on her wellies and running over with a basket, giggling delightedly. Had she treasured them enough? Those moments before her little girl had disappeared? Should she have hugged her more, breathed her in? Stored those magical moments to help her get through this more barren season?

She shook her head. She was being ridiculous. Self-indulgent. She set her coffee down on the bench and stood up. She'd do it now, to avoid having to think about it. Grabbing one of the metal baskets from the hallway, she strode over to the chicken run as if telling the chickens that she, not they, were in charge here. They stared at her, their sharp little eyes far from convinced.

'This is it, girls,' she said to them, unhooking the little metal clasp and letting herself into the run. The chickens began to mumble and cluck around her. One particularly stringy bird – they'd nicknamed her Gollum – made her jerky way towards Leah and began worrying at her leg. 'I thought chickens were supposed to be harmless,' she said, trying to nudge it away. 'Not now, Gollum.'

Gollum looked up at her as if to say, *Well, you called me Gollum – do you expect me to like you?*

'I'm warning you,' she said to the chicken. 'No sudden movements.'

Gollum's eyes seemed to glint as if the chicken had understood and Leah had the sudden urge to run. To leave it all to Nathan on his return.

Instead, she crossed the poo-and-straw-peppered grass at the bottom of the run and reached into the darkness of the hen house – feeling a little like a contestant on *I'm a Celebrity – Get Me Out of Here!*

Soon she'd found a warm shell under some straw; she withdrew her hand and triumphantly placed the egg in the basket. Another rummage, another egg – this one cooler and garnished with poo. *Great*, she thought to herself, *really living the dream here.* Gollum continued to worry at the leg of Leah's jogging bottoms and she wished she'd gone for her wellies instead of grabbing her easy-to-slip-on crocs. She reached forward again, her hand rummaging in the straw. One more egg. Probably that would be it. At least, it would do.

She added it to the basket and stepped back, only to feel her foot touch on something soft. A sound – more like a scream than a squawk – filled the air. 'Gollum! Oh, sorry,' she said, realising she'd stepped on the bird's tail end briefly.

But Gollum must have decided enough was enough. With a loud crow, she fluffed up her feathers, flapped her wings and lunged forward, pecking Leah on the leg.

'Ow!' she said, kicking at the bird. 'Get off!'

If anything, Leah's attempt at self-defence simply seemed to anger Gollum more. The bird flapped her wings again, this time raising herself up a little and managing to plant a quite painful peck on Leah's hand. 'Gollum!' she said, 'stop it!'

But it was too late. The other hens had noticed.

Chickens might not be the friendliest of creatures, nor seem as if they have each other's backs. But something about the attack seemed to spook the other, usually more friendly, birds. Another fluffed and pecked, then another. They chattered wildly as they closed in. 'Get off!' she said, trying to shake her leg in their direction. 'Get off or I'll... I'll...'

The chickens, now worked into a terrified, angry frenzy, paid no notice.

Soon, Leah was racing for the wire door, chickens in hot pursuit. She suffered four peck wounds and a number of scratches, nearly trapping Gollum's wing in the door in her attempt to escape. Her hands were shaking as she pushed the small, metal hook back into the eye of the door lock and finally secured the birds in their run.

Her heart was hammering as she examined her wounds, then sighed as she realised the basket, with its three measly eggs, was still sitting in the centre of the run. Sod it, Nathan would have to fetch it.

In none of her investigations into chicken rearing had she come across any stories of chickens attacking their owners. Roosters, yes. But chickens? Nathan had reassured her that her fear was unfounded. Well, now she had the bloodied evidence to prove him wrong.

Making her way back to the house, she felt a couple of self-pitying tears well in her eyes. It wasn't the peck wounds making her cry – they were superficial at best, and she'd had a booster tetanus shot the year before. But when your husband seems off with you, your teen girl appears to hate your guts, then you get attacked by a flock of chickens, well, it does nothing for the self-esteem.

Moments later, she wrenched the front door open and stepped back into the warmth of the hallway. Scarlett was there – unusually early – dressed in a towelling dressing gown and a pair of trainers, hair in a towel. She looked at her dishevelled, slightly tear-stained mother and crinkled her nose. 'What happened to *you*?' she said, accusingly.

'Gollum.'

'What?'

'The chickens attacked me,' she said simply.

'God, Mum,' Scarlett said, her face anything but sympathetic. 'You can't do anything normal, can you?'

5

In the end, it took them three days to rotavate the patch of garden they'd planned. The motor of their rotavator – a small model that had seen better days – cut out several times, the ground was hard and they just couldn't get into a rhythm. Still, it was nice to look at the garden from the warmth of the living room, despite its clutter, and congratulate themselves on a job well done. Or well enough done.

They'd tried to persuade Scarlett to help them on the Sunday when they'd finally made a start, a day later than planned, but she'd made an excuse about homework and disappeared to her room. 'How come she only seems industrious,' Nathan had puffed, 'when we need a bit of help?'

Now, it was three o'clock on Tuesday afternoon and they'd just finished the last couple of beds. Nathan had disappeared upstairs and Leah had just made a cup of tea for each of them, then settled down in the living room again with *Great Expectations*. She'd made a little progress in the book, and was just refamiliarising herself with Miss Havisham's revolting living arrangements when she heard a creak on the stair.

'Tea's next to the kettle,' she called, simultaneously wondering who exactly was tending to Miss Havisham's extensive land while she moped around with her broken heart, still wearing the wedding dress she'd had on when her lover had abandoned her. If the mad old woman had had to wield a hoe herself once in a while, perhaps she wouldn't have got herself into such a state, Leah thought, imagining how such a comment would go down with Grace. She tried to think more of the literary symbolism, but it was hard when, at times, she wouldn't mind doing a Havisham herself – downing tools dramatically and completely surrendering to her feelings like a toddler. Only she'd keep both her shoes on, she decided. When even the chickens are out to get you, you need to be prepared to run at any moment.

The door opened, and with a waft of sweet-smelling shampoo, her husband appeared in the room, several shades lighter than when he'd disappeared up the stairs twenty minutes before, covered in mud. 'You look nice,' she said. 'I'll jump in the shower when I finish this chapter.'

'No rush,' he said, his eyes travelled to the window and she followed his gaze. The afternoon was blue-skied and bright in a way that made it seem welcoming until you stepped outside and realised that you were ten seconds away from hypothermia. 'Actually I'm just... I've just got to... pop out.'

'Oh?' she looked up. 'You didn't mention anything?'

'No,' he said, his eyes moving from the window to his shoes but barely resting on her at all. 'I wasn't sure if we'd finish in time... but, well, I'm just... I need to...'

'In time for what?'

He coloured. 'Well, there's, um, a *vide-maison*. Saw an ad on Facebook this morning. Someone's selling some of their old junk.' He laughed, a little stiffly. 'I thought I'd see if they've got any garden tools we might make use of.'

She looked again at his apparently ironed shirt. Did they even have an iron? 'Bit overdressed for a *vide-maison*, aren't you?'

'Well, I might have a little walk around the city after. See a bit of life,' he said, shrugging. 'Remind myself there's more to me than being a failed farmer.' He grinned, but there was a sadness in his eyes.

'Oh, come on,' she said. 'We'll make a farmer out of you yet!'

'Ha. Well, I live in hope!'

'You should have said you wanted to go out!' She set the book down, dog-earing it first in her haste – something she knew would earn her Grace's wrath. 'I'll get changed and come with.'

'But you were looking forward to relaxing this arvo, you said?'

'I know, but...' Was it unreasonable that she felt a bit put out? She had said more than once over the weekend that she was looking forward to putting her feet up when the beds were done. But something felt off.

'Is everything alright?' she asked.

His brow furrowed. 'Of course it is.'

She had a sudden, odd, urge to ask whether he was annoyed about something – the carrots again? The chickens? – but managed to suppress it. 'OK,' she said, uncertainly.

'Do you want me to pick anything up?' he asked her.

'No, I'm OK.'

'Ok, see you soon.' The door slammed and moments later, almost as if he'd hurried to get there, the car door shut and the engine started.

Once he'd pulled away, the house settled around her. It was odd, when she was here on her own, how the house felt different. How she had a sense of its empty rooms, the coldness of its stone walls when she knew there wasn't another living, breathing human inside.

They'd recently talked about getting a dog – and despite never having owned one before, she was tempted. It would mean there was always someone – well, something – around. But she wasn't sure, especially after the chicken incident. *Could all animals smell fear?* she wondered.

She sipped her tea, picked up her book again and tried to concentrate. But when she turned a page and realised she had no idea what she'd just read, she set it down again and decided to shower. Scarlett would be home from school in a bit – perhaps she'd use the time to try to reconnect with her daughter? Maybe they could pop out for a coffee, or stick on a film together? If not, *Countdown* would be on soon – her go-to comfort TV ever since they'd invested in a British TV package. The familiar-faced presenter might not actually know she existed, but at least he was friendly whenever she turned the TV on, and didn't screw up his nose at the sight of her, or disappear out of the door when she flicked onto his channel like everyone else in her life seemed determined to do.

As she stepped out of the shower forty minutes later, she heard the unmistakable sound of the front door slamming, shortly followed by a bag being dropped heavily from a shoulder. 'Scarlett!' she yelled down. 'Fancy going to get something from the patisserie?'

There was a pause. 'If you want,' came the eventual answer.

It wasn't the most enthusiastic of yeses, but it was nice to know that Scarlett still craved her favourite *millefeuille* more than she disliked her mother. Leah imagined a set of old-fashioned scales: custard filled pastries on one end, her daughter's negative impression of her – which she imagined as a heavy, black tangle of jagged metal – the other. The day she offered Scarlett the chance of a sweet treat and was rejected was the day she really had to worry, she decided. Scarlett was going through a phase, was all. Perhaps

Nathan was too – just needing to get out a little bit more. Maybe even Gollum was getting itchy feet?

If you can't beat 'em, she thought, looking at herself in the mirror, *join 'em*. And she'd go for her favourite lemon meringue and sod the calories. She'd earned them.

She wiped the steam from the mirror with her hand, leaving it shiny, but coated with droplets and runnels, and took in her reflection. Forty-five. It was hard to believe. Not because she didn't look it (although in the right light and to someone with pre-op cataracts, she might pass for five years younger), but because it seemed now that she was here, the years before had passed in a flash.

At least once a day, the thought would strike her: *I'm forty-five! Forty bloody five.*

She ran a brush through her damp hair and watched it fall into gentle, thick strands. Then she quickly rubbed some moisturiser on her skin, dabbed on a light foundation and blasted her chestnut hair with the dryer, quickly and expertly fashioning it into her habitual style – the 'just hanging there' look or 'neglected but serviceable'. She would do. The pastries were calling.

In her bedroom, she dropped her towel and pulled on clean underwear, then stepped into a fresh pair of navy jeans – smart ones that hugged her hips – and a warm, black, polo-neck jumper. She pulled on her knee-length, black boots and inspected the result in the wardrobe mirror. She looked OK, she decided. Definitely an improvement on the muddy, sweat-soaked, pre-shower version.

She grabbed a smart, wool, waist-length coat from her wardrobe and took to the stairs. 'Scarlett!' she called on her way down. 'Are you ready?'

Scarlett appeared from nowhere in front of her, a ghoul hovering in her line of vision. 'You don't need to shout,' she said.

She, as always, looked stunning – she'd shed her carefully chosen school clothes like an unwanted skin and pulled on the pair of jeans Leah remembered having seen crumpled on her bedroom floor earlier, paired with a hoodie of Nathan's that read *Varsity* on the front. Somehow, Scarlett made these dubious fashion choices look both chic and flattering.

Scarlett would never accept that she was beautiful. She shrugged off compliments and thrived on finding tiny flaws to beat herself up about. Yet, with her luminous skin, dark hair and blue eyes, she looked almost ethereal. Leah remembered herself at that age: a home perm, temporary red hair dye and a fringe she'd cut herself. She'd hated the way she looked too, as a teen, but unlike her daughter, she'd had every reason to.

'Coat?' she said, and was admonished with a look that was colder than all the days they'd endured in February put together.

'I've got a jumper on!' her daughter said with an eyeroll.

'But it's...' she began, and was treated to another look. 'Never mind,' she said, opening the door and noting, slightly gratifyingly, Scarlett's eyes widen as the reality of the cold air flooded in.

Nathan had taken the Scenic, so they were forced to jump in the doddery old Clio they'd bought as a backup. Still, they were only going to the patisserie, not right into Bordeaux after all.

Their house was on the outskirts of the city in a small enclave close to *Mignoy*, far enough out to be affordable and have land to work on, but close enough to be able to drive to the centre with ease. 'It's the best of both worlds!' Nathan had exclaimed when the listing had appeared on the website they'd been favouring. And it was, sort of. But what had seemed like a dream property on screen hadn't turned out to be quite so charming in the flesh. The house had been uninhabited for five years, and had smelled of old carpets at first. The garden had been larger than they'd anticipated – which they'd thought a plus at the time – but Leah was beginning to see the acreage in terms of the work it represented rather than the space and potential.

They'd viewed the house on a sunny day in June – enjoying the sort of optimistic weather that makes you feel capable of anything and which makes small problems seem easily surmountable. But when they'd arrived that September, winter was lurking just behind the corner, waiting to demonstrate the realities of living in an old, draughty house and planning a garden into which you could barely drive a spade.

They'd worked hard since then and the house had begun to look – and smell – better. They'd had some radiators replaced, updated the bathrooms. Nathan had even had a go at tiling the kitchen floor – and as long as they kept the breakfast bar in situ to hide the unfortunate crack, it looked practically professional. Not a patch on Grace's reclaimed vintage paradise, but good enough at least.

The land had been a different matter. At the front, their house had a traditional, slightly overgrown, front garden, with a central path leading to the front door. So far, so normal. But it had come with land that stretched out in a strange half-triangle shape at the back. Most of it had now been rotavated into beds. Shoots and mounds of earth and a pile of manure and discarded spades scattered the area. The chickens chattered in their run by the fence on the left-hand side.

When they'd talked of 'living off the land' and 'having a peaceful existence', she hadn't realised the two ideas were oxymoronic. You could do one or the other. The land, whilst tranquil and manageable from a distance, or in your imagination, was a hard taskmaster. One mistake, a crop would fail. One missed day, and something would wither, weeds would take over or you'd miss the perfect moment for harvesting something or other. And the watering! They'd installed two water butts for the purpose, but still had to use their 'grey' water – sourced from the bath or a bucket system Nathan had managed to fashion at the back of the washing machine – to keep everything hydrated.

The endless gardening had been great for her arms – her emerging bingo wings had retreated from whence they came. But in terms of enjoyment and 'living the dream', it wasn't exactly what she'd envisaged. More hard work, less red wine and definitely more blisters.

'Are we going then?' Scarlett was standing just ahead of her on the drive. 'You've gone weird.'

Leah realised she'd been staring out over the garden and flushed. 'Sorry,' she said, wishing almost instantly she hadn't. It wasn't OK for Scarlett to call her weird. Just because she might agree with the description didn't mean she should endorse her daughter using it on her.

The engine started second time and, with a blast of heat and a stink of petrol (which for some reason, she rather liked), they trundled up the drive and onto the road. '*Les Cerises*', the small boulangerie-patisserie that made up one of a few scattered shops on what passed as a high street in their suburb, was housed in a small, sand-coloured premises which formed part of a row of once houses, now repurposed into a brasserie, pharmacy, small shop and a boutique clothing store.

The owner had optimistically set a couple of tables in the freezing sunshine for punters who fancied dicing with the risk of death by winter, but once Leah had parked the Clio haphazardly in the nearby parking area, they walked in through the door, their sights fixed firmly on the inside.

It was a small enterprise – with just three indoor tables, one of which was taken up by a guy reading the local paper, so Leah went to set her handbag on the chair of the table closest to the window, with daylight and view of the high street.

'Do you mind if we sit there instead?' her daughter asked her, pointing at the other empty table towards the back and away from the window.

'Sure,' Leah said, picking up her handbag and obediently taking it to the table. Scarlett slid herself into one of the empty chairs. 'Millefeuille?' Leah asked.

'Macaron.'

'Oh.' The unexpected choice threw her. 'Sure, what colour?'

'Flavour.'

'What?'

'It's not what colour, it's what *flavour*!' her daughter explained impatiently.

To be honest, it's also a colour, Leah thought but didn't say. 'OK, what flavour?' she asked, holding onto her patience by a thread.

'Pink.'

Leah gave a tight smile and went to stand at the counter. To her left, in a kitchen area, she could see two people working – icing cakes, kneading pastry. The smell of sweetness and coffee hung in the air, making her stomach growl.

As the customer before her left, she stepped forward and made her order – a coffee, a mint tea, a pink *macron* and a *tarte au citron*.

The woman nodded. '*Un Macron?*' she said, with a small giggle.

'*Oui, un macron.*' Leah repeated. '*Fraise,*' she added.

She glanced over at Scarlett and was surprised to see her daughter staring fixedly in the opposite direction, the top of her ears red.

'Ah but we do not serve 'im,' the woman said, breaking into English.

'But I can see...' she pointed at the array of colourful macarons arranged beautifully under the glass viewing pane.

'Ah un mac-*a*-ron, *madame*,' the server said, her eyes sparkling with mischief. 'But you have asked me for, how you say, the president of France, with some strawberries.'

'Oh.'

'And I do not have 'im in stock right now. And I am not sure what 'is wife will say if I try to cover 'im with fruit, *non*?'

Leah laughed. 'Sorry, mac-*a*-ron,' she said, catching the woman's humour. '*Je préfère l'option végétarienne!*'

She was still smiling when she made her way back to their table, two cups and saucers rattling and threatening to spill on their delicious treats. She set the tray down. 'Well, that was embarrassing,' she said, not really meaning it.

'For God's sake, Mum,' Scarlett hissed. 'Why do you have to do that all the time?'

'Do what?' Leah felt her humour seep away.

'Well, your accent, and saying Macron instead of macaron. I thought I'd be safe!'

'What do you mean?'

'Well, you know I like millefeuille, but you say it like mille filley – it's so embarrassing,' Scarlett said, taking a bite out of her mac-*a*-ron and scowling. 'So I thought, I know, I'll ask for something else. And you did that.'

'Scarlett! It was nothing. And it was funny, if anything.'

Scarlett's expression made it very clear that she did not share the joke. 'But why do you have to talk like that?'

'Like what?' If anything, Leah felt rather proud of her French. Sure, it wasn't perfect, but three years of lessons had meant she could negotiate most situations and be understood.

'Like – I dunno – like you're on holiday or something!' Scarlett said. 'It's so embarrassing!'

'My... my accent?'

'Yes!' said Scarlett, screwing up her face. Three years of complete immersion, added to the fact that she had still been very young when they've moved, meant her daughter spoke French flawlessly in an accent that sounded local. But, as she'd been in her forties by the time she'd started learning in earnest, Leah knew she'd always sound a little like an Englishwoman speaking a foreign tongue. And she was OK with that.

She felt herself get hot. But she'd taken her daughter out to bond with her, not fight. She could very well do that at home. She held her patience and tried to change the subject. 'Love this café though,' she said.

Scarlett nodded. 'It's alright.'

'I just...'

The bell on the door pinged.

'My shoe!' Scarlett said, disappearing towards the ground. 'I'll just...' She began fiddling with her trainer.

Waiting for her to finish her sentence, Leah took a sip of coffee which was warm and sweet. She used the tiny fork she'd been provided with to break the crust of the lemon meringue, feeling it crumble satisfyingly onto the plate. Lifting a forkful to her mouth, she sighed as the tang of lemon and the sweet, crumbly mess of pastry melted on her tongue. This was simply to die for.

She'd always imagined life in France would be like this. Not just sitting and scoffing cakes all day, but taking time out, exploring little cafés and quaint high streets. Enjoying a slower pace of life and having time to appreciate the smaller things.

When they'd first arrived, it had felt like bliss – for a while. They'd relished the fact they were no longer slaves to their alarm clock, enjoyed planning the garden at leisure, shopping for DIY materials or seeds. Going on recces to local markets to try out the produce. Leah hadn't even minded her shifts at the laptop – after all, she was still in France and enjoying the beautiful scenery whilst typing. But over time, they'd had to get real, had to actually try to make their plan of sustaining a life here work and she'd begun to realise how unrealistic it was. She was worried she might never be able to quit the copywriting. Yet Nathan was so fixed on their project, his self-esteem somehow so tied in with making this a success, she just couldn't raise the subject with him.

'It'll be hard graft for a while,' Nathan had told her as they'd rotavated their first bed. 'But once things get going, I reckon the garden will almost take care of itself!' She'd believed him – why wouldn't she? He'd been senior to her at work and had always seemed to know what he was doing there. She had simply transferred her faith in him (based on his being an editor) to this new situation. Ill-advisedly, as it turned out.

Because three years on, she was still up at dawn, muscles aching, trying to be positive about a day of planting or plant care. Or looking up endless egg recipes online and pretending they tasted different from each other; desperately trying to become self-sufficient rather than nibbling away at their 'savings' – the equity they'd had left over after moving. She tried not to think about whether they'd be properly set up for business by the time they ran out of funds. Plus, she...

A movement below the table interrupted her train of thought. What on earth was Scarlett doing? She was still under the table, still fiddling with a lace that looked perfectly fine to Leah as she glanced down.

'Scarlett?' she said. 'Are you alright?'

'Yes, shut up, OK?'

Leah was about to admonish her daughter in no uncertain terms, but a movement near the counter caught her eye. Two girls of about Scarlett's age were there, buying takeaway hot chocolates and chattering with each other. Was Scarlett hiding from them?

She waited until the door clanged shut behind the teenage customers before saying. 'They've gone, Scarlett.'

Scarlett emerged from her under the table hiding spot looking... well, scarlet.

'What's going on?' Leah said, fixing her daughter with knowing, yet hopefully understanding, look. 'Is everything OK?'

'What? It was just my—'

'Scarlett – you were hiding!'

'Yeah,' her daughter admitted, shoulders slumping.

'What's going on? Do you know them from school? Scarlett – are you being bullied?' This would explain, Leah thought, the temper, the locking herself away. The way Scarlett was speaking to her these days – it was classic lashing out due to stress/fear. How had she been so blind... how had...?

'No, I don't know them.'

'Oh.'

'It's you.' Scarlett said flatly.

'Me?'

'I just...' She shrugged a shoulder and began to play with the edges of the macaron. 'Going out with your mum. It's kind of lame.'

'Oh.' It was hard to know what to say. Leah remembered being embarrassed of her mum, occasionally, back in the day. But her mum had been... well, old-fashioned. And Leah was... Leah looked down at her outfit. She'd thought she looked pretty chic.

They finished their pastries in silence, before making their way back to the car.

6

'Mum!'

The shock of Scarlett's sudden yell almost caused Leah to swerve from the road. But there was nothing there – no oncoming vehicle, no animal cowering in front of the car. She looked at her daughter with thinly disguised annoyance.

'What is it, Scarlett!' she snapped. 'I nearly crashed the car.'

'Sorry, Mum,' Scarlett said, her eyes wide. 'I just... it's just I think I saw Dad?'

Nathan? Perhaps he was on his way home too, Leah thought.

'Well, you do know your father lives around here, right?' she said, half mocking, half annoyed. 'He's probably coming back from the *vide-maison* he went to.'

'But he wasn't in his car.'

'Oh?' Still, it wasn't so surprising that Nathan might have stopped at a shop or something on the way home. It was hardly walking around the city centre as he'd claimed, but he was a free man. He could go to the DIY store or delicatessen without getting her permission. 'Well, he's probably...'

'No, Mum. You don't understand,' Scarlett's hand touched her arm. The contact was rare – Scarlett barely ever hugged or even touched her these days – and somehow shocked her. 'He was with a woman. It looked like they were... he had his hand on her shoulder.'

'A woman?' Leah frowned. Again, it was hardly a complete surprise. They knew several people locally, of both sexes. He'd probably bumped into someone and was saying a quick hello. It was just the combination of the tap on her arm and Scarlett's scream made Leah feel a little... odd.

'Yeah, and they were kind of... they looked sort of close, Mum. Like... together close.'

'Oh, don't be silly!' Leah said, far too brightly. 'It'll just be one of the neighbours or something!'

She drove on for a moment, brow furrowed. She couldn't shake the odd feeling – probably the result of the adrenaline rush caused by Scarlett's sudden cry. But perhaps it would be nice to say hello. Ask how he'd got on at the sale.

'Shall we go and say hello?' she said, doing her best not to show her worry on the surface. She reversed in someone's driveway, trying to ignore the barking dog that seemed to be threatening to rip them both to shreds if they so much as opened a door, and began to drive back along the road. More slowly this time.

'Uh-oh, are you checking up on him?' Scarlett said, with a grin that appeared slightly malevolent.

'What?' Leah said, her voice coming out a little more squeakily than she'd expected. 'Of course not! I'm just... But seeing as you noticed him. I want to see if he's managed to pick up some... uh, bananas.'

'Right,' said Scarlett, unconvinced. 'And nothing to do with the woman he had his hands all over.'

'He had his what?'

'Oh, you know what I mean. They just looked, I dunno. Cosy.'

Was this all some elaborate hoax, or was her daughter serious?

'Whereabouts was he?' Leah demanded.

'Mum! He won't—'

'Whereabouts...' she interrupted, fixing her daughter with a stare – as much as she could when driving a car, 'Was. He?'

'Just outside the *tabac*.'

'Right.'

Forgetting there was a speedbump and almost launching the car into the air, Leah drove back up the road they'd just negotiated, eyes scanning for her husband and whoever 'she' was. She was being ridiculous checking up on him like this. It was just... The aftershave, the clean outfits. Popping out and not wanting her to come? But Nathan wasn't like that, surely? He valued their marriage, their family, too much.

She wanted to see for herself what the woman looked like, whether Scarlett's shout out had been one of horror or simply surprise. Whether it was an innocent situation or not. Her heart told her this was ridiculous, but somewhere in her gut, something churned. She'd known something was wrong. Hadn't she?

Within minutes, they'd scanned the whole of the tiny road and turned around. There was a smattering of locals – children with their mums, people walking dogs. A group of schoolkids walking and talking animatedly. But no husband.

Leah tried to breath more slowly. 'Scarlett,' she said, trying to keep her tone as light as possible – although in all honesty, it was probably too late to try to appear nonchalant. 'Are you sure it was your dad?'

'Pretty sure,' Scarlett said. 'Although... I only saw the back of him, mostly. Then I looked back, but it was hard to...'

'So you saw a man with short, brown hair,' she said, trying to keep her voice steady. 'From the *back*?'

'Well, yeah.'

'But you were sure it was your dad?'

Scarlett shrugged, blushing. 'Well, maybe I got it wrong.'

Shaking her head, Leah turned the car around and drove the ten minutes to home. Scarlett was, of course, just being an overdramatic teen. But what about her own behaviour? Turning the car like that, rushing back?

A month ago, if someone had suggested Nathan might be having an affair, she'd have laughed her head off. 'What, with a local farmer?' she'd have howled. 'With one of his precious carrots?' He'd spent most of his time digging over the land, or planting things, digging things up, sourcing manure (and unless he'd met a ravishing donkey owner who offered manure 'with benefits', she was pretty sure she was safe). He'd slobbed around in old jeans and tracksuits, causing her to complain that he could occasionally make more of an effort. He was the last person she'd ever suspect of having an illicit liaison.

But in the last little while, something had definitely shifted. He'd been spending more time on his personal grooming and less time at home. Those trips out. It was nothing, probably. But clearly if her actions in trying to chase him down and confront him outside the *tabac* were to be believed, she was not feeling completely confident about things.

She pulled up in the drive, disappointed that the Scenic still hadn't made an appearance – if Nathan had been home, it would have confirmed once and for all that Scarlett had been mistaken. In silence, they got out of the warm car into the freezing air, already tinged with a wash of grey as the light faded from the day.

'You alright, Mum?' Scarlett said.

'Yes, why wouldn't I be?' she replied, probably a little sharply.

'I dunno,' came the response. Her teen had returned to normal service.

She unlocked the door and let Scarlett rush in ahead of her –

finally accepting, at least inwardly, that a coat would have been a good idea. Then, despite the bitter air, Leah sank down onto the steps and sat, looking over the land that had started as a dream but had begun to feel like a curse.

Most of the rotavated runnels of soil lay barren, with no green shoots yet protruding through the mud to indicate what they'd planted beneath. In the far bed – the one that had started it all – green stalks and shoots stood defiant against the cold, ready to be pulled up. Each one, she'd found, was a little like a lucky dip. Sometimes the crop would be abundant (or at least comparatively abundant). Sometimes there would be a couple of small, apologetic carrots. Sometimes there would be nothing at all.

There was a crunch and the sudden glare of headlights as the Scenic carrying her – probably not errant – husband returned. Nathan got out of the car and looked slightly startled to see her sitting there.

'Everything alright?' he asked.

'Yeah, just thinking.'

He moved to the back of the car and opened the boot, drawing out from its interior an ancient rake and a more modern strimmer. 'Did well at the *vide-maison*,' he said, excitedly.

And she felt herself smile at last.

7

MARCH

Grace had excelled herself.

As Leah entered the room for the first official meeting of 'The Bordeaux Book Club', she almost gasped at how lovely everything looked. Her friend had set out enormous glass goblets for the red wine, even a lace tablecloth for the low table in the centre. A corkscrew lay on the side – one of those old-fashioned ones with just a twist of metal and a wooden handle – and two bottles of red wine sat open and airing alongside.

The rest of them were already there: George, this time dressed in jeans and a generous woollen jumper; Monica, in baggy jeans and a sweatshirt; and Alfie with tracksuit bottoms, a hoodie and enormous, white trainers. Each clutched a copy of *Great Expectations*.

Leah sank gratefully into the armchair proffered by Grace and set her bag by its side. She felt exhausted; she'd been dreaming a lot recently and her sleep had been uncharacteristically fitful. It wasn't even as if she was even dreaming about anything interesting. No deep-buried fantasies and hardly a nightmare. Last night's instalment had featured her packing a picnic, but being unable to find the cool box. It was a boring, mundane, mum dream, yet she'd woken with her heart racing, covered in sweat.

'Alright?' George said, reaching for one of the bottles and pouring her a glass of wine. Leah glanced up at Grace and saw her friend's face was fixed in a strained smile as she watched the audacious move.

'Fine thanks. Cheers,' she said, as she took the glass and sipped from it gratefully. The wine was rich, full-bodied, but more importantly, it slid down well and filled her body with warmth. She felt herself begin to relax. 'Wow, Grace, this wine is lovely!'

'Anyone else need a top-up?' Grace, who'd recovered her equilibrium after George's faux pas, reached for the second bottle. 'It really is a gorgeous blend,' she said. 'Straight from the cellar in *Saint-Émilion*, and one of their finest, I think you'll agree.'

There was a murmur of vague agreement from the rest of them, although it looked as if Alfie, who'd made his way through about three quarters of his, might nod off at any moment.

Leah had been looking forward to this evening – had even found the time to read the book twice. In all honesty, she'd forgotten how much she loved *Great Expectations*. Or perhaps it wasn't that. Perhaps she hadn't loved it as much in the past, but this present version of herself had found something new in the old pages. In the past, she'd rooted for Pip – the small boy who began the book as a poor orphan, cared for by his mean sister, then unexpectedly found himself offered a brand-new life by a mysterious benefactor. She'd loved visualising him go to London and mix with the upper classes. But this time, she'd seen the selfishness in his behaviour. How the moment his fortunes had changed, he'd been happy to reject the man who'd been a father to him and felt ashamed of his lowly roots.

She'd googled a few articles to try to find out how old Pip was meant to be at this point – the answer? Fourteen. It sounded about right. Peak rejection time. No wonder he'd seemed embarrassed of his past. Teenagers.

'So!' said Grace, perching herself on one of the upholstered, wooden chairs.

Leah felt momentarily guilty for sitting in one of the softer, lower armchairs and leaving her host to perch on something less comfortable. Then she realised of course that this was what Grace wanted. She sat tall, at least a couple of foot higher than the rest of them.

A silence settled over them.

'What did we all think?' Grace prompted.

'Yeah, it was good,' said Monica, earning herself a look of disapproval.

'Good?' Grace said, an eyebrow cocked. 'I should say so! Was there anything specific you enjoyed or related to?'

Monica looked at her text. 'I liked the bit in London,' she said. 'You know, when Pip's trying to become a gentleman. Must be hard. Trying to be a new sort of person.'

Grace nodded. 'Yes, I tend to agree. I'm sure Dickens wanted the reader to sympathise with young Pip there.'

'I don't know. I couldn't help but see Pip as selfish,' Leah found herself saying. 'The way he turned his back on everyone and everything he knew – and for what? False friends, high society and strutting around in fancy clothes – just leaving his sister and Joe to rot!'

'But you can't fully blame him,' Monica said. 'The times he lived in... Well, he was kept down by his class. He had to sort of shake people off so that he could properly enter high society.'

They all nodded their agreement.

'His brother-in-law, Joe, is so lovely, though,' Leah said. 'I mean, Pip was looking for something more – more money, or whatever, but the way he treated that man who'd taken him in...' She found herself feeling slightly tearful. What was wrong with her at the moment? She took a large gulp of wine.

'He gets his comeuppance in the end, I suppose,' George said. 'You know, when he finds out that the money came from a criminal not from someone upper class. And Estella as his love interest isn't exactly a recipe for happy ever after – not the best prize for him.'

'Not that a woman could be considered as a possession, of course,' Grace interjected.

George flushed. 'No, not by me anyhow,' he said, hurriedly. 'But...' He waved the book and trailed off.

'They were different times.' Leah nodded.

'What do you think Dickens is trying to tell us in this tale?' Grace prompted. 'That we ought not to trust our instincts? That we ought not to seek better for ourselves lest we fail?'

Leah had not heard Grace use the word 'lest' before. She must really mean business.

'Maybe more to appreciate what we have,' suggested George. 'Like, I know at the start of the book, his sister's a right... um, cow, but he's got Joe. He's got a profession ahead. Then he's taken in by this money...'

'But to be fair,' Monica said, 'he doesn't know the money's not from Miss Havisham, the rich old spinster he meets as a kid. He thought he was going to be a legitimate heir; be welcomed into proper society.'

'Yeah, but Miss Havisham!' George said. 'Who'd want to take money from her? Some screwed up old bint rotting away in her old wedding dress. She only gets away with it because she's got money and status. Can you imagine her these days?'

'Maybe these days, she'd have had a bit of trauma counselling?'

Alfie suggested. 'Like, she's sort of allowed to get in that state after what happens to her – being left on her wedding day – because she's rich and because maybe people didn't understand...' he took a deep breath as if to refuel, '...sickness then. But maybe her money becomes a bit like a cage for her – it, like, traps her. She doesn't have to do anything. Go out to work. Mix with people. So she kind of... rots away?'

Monica looked at Alfie and smiled. 'That's such a good point,' she said. 'Miss Havisham is a bit... weird. But she's not exactly living her best life, right?'

Leah saw one of Grace's 'looks' drift across her features. She assumed it was either the 'whatever' or the 'living her best life' reference. It was the schoolteacher in her, judging their choice of words.

'Yeah, I get that,' said George. 'But Joe is such a great guy – a great dad to Pip. He's kind, he loves Pip, he stands by him through thick and thin. Then, just because he works with his hands, just because they don't have much money, Pip shrugs him off.' He took an enormous gulp of wine as if this had been hard to say. 'There's nothing wrong with working with your hands,' he concluded, causing them all to momentarily glance at his weathered fingers, which looked out of place against the delicate crystal.

He sees himself as Joe, Leah thought. *Because of his work*. But she'd also identified with Joe because he'd been rejected by his surrogate son. She wondered whether the others had identified with anyone. But found herself unable to ask – because if she mentioned anything, she'd have to tell them all about Scarlett's behaviour and how it made her feel. And she felt shy about it, somehow. As if, once she acknowledged it, then it would become a permanent fixture. As if telling everyone how Scarlett was behaving towards her would make them judge her effectiveness as a mother.

'I'm just glad I didn't live then,' Alfie piped up, his voice quiet. 'At least now people have a chance. You know, to make their own fortune. They're not held back by, well... class or whatever. Or if, like, they're a bit poor, it doesn't matter. Not to the way people see them.'

Leah found herself smiling at his innocent take on the world. She wanted to tell him about invisible barriers that still lurked in workplaces and society. Barriers that you can't see until you hit them smack in the face. But she held back – it was nice that this young man had such an optimistic view of life. Or perhaps it was growing up in France. All that fraternity and solidarity. Maybe things would be different here, for Alfie.

An hour later, the books had been set down (or in Alfie's case, dropped to the floor at the side of his chair) and they had moved on to talking about wine, and France, and anything other than a young boy with a mysterious benefactor.

'So, what brought you to France?' Grace was saying to George. Leah noticed her friend's cheeks were flushed – perhaps too much of the *Saint-Émilion*?

'Oh, I'm just here on a temporary visa,' he said. 'Helping a mate with some renos.'

'Renos?'

'Renovations.'

'Oh, of course. And what do you think? Would you be tempted by *la vie en France*?' Grace continued, leaning forward in her chair and rolling her 'r' like a pro. 'Think you might make it permanent?'

'It's alright,' he shrugged. 'I guess people seem pretty chilled round here. And the food's pretty good. Don't know if I could stand living here full time though.'

'Oh.' It was hard to tell whether Grace was disappointed or insulted.

'Not that it's not, like, beautiful and everything,' he said hurriedly. 'I just I think I'd feel a bit weird living here on me tod.' They were all silent for a moment as he realised his second faux pas. 'You know,' he continued, 'some people like living on their own. It's just me... for me, it would be... well, it wouldn't be ideal. But if I did come here, I'd be more likely to do a Leah – plant my own stuff, live the good life. That kind of thing.'

Leah felt herself go red. 'Yeah, it's hard work though,' she said.

'I bet.'

A silence settled over them.

'You know,' Monica piped up. 'I get what you mean – about it being a kind of lonely place. I know I'm here with Bella, and I'm married, so not strictly alone. But Peter's off three, four weeks at a time and I'm rattling around in this enormous apartment. It can be... yeah, it can make you feel weird.' She tilted her glass slightly towards George as if clinking it with his from a distance, then took a sip.

'How is Bella?' Leah asked.

'Yeah, good thanks.'

'And Peter's...?'

'Off flying around the world,' Monica said, with an eyeroll. 'Everyone thinks it's so romantic,' she added after a sip of wine, 'being married to a pilot. And, well... there is the uniform and that,' she glanced away, clearly a little embarrassed. 'But it's a bit shit too when you're stuck at home with a baby who just won't feed.' Her voice broke slightly on the last words and Leah and Grace exchanged a look.

'Oh, it's so, so hard at first,' Leah said, quickly. 'Honestly, it does get easier.'

Monica gave her a grateful, tearful smile. Leah tried to assemble her face into a look of confident reassurance. But she couldn't help but wonder if she'd given her new friend false hope. Things did improve after the baby months. But they went downhill again once teenage hormones were thrown into the mix.

'What about you, Alfie?' asked George, making the young man – who'd been sitting quietly – jump slightly. Leah noticed that the red wine had stained Alfie's lips and given him the look of having applied lipstick in the back of a taxi. She wondered whether she should say anything, but decided against it. The last thing the kid needed was any more reason to feel self-conscious.

She'd been a shy child and teen herself, only really coming into her own in her thirties. Still, on the inside, she felt the reluctance of an introvert – but had found ways to push herself forward. Like a fitness fanatic set on a goal, she forced herself out of her comfort zone hoping that in time, that zone would expand. It had, a little, over the years.

'I've been here since I was about five,' he said. 'Just me and my mum. I can't remember living in England.'

'I bet you're a whiz at the language,' Grace said.

Alfie nodded, flushing. 'I'm OK,' he said.

'And you're still living with...?'

'My mum,' he said. 'Dad's not around.'

Grace nodded, shuffling on her chair in a way that betrayed her discomfort. She took a sip of wine. 'Did I tell you all,' she said, 'that the grapes in this particular vintage were crushed the traditional way? Underfoot?'

George laughed. 'I thought there was a bit of a taste to it,' he said. 'Bit of sweat in the mix, I reckon.' He swilled the wine and gave it a sip. 'Salty.'

The humour did not land well with Grace, although the rest of them giggled. 'It's all very hygienic,' she said, a new edge to her voice.

George grinned. 'Oh yeah, I know,' he said. 'Mind you, it gives a whole new meaning to the idea of a "cheese and wine" evening...'

Another hour, another bottle and they were standing collectively on the front porch waiting to be picked up. Leah had resolved just to have half a glass so she could drive herself home, but had lost her resolve after the first few sips. George – also almost certainly over the limit – had been admonished by Grace when he'd reached for his car keys. 'I'm fine!' he'd argued. 'Just a couple of glasses.'

But she'd insisted, and Leah had been glad. Sometimes it was good to be forthright and unafraid; she might well have let him wobble off to his car, not wanting to upset him. And it might have been disastrous.

Now as they waited for various taxis and lifts, Leah was reminded of standing outside the youth club as a teen, waiting for her mum to turn up and embarrass her and rescue her in equal measure.

Poor Mum. Had she really been old-fashioned, embarrassing back then? Or had Leah, with her enthusiastically adopted nineties style of baggy jeans and those bright-white trainers with the enormous tongues, actually been the problem herself? Looking back on old pictures of herself as a sulky girl in dungarees or double denim, she saw traces of Scarlett. She looked miserable, moody, angry even. But all she remembered about that time in her life was being frightened, paranoid that she wouldn't keep up, that people would laugh at her.

Still, so terrified that she'd pushed away a woman who'd always been by her side, because – why? – her shoes weren't right? Her clothes weren't 'on trend'?

Perhaps there's a little bit of Pip in all of us, she thought.

'So, let me know if you have any problems sourcing the book,' Grace told them, as if they were children and she the teacher in charge.

It had been Monica's choice. She'd told them she'd been

debating all week between a modern murder story that had soared up the charts, and one of her favourites, a pioneering yet classic Gothic novel. 'I think I've decided on *Wuthering Heights*,' she'd said, 'if that's not too old fashioned for anyone.' She'd blushed a little and tucked a strand of silky hair behind her ear.

They'd assured her that of course it was fine, and it would actually be a lot easier to source than something new – especially if they wanted to pick up a second-hand copy. Grace – of course – already had two copies of the text on her shelf. She'd pulled one free, almost sending a pile of badly stacked texts tumbling, and gave it to Alfie. 'Save you the trouble,' she'd said with a smile and he'd taken it gratefully. A couple of books hit the floor and instead of picking them up, Grace had simply kicked them towards the bottom shelf and beamed as Alfie flicked through the text.

'What's it about?' he'd asked, looking at the brooding painting of a black-haired man on the cover.

'It's a love story,' Leah had said. 'One of the most celebrated love stories in literature.'

'OK,' he'd said. 'Sounds like my Mum would like it.'

It was hard to know whether he'd meant this as a slight.

There was the sound of a motor and a white van arrived to pick up George. The bloke driving looked to be about twenty and gave them an enthusiastic wave. They waved back dutifully. Monica was next, getting into a taxi she'd booked on an app. Finally, an old Citroen pulled up and a beautiful young woman with long, brown hair got out. She was wearing skinny jeans and a jumper that while suited to the weather at the top, was cut off entirely to expose her midriff. '*Allez!*' she said to Alfie with a smile. He grinned, said his goodbyes and disappeared into the passenger seat.

'Wow,' Grace muttered just loud enough for Leah to hear. 'Do you think that's his girlfriend?'

Leah looked as the pair gave each other a quick peck in the front seat. 'Maybe,' she said.

'Wonders will never cease,' said her friend, her smile fixed as they waved the little car off.

Then it was just Leah and Grace, shivering on the front porch in the icy air.

8

Back inside Grace's living room, they began to clear the glasses and bring them carefully to the kitchen. 'I'm really sorry,' Leah said, 'Nathan reckons he'll be here in a bit.'

'It's not a problem,' smiled Grace.

Grace stacked everything expertly next to the sink. 'I'll get to it all tomorrow,' she said, although Leah suspected the minute she left, Grace would be shining her glass and returning it to her immaculate dresser. She wondered whether Grace was simply being kind – not wanting her guest to put herself out. Or whether, in reality, she simply didn't trust Leah to handle her expensive goblets without smashing the lot.

Grace was houseproud to say the least. But with good reason – she'd shown Leah pictures of what it had been like when she'd first arrived, and how over the decade and a half since, she'd brought the old house back to life on her own. And it was truly beautiful – home interiors magazine levels of beautiful. Leah loved it, but always felt it threw her own living situation into sharp relief – made her realise just how scruffy their house was.

Leah scrolled through her phone. When she'd called Nathan,

he'd said he'd be able to come and get her 'in a bit' but hadn't been specific about how long that might be. 'I'll text you when I set off,' he'd told her, his voice registering a little annoyance.

She understood. Tomorrow, they'd have to drive back again to collect the car – and really, she should have thought about it before she filled herself with wine. She could have arranged the lift in advance, or booked a taxi home, so it was inconvenient. But Nathan wasn't usually one to mind that sort of thing. Perhaps he was tired, she thought, checking her WhatsApp again and finding it empty of anything new.

'Everything alright?' Grace asked, setting down a cup of mint tea in front of her.

'Thank you,' she said, 'yes, it's all fine. I think Nathan's just... well, a bit busy at the moment.'

Grace seemed to have a similar skill in eyebrow communication as her husband, Leah noted, as her friend's left brow shot up at least an inch into the furrows of her forehead. 'Husbands, eh,' she said, clearly hoping that Leah was going to spill the tea. Metaphorically, at least.

Leah wondered suddenly why she was holding back. Sure, Grace knew everyone, spoke to everyone. But as far as Leah knew, she wasn't a gossip. Only she'd never really spoken about their relationship before to her friend – just superficially, or in a light-hearted way. Perhaps she'd been scared of Grace's judgement. Grace was so fiercely independent that Leah sometimes wondered whether her friend saw giving part of yourself to someone else as a sign of weakness.

'Uh, it's just I think he might be a bit cross with me right now,' she admitted, raising the tea to her lips before realising on impact that it was still too hot for consumption. She set the cup down into its saucer with a clatter.

'Cross?' Grace prompted.

'Well, maybe. Or something like that.' She explained the carrot catastrophe, told her friend how Nathan seemed to want to spend time on his own more than he had in the past. That he kept popping out, mysteriously, and at short notice. She stopped short of mentioning the outfits, the aftershave, the sense that he wasn't being completely honest with her. It was too clichéd, somehow.

In the two weeks that had passed since the *vide-maison*, Nathan had 'popped out' four more times. Which wasn't much at all. But each time, he'd showered first, emerged in stiff jeans or chinos, a neatly ironed T-shirt. And each time, he'd made an excuse as to why Leah shouldn't join him. 'I'm just going for a wander,' he'd say. 'You'd hate it.' Or, 'I'm off to the DIY store – not really your cup of tea.'

He'd been as gentle and affectionate was as usual, but there was a kind of distance about him that she couldn't quite put her finger on. It was possible it was all in her mind – brought on perhaps by Scarlett's 'sighting' of him with some woman. It was possible that she was tired, worried about their finances and rapidly draining savings, or that she felt down because spring was dragging its feet and the weather remained mostly gloomy and wet.

She trusted Nathan, she really did. And if he'd only properly fill in the 'gaps' – answer the questions about what exactly he was up to – she'd feel better. But his vague reassurances were making her paranoid.

'He's probably sulking,' Grace concluded. 'You know how men are.'

'But it can't be the carrots, surely?' she said. 'I mean, that was weeks ago now. It's just... I can't think of anything else that might have upset him!'

'Don't underestimate the impact of the carrot situation,' her friend advised. 'Think about it – he's gone from a pretty amazing job: lots of status, that sort of thing. Now he's running a veg patch. They weren't just carrots. They were his achievement – a symbol of how things were going for him. And you kind of crushed that.'

'Oh,' Leah said, feeling suddenly guilty. She was often a little envious of Nathan, the fact he was living the life they'd dreamed of living – working the garden, trying to build something akin to self-sufficiency – while she still worked online a few shifts a week and had to be stuck to the laptop for set hours. But she hadn't imagined what it must feel like to put all your eggs – or carrots – into one basket, a basket that also held your self-esteem.

'Don't get me wrong,' Grace added, 'it is ridiculous and I'm completely with you – but men, they can be quite needy about these sorts of things.'

'I suppose so.' Leah always tried to take Grace's thoughts on men with a large pinch of salt – or glass of wine.

'Believe me, when Stephen and I were first here, he got in a sulk about paint colours that lasted about three weeks,' Grace confided, in a rare moment of self-revelation. 'He was head of finance in some huge firm in London – not sure if you remember that – and used to being the boss at work. I married his 'home self' – the bit that was left over after a week of bossing his secretaries or the junior solicitors around. He was as laid-back as you like back then. Only – when we got here, I got the whole package – home Stephen and work Stephen – and it was a different story.'

Leah listened interestedly. Despite their knowing each other for three years, Grace had never really opened up about what had broken her relationship up. 'France didn't suit him,' was all she'd ever got out of her. Leah wondered whether it was the wine or her own admissions of 'trouble in paradise' that was driving the conversation.

'Different story?' she prompted, taking a sip from her now cooler tea.

Grace waved a hand. 'Oh, he wanted to be in charge of everything. Before, it had been me when it came to the house stuff. He'd left the colour scheme, curtains, everything to my choice. But when it was all we had – well, he used to get quite disgruntled about it all.'

'Is that why he...' Leah began, pausing and wondering whether she ought to ask at all.

'Left?' Grace said, looking at her pointedly.

'Well, yes. Is it?' she asked, wondering whether couples really split up over paint colours. Or carrot crops. And whether she ought to worry.

'Oh, not entirely. Not really. In the end, he chose being a city hotshot over life with me,' Grace said, shrugging her shoulder as if it was no big deal. But her eyes were moist. 'It's just a blessing we hadn't any children to screw up,' she added, swatting a tear from one eye as if annoyed at its presence.

Leah thought of Scarlett. How she might be if her parents broke up. But she shook the image away. She was just feeling a bit vulnerable at the moment. 'Do you ever...?' she began.

'Miss him?' Grace asked. 'No, not at all. Better off without.' Her voice was firm and the phrase sounded slightly rehearsed.

'What about...?'

'Finding someone else?' Grace finished. 'No, I think I'm better off without another old man to look after.' She took a sip from her tea and fixed her eyes on Leah. 'Seriously, I spent most of my adult life in relationships. And I never really thought what it would be like to be... well, on my own. But I've come to like my own company. Plus, I have Hector. Male cats require far less maintenance than their homo sapien equivalents.'

Leah found herself laughing. 'Hector is definitely that rare thing – a low-maintenance male,' she said, reaching out to stroke the cat who'd settled himself in a neat ball on one of the rattan chairs. She doubted he'd mind how many bags of carrots she bought. Perhaps Grace had a point.

'Indeed, plus I'm not sure what his highness would make of it if a new man came and usurped his position,' Grace told her.

Hector opened one eye and looked at them both with undisguised disdain. They laughed.

The conversation moved on to less personal topics – Grace's involvement with a bake sale, the fact that the weather was bleak for March. But Leah's mind kept returning to Grace's relationship. How she'd chosen to stay in France after Stephen had left. Would she do the same if Nathan left, she wondered? Would she be able to make a life for herself here without him? But she couldn't imagine life without him anywhere, France or not.

'Do you ever think of moving back?' she blurted, just when Grace was telling her about the latest trials and tribulations in the knitting circle.

'Back? To England, you mean?'

'Yes.'

'No. Never. Why?' Grace's sharp, inquisitive eyes fixed on hers and she had to look away.

'I just wonder sometimes whether France... suits me. I mean, it's romantic, isn't it, from a distance. The idea of being self-sufficient, not answering to anyone. But in reality, it's...'

'Bloody hard work?'

Leah laughed. 'Exactly. Bloody hard work.'

Grace shook her head. 'But it doesn't have to be.'

'What do you mean?'

'Well, have you thought whether it's France you're not taking to, or all this "living the good life" stuff,' she said. 'Allotments can be hard taskmasters.'

'True.'

'I know I'm lucky,' Grace said. 'I'm retired now – have my teachers' pension. It's not a full one, but it does me, what with the settlement from Stephen. So I've got... well, things are more flexible for me. But I think I'd be here no matter what.'

Leah nodded.

There was a sound of car on gravel outside and they both instinctively rose to their feet.

'Anyway, I forgot to ask,' said Grace as Nathan knocked on the front door, 'how's that gorgeous daughter of yours?'

'Oh she's... fine,' Leah said, fixing her face into a smile.

'Glad to hear it.'

As they moved – silent now – towards the front door and Leah lifted her coat from the rack, she told herself it wasn't exactly a lie. Scarlett was fine. She wasn't ill. Nothing was demonstrably wrong. Her school grades were OK. She had friends.

It was her demeanour around the house, still angry, sullen, embarrassed at times. Plus, she'd also developed an air of sadness around her. As if she was carrying a secret, or thinking about a personal worry. Try as she might to get her to open up, Leah had got nowhere.

Maybe it was her. Maybe this was the anxiety that people talk about that comes during peri-menopause, she thought as she buttoned up the black, wool coat. Which was more likely? That both her husband and daughter had started being 'off' with her and keeping secrets, or that she had developed a mild case of paranoia and anxiety and was reading things into situations that simply weren't there. She'd have to get her hormone levels checked at her next GP appointment.

Grace opened the door just as Nathan raised his hand to knock again and he almost punched her in the face. They laughed and Nathan looked at her with what seemed to be affection. 'Grace,' he said. 'I take it you've been leading my wife astray again!' He was wearing his work trousers and an old coat, but he'd taken the time to slip off his wellies and sported a bright-white pair of trainers.

'What can I say?' Grace flirted. 'She's easily swayed.'

'Or sway-ing?' he joked. 'Heard the red wine was delicious!'

Grace laughed. 'Well, you know I have impeccable taste.'

The mood shifted as Leah and Nathan turned together to the car. To an outsider, it would be imperceptible, but Leah felt it from the turn of Nathan's shoulder; the fact he walked ahead of her down the path.

'Sorry love,' she said as she followed him to the car. 'I didn't mean to make you come out.'

'No problem. Next time, we'll arrange lifts in advance, though. Save me driving the Clio on the ice,' he said, still friendly but without the sparkle he'd had when talking to Grace. She sensed he was a bit annoyed at the unexpected journey.

'Yeah, sorry,' she said again.

'No harm done.' He led her to the little, white car and opened the door for her. '*Madame*,' he said, giving a little bow. She laughed and slid into the seat gratefully. The car smelled, as usual, of spilled petrol and old crisp packets. She began to wind down the window, then thought better of it. Her nose would soon adjust but someone needed to send Mother Nature a memo, because – temperature wise – spring had definitely not yet sprung.

Nathan made his way around to the driver's side, climbed into his seat, turned the key and moments later they disappeared into the darkness, Grace – still on her front step – waving them away.

9

Grace was freezing by the time she re-entered the hallway, her body shivering as she gratefully felt the warm air hit her. Hector appeared in the doorway of the living room, looking at her with his usual disdain. 'What?' she said to him. 'Like you'd have said anything?'

He padded off into the kitchen and she followed, picking up a glass that somebody – probably George – had left on the hall table. He'd at least put it on her address book to spare the wood, but now there was glistening wine ring on the front of her beloved black leather. She'd clean it tomorrow.

In the kitchen, she opened the fridge and grabbed the can of cat food, filling up Hector's bowl as he gratefully rubbed himself against her legs. 'As men go, Hector, you're not too bad,' she told him, scratching him behind his ears in the way he loved.

Grace hadn't thought much of it when she'd spied Nathan in a café in central Bordeaux the other day. He'd been sitting, chatting animatedly with a woman. She'd almost gone over and said hello, but had been in a hurry and – besides – the pair of them had seemed to be deep in conversation. She'd assumed the woman was a friend, a visitor, a sister, and that Leah would no doubt fill her in on the details when they next met. And for all she knew, the woman could have been someone entirely innocent. But having Leah share her doubts had made her look back and question her memory. Had they been a little too animated? Too close? Had their hands almost touched across the table? She couldn't remember, but what she had noted was the woman was beautiful, young and was wearing an inadvisably short skirt, in her opinion at least.

She tutted to herself as she began to stack the glasses and plates carefully next to the sink; now she was left feeling as if she'd kept something from Leah. But if she'd mentioned it, in that moment when Leah was clearly feeling so vulnerable, her friend might have jumped to all the wrong conclusions. It was probably innocent. It was probably nothing.

She ran warm water into the larger of her two kitchen sinks and added washing up liquid, watching as it foamed in the moving flow. Then took her red-topped scourer – the one appropriate for delicate glass – and began to gently wash the first goblet.

She'd told herself it was nothing with Stephen too. When she'd begun to feel him pull away from her, six months after they'd embraced what was meant to be some sort of long-held dream. He'd been the force behind their move to France. It was he who had found the house, sold her on giving up work and finding a new way to make a living on the continent. And she'd bought into it – giving up her job as a primary teacher and, once they'd arrived, starting to put out feelers for tutoring.

His 'dream' had been to quit his role as head of finance for a corporation in the city, and instead spend time decorating their new home, before starting a business of his own. He hadn't been entirely sure what he wanted to do, but had been in love with the possibilities. 'Don't you see?' he'd told her when first raising the idea, 'That's the whole point. We can do anything we want!'

Their cost of living had plummeted on moving to France – giving them plenty of breathing space. Groceries had been just as expensive – if not more – but the house they'd bought with its five bedrooms and well-converted interior had cost a fraction of the price of their London apartment. They'd had plenty in savings when they'd come across – enough to ease the passage and give them at least a year or more to figure everything out comfortably.

Stephen had had a hankering to renovate a property for years. The apartment they'd lived in, close to Canary Wharf, had been perfect – smooth walls, windows that showcased the city, a kitchen that was so modern, it had taken Grace about a month before she'd dared to use the oven. But he'd often moan that it was 'too modern' and even 'too perfect.' And when he'd told her about his French dream, he'd explained how he felt transforming a property with his bare hands would fulfil a part of him that had lain dormant for so long. 'Dad was an architect,' he'd said. 'Mum still paints – and you know, she could have made it big if she'd known how to market herself. And there's me, slaving away in an office all day. All that creativity, wasted.'

Back then, Grace had looked into his enthusiastic face and whispered, 'Why not?' They were in their forties – still young enough to have the energy for a change. They'd hoped for a baby – still did, despite the odds being stacked against them. But it wasn't happening right now, so why not make the most of the fact they were 'child-free'? They didn't have responsibilities, and they did have skills and energy. She'd never considered moving abroad, but his enthusiasm had carried them both forward.

She closed her eyes momentarily, picturing the day when she'd come back from tutoring – proudly having secured her first pupil in France – to find him sitting at the kitchen table. It had been autumn and the room was gloomy. At first, she hadn't even seen him sitting there, so when she turned on the light, she'd let out a little scream. Then laughed: 'Stephen!' she'd said. 'You'll be the death of me.'

Then he'd told her to sit down.

She'd known instantly that something was wrong and her mind had rushed to the possibility of him being ill, or that someone had died. Heart thundering, she'd dropped her bag and sat down in front of him. 'What?' she'd said. 'What is it, love?'

'I've had enough,' he'd said, and at first she'd assumed he meant of her.

'Why?'

'This place,' he'd gestured to the half-painted kitchen. 'It's killing me, Grace.'

She'd often thought back to his choice of words. *It's killing me.* What he'd really meant, she'd concluded over the years, was that it was too much like hard work. He hadn't been willing to think outside the box, to consider a different way of living over here, with her. He'd simply wanted to throw in the towel when he realised that tiling and painting and all the things he'd assumed he'd be an instant pro at were more difficult than he'd thought.

'What do you mean?' she'd asked at the time.

'I want to move back,' he'd said.

She'd taken a moment before responding. 'We've hardly given it any time! Come on, you're just...'

But he'd shaken his head. 'I've got a job interview, Friday,' he'd said. 'I'm flying back tomorrow. If I get it, they want me to start right away.'

It had felt a little like a punch to the stomach. The casualness of it. And how long had he been feeling like this without telling her? She'd noticed that he hadn't touched a paintbrush for a couple of weeks, but had assumed he was just taking his time, thinking. And she'd concluded that they hadn't come here to rush, to create a perfect home and simply live in it like before; that renovations like theirs took time and care.

But all along it had been something very different.

'But what about us?' she'd said.

He'd reached his hand over then to cover hers. She'd let it sit there, not sure whether to pull hers away from him. 'Of course, I want you to come back with me, love,' he'd said, completely confident that he could turn her life upside down on a whim, then change his mind and that she'd simply follow.

'But,' she'd said, her voice prickling with thinly disguised anger, 'what about what *I* might want?'

His eyebrows had shot up. 'Look, love. I know, I'm being impulsive, I guess. You know me!' he'd grinned – seemingly quite pleased with himself. 'So it hasn't worked out. So what? We can go back to London, start again. You'd get a job easily... you—'

'Stephen,' she'd said firmly. 'I gave up a job I loved for this. I said goodbye to colleagues, friends, kids...'

'I know, and I appreciate—'

'I've started to make inroads here, set up a tutoring business!'

He'd scoffed then. 'What, *one* pupil? I think they'll probably survive.'

That was when she'd withdrawn her hand. 'It's not that, Stephen. I've... well, I want to give this life a chance. I think you should too. It's been, what, six months? And you've discovered you're no good at installing kitchens. So what? We own this beautiful house, in a beautiful place, and if you give it a little more time, you'll find...'

'This job,' he'd said, reaching again for her hand but removing his from the table when she failed to meet him halfway, 'is the opportunity of a lifetime!'

'And what would you call this?' she'd said, gesturing around their half-painted stone kitchen, the garden outside that stretched almost to the horizon.

He'd paused. 'I think...' he said, 'I think it might have been a midlife crisis.'

She'd shaken her head slowly.

'What?' he said.

'I can't.'

'What?'

'I just can't.'

She'd since wondered whether deep down, she'd known that something wasn't right between them. That there wasn't a true balance in their relationship. Whether their infertility and the stress of recent months had driven him further away.

She set a glass down on the drainer and reached for the next. This one – Alfie's – still had wine in it and she poured it down the smaller sink, shaking her head at the waste, before dunking it under the warm, washing-up water.

It hadn't been a love of France that had stopped her simply following Stephen back – although she had since fallen in love with the country. It had been the sudden realisation that in making his decision to quit the life they'd only just started, he had simply assumed she'd follow him wherever he went, whatever he decided. That her life wasn't as important to him as his own.

She'd looked at him, her eyes fixed, firm. 'I want to give this a proper go, Stephen. We've only just arrived. It's beautiful here. We have enough money to live for maybe a couple of years without worrying about getting any sort of work. Why not make the most of it? We're still relatively young. It could be a gap year at worst, and maybe the start of a new life at best.' She'd looked pointedly at him. 'And we don't have to give up on... well, a family. Not yet.'

He'd shaken his head. 'Darling, you don't understand. The interview is with Grayling.'

Grayling was a multi-billion-pound capital fund, inhabiting the top floor of the building Stephen had worked in before. She knew that he'd sometimes dreamed of a job there.

'I do understand,' she'd said softly. 'But can't you see my point of view? After giving all that up – I'd... I just want to see what sort of life we can make out here. Whether it might be better. To properly live it.'

'I just can't,' he'd said. 'I made a mistake, and you know what I'm like. Once I've decided.'

'But I'm your wife!'

'I know.'

'What about *us* deciding? What about... what about me?'

His brow had furrowed. 'Look, if it's money you're worried about, don't be!' he'd said. 'I'll earn enough to support us both, easily...'

'But I gave up my job for this, Stephen. I have to at least...'

He'd snorted. 'What, that thirty grand a year job that was wearing you out?' he'd said. 'Come on, Grace. Seriously? I'm willing to bet it wasn't so hard for you to give that up. And in the unlikely event that we do become parents, you can put your feet up and I'll bring home the bacon.'

And she'd known two things at that moment. That her husband didn't understand her, her passion for teaching that went way beyond the salary; that her husband didn't value either what she did or thought.

She'd taken a breath then looked up at him. 'OK.'

'OK?'

'OK, you go,' she'd said.

'And...'

'And I'm staying here.'

He'd looked astonished. 'Come on, love. Seriously? You living out here on your own? In this place? I don't think so.'

'Why not?'

He'd shaken his head. 'You like your home comforts. You'd be lonely, just for starters,' he'd said. The hand had reached out again but again found hers unwilling to meet it. 'Come on. You'd never have moved here if it wasn't for me,' he'd added. 'This was *my* idea. You just followed.'

She'd felt her cheeks flush.

'You don't belong here any more than I do,' Stephen had said, dismissively.

'How do you know?' she'd said. 'You've insulted my job – which I happened to love. And yes, I did give it up, to come here for you. But I'm perfectly capable of living here without you. I'm perfectly capable of living a decent life here. And I don't think we should give up on this without giving it a proper chance.'

'Love...'

'I'm asking you for six more months,' she'd said, feeling herself flush as she realised what she was about to say.

'I can't. It's Grayling, Grace. I'm not sure you understand...'

'I'm not sure *you* understand,' she'd said, her voice wobbling a little. 'But I'm telling you now. If you love me, you'll stay. You'll give me this little bit of time to try. Because I gave up everything for you and I don't see why I should do it again, just like that. Just because you decide one day that it's not for you.'

'You're just feeling emotional.' Stephen had shaken his head sympathetically.

She'd felt her temper rise. 'I'm just asking for a few months.'

'But...' he'd said. 'It's Grayling.'

'Stephen,' she'd whispered. 'It's Grayling or me. Grayling or us.'

'Well, now you are being hysterical.' His blue eyes had flashed with something close to anger. 'I get it, OK? You've made your point. I've messed up. But don't do this, Grace.'

'Do what?'

'Sabotage my career just to make a point. I'll make it up to you, OK? Whatever you want. A car? Holidays? Just don't be difficult on this. Please.'

When he'd left two days later, she still wasn't sure he understood exactly why she'd refused to come with him. 'Come for the trip,' he'd said. 'I might not even get the job'. But that wasn't the point. She'd realised he hadn't factored in that she was a living, breathing human in her own right, rather than just an extension of him. And she saw that she'd been another check on his list of life goals, rather than an equal.

Grace had cried for a week.

Then she'd got up, brushed herself off. Had her hair done. Gone to a DIY store. Watched YouTube videos on how to paint, how to plaster, how to repurpose furniture.

And within a year, a whole new Grace had come to life. And she wasn't going to follow anyone, ever again.

10

'Do you want me to collect the eggs?' Leah asked Nathan, handing him a cup of tea. Two weeks had passed since her talk with Grace and although he'd popped out a couple of times during the fortnight, her fear about him having an affair had more or less dissipated. It helped that each time he had disappeared, he'd returned with something – a box of treats from the patisserie; some new mugs from the pottery shop – that proved (if proof were needed) that his trips were purely innocent.

'I just need a bit of time out sometimes,' he'd said when she'd questioned him about it. 'You must understand that? Just see a bit of life! Forget about the garden?'

She did. She had the group, her reading, French classes that she attended sporadically. She sometimes went to gardening club with Grace. She was working through *Wuthering Heights* – a book she'd last read aged seventeen and was looking at from a whole new perspective now she was undoubtedly older and possibly wiser (because, really, who did Heathcliff think he was?). She should probably start arranging more activities for herself too – it wasn't healthy for them to simply live at home, working on the land, eating the meagre results of their labours.

It was natural for Nathan to want to carve out a bit of life for himself separate from their family. He'd been slow to learn French, finding it difficult to conjugate his verbs and preferred to work his way through online courses and apps rather than join a group as she had. It meant that in the years they'd lived here, he had become a bit isolated. Really, she ought to be pleased he was getting out and about.

Scarlett hadn't mentioned the fact she'd seen Nathan with a woman since their car screeching dead-end over a month ago, and Leah suspected her daughter had felt embarrassed about her faux pas. She hadn't spoken to her about it since, either; talking to Scarlett was becoming increasingly difficult – her daughter's one-word answers to her cheery questions were deflating at best – and she was on a mission for self-preservation. She stuck to safe topics like, 'What would you like for dinner?' and slightly riskier but necessary questions such as, 'Have you done your homework?'

Nathan straightened up, grimacing as his back gave its habitual spasm, and stuck his fork into the earth. He took the tea and they both watched as the fork started to lean slightly in the soft soil and gently give into gravity until it was prone. 'Know how it feels,' he said, and they both laughed.

Spring had finally made itself known and the air was bright and fresh. Trees were beginning to break out in blossom seemingly overnight, creating a riot of pinks and bright whites. Insects were beginning to buzz in the undergrowth and crickets sometimes chirped into the evening. She loved summer, but spring was her favourite season – because it was on the cusp of everything, as if nature was giving a preview of coming events.

She watched as Nathan sipped his tea, then she made to walk towards the coop.

'Don't be an idiot,' her husband said, taking the basket from her firmly. 'I'll get them.'

'But I ought to...' she began, secretly incredibly relieved that he'd yet again taken on the task. She wasn't sure whether chickens had big enough brains to hold a grudge, but if they did, Gollum had certainly had it in for her since she'd stepped on the bird's tail. The angry chicken seemed to eye Leah through the wire whenever she got close, with barely disguised hatred.

Leah felt stupid, of course, to be afraid of a bunch of hens. It was ridiculous, really, that she felt so relieved whenever Nathan brought the basket of eggs to her and she knew that the job was over for the day. Then as the time to collect or change straw or feed their poultry approached, she began to feel apprehensive. She'd overcome it, she'd decided. But there was no rush.

She smiled as she watched Nathan stride across the garden, basket in hand, like a conquering hero. He opened the door without hesitation and the chickens scattered in his wake. Even Gollum seemed to look at her owner with a degree of respect. Moments later, he was back, four eggs in the basket. She handed back the rest of his tea. 'Thank you,' she said.

'At your service, ma'am.'

She laughed. 'You know what, you're pretty sexy for a farmer,' she quipped. 'My hero.'

He laughed again and grabbed her around the waist. She felt the electric charge of it – how long had it been since they'd touched? They were so exhausted sometimes from digging, or battling Scarlett, or chicken attacks, that they fell into bed and virtually passed out each night. She wrapped her arms around him in return. 'Love you,' she said.

'You too,' he said, leaning in and giving her a soft kiss on the lips. Then he straightened up, grimacing again. 'Going to try for some potatoes,' he said, picking up his fork and looking at her, his eyes suddenly uncertain.

She felt a frisson of unexpected anxiety. 'That's lovely,' she said. 'I can make frittatas.'

'Yum.'

'Or, as they'll probably be sma— um, *new*,' she added carefully, 'maybe with a bit of salad?'

'Perfect.' He turned to walk towards the potato bed.

'But,' she gabbled, 'you know, if there aren't many. Or well, *any*, it really doesn't matter. I can... well, I'm enjoying omelettes so much. They seem to suit the weather, don't you think?'

He mumbled something, but continued to walk purposefully to the back of the garden where the large, green leaves protruding from the earth had doubled in size in the past fortnight. In all honesty, Leah was keen to leave them longer – to ensure sufficient growth. But Nathan had a penchant for new potatoes and was probably hoping to find a crop of small, white, fresh specimens to steam and have with butter.

She watched him, her heart racing (who knew digging up potatoes could be such a white-knuckle experience?) before turning and carrying the eggs carefully up the garden and into the kitchen. She set the basket on the side and looked at the straw and poo-flecked eggs. You weren't meant to wash them until just before use – it removed some sort of protective coating and let bacteria in, according to Google – but she failed to see how much protection a bit of poop on the shell could give.

She boiled the kettle and picked up her discarded copy of *Wuthering Heights*. Strange, how she'd loved the hero, Heathcliff, so much first time round. She'd remembered him as dark, brooding, lovelorn and passionate. 'But he's a bully,' she said to herself turning the page and feeling almost sick at his threats against the girl he'd married, Isabella. How she'd found anything attractive about this strange man-baby with his endless quest for revenge and power, she wasn't quite sure.

'How can you fall for that man?' she thought as she read Cathy's words. 'How can—'

At that moment, Nathan came into the kitchen, brandishing a huge bunch of potato stalks. At their end wobbled ten or twelve tiny potatoes. 'Look!' he said. 'Looks like we'll be dining in style after all.'

It was so great that he was developing more of a sense of humour about it. She'd been quite worried when the whole carrot-astrophe had happened. It was par for the course, as far as she understood, for early potato crops to be rather meagre. And meagre was the word, she thought, looking at the potatoes still being held aloft by her grinning husband.

'Oh love,' she said, laughing. 'You know what they say, size doesn't matter, eh!'

'What?' he said, his face registering confusion at what was a fairly obvious joke.

'Don't worry, we can always freeze some if there are leftovers!' she quipped again.

He looked at the dangling potatoes as if she was making a serious point. 'I don't think...' he began.

'Do you mind if I take a pic?' she said, picking up her phone and abandoning the devilish Heathcliff next to the cutlery drawer. 'It'll be hilarious on Facebook.'

Nathan's face went rather pale.

'Are you OK?' she asked, snapping the picture quickly then moving to take the bunch of potatoes from him. She'd make a little potato salad or something. They could show Scarlett and have a good giggle about it. Then next time, hopefully, the crop would be bigger.

It was their third year of growing and they'd had a few

triumphs. But more often and not, their crops had been on the sparse side. They'd learned a lot about when to water and when not to. About hosepipe bans and water butts. About natural fertiliser and the sort of plants that just won't grow in their clay-rich soil. Yet still, they were not close to anything resembling self-sufficiency. Sometimes she'd wake up, her heart thundering, wondering what they'd do if they never managed to nail the gardening thing.

So it was nice to laugh, to take a break from worry and turn disaster on its head.

As she reached for the bunch, Nathan moved his arm higher, pulling them out of reach.

'Nathan!' she laughed. 'Come on! I'm going to have to work like a trojan to get those all prepped for lunch!'

Her husband looked at her, the potatoes still out of reach.

'Do you think we should invite the neighbours to help us finish it all?' she added, jumping a little, because obviously he was playing some sort of game. Her hand grazed the side of the stalks but she failed to grab one. 'Nathan! Come on. Stop being an idiot.'

In a sudden move that made her jump, Nathan slammed the potatoes down on the breakfast bar, scattering crumbs of earth and leaves and crushing one of the tiny potatoes in the process. 'That's what you think I am, isn't it?' he said, in a dark tone that made her look at him with surprise.

'What?' she said, uncertain now.

'You think I'm an idiot.'

'Don't be silly – I was just. You were holding them... so...' she said, unable to read his facial expression and slightly confused.

'Not that,' he snapped. 'Taking the piss out of me, my potatoes.'

'But...' she looked again at the tiny vegetables. Had she missed something?

'I was happy,' he said, the 'happy' coming out in almost a sob.

'For the first time in what – months? – we'd got enough to make a meal. And all you can do is laugh at me.'

'Enough for a...' she looked at the potatoes doubtfully.

'See!' he said. 'This is what I mean! You're meant to be supporting me in this. And what are you doing instead? Taking pictures so you can laugh at me with your friends on Facebook. I suppose...' he said, drawing himself up. 'I suppose you're going to get some potatoes from the *supermarket* now.'

He was so very angry. So angry that it was hard not to let the corners of her mouth turn up with a mix of incredulity and surprise. 'Nathan, I thought you were... you said dining in style. I thought you were... I thought you were joking,' she said.

'Oh, sorry if I can't meet all of your potato needs,' he said, sarcastically. 'There are twelve of them there! Twelve! That's, well, four each!'

Four potatoes did sound like a lot, she reasoned, until you looked at their size. Had he really thought she'd be pleased – proud? She felt suddenly guilty. 'I'm sorry, I just...' she said. 'I misread the tone, is all.'

He sank onto a bar stool. 'Yes, but don't you see,' he said, 'you revealed what you really think. You think my growing is pathetic. You think I am pathetic.'

'Hey!' she wheeled around and cupped his face in her hands, forcing him to look at her. 'I do not think you are pathetic, Nathan. I'm sorry. You're right. Four potatoes each is quite... something.'

He looked at her. 'Do you realise,' he said, 'how emasculating it is to have my wife mock my potatoes?'

Sometimes she wondered whether her mouth was being controlled by her at all. Because honestly, why would she smile at a time like this? But her lips seemed fixed on the idea of stretching out despite her trying to keep a straight face.

He pushed her hands away. 'Maybe if you believed in me more, I'd be better at it,' he said.

'Oh, come on!' she was annoyed now. 'Nathan, you're not being rational.'

'So, now I'm mad as well?' he questioned.

'Let me make you a cup of tea,' she suggested. 'We can talk about it.'

'No,' he said. 'I'm going out for a bit.'

'Again? You only went out yesterday... You...'

'Well,' he said, getting majestically to his feet. 'Someone has to buy potatoes, I guess.' He made to put his hand in his pocket, perhaps to check for money, but managed to knock the basket of eggs with his elbow. They both watched, transfixed, as the rounded basket base rocked on the wood, gaining momentum until it tipped, spilling its contents messily onto the floor.

'And I suppose that's my fault too, is it?' he demanded.

It was. But she thought it was better not to say anything. 'Look, I'm sorry,' she said instead. 'I'm sorry if I upset you.'

He shook his head. 'You didn't upset me. You just showed me the truth. That you don't believe in this. In what we're doing.'

'I do...' she felt her voice waver. Did she? She had to admit that after three years in France, she'd begun to wonder whether they hadn't made a giant mistake in thinking they could make do – even make a living! – off their own land. She was scared of the chickens, reluctant to get any other animals. If she was honest, she didn't even like carrots that much.

But she had to be positive about it; it meant so much to Nathan that they live this life.

Nathan looked at her, shaking his head slowly as if he'd just caught her out in a terrible lie. 'Well, thanks,' he said, backing from the room. 'Thanks for your faith in me.'

Moments later, the car revved up and he was gone.

Wiping the eggs from the floor with a cloth, feeling their gooey stickiness against her fingers and trying not to retch, Leah still didn't feel entirely sure what had just happened. She looked at her copy of *Wuthering Heights* – unlike Heathcliff, Nathan (thankfully) wasn't prone to outbursts. So why this? Why now?

And where exactly had he raced off to when things had gone wrong?

She sent him a text saying simply:

Hope you're OK.

She stopped herself from apologising because, honestly, she hadn't really done anything wrong. They'd talk later; it would be OK.

In a bid to get her mind off it all, she made a coffee and took it and her book out to one of the wrought-iron chairs they'd bought and intended to paint. Looking over the sun-drenched back garden and the fields beyond, she felt a sudden sense of peace wash over her. All was virtually silent, save for the chittering of birds and the odd car crawling past on the road outside. It was still early, but there was a warmth in the sunlight as it played on her skin and promised a lovely day ahead. She had some free hours before her copywriting shift began later this afternoon, and she was going to make the most of them.

If she'd looked up at that moment, she'd have seen Scarlett's face at the window, her features concerned, looking down at her mum sitting alone in the garden, the hole in the earth where the potatoes had been, and the abandoned fork left by her father lying forlornly on the earth.

11

APRIL

Leah slid the Scenic into the space with such ease that she wished someone had been filming it for posterity. Usually, when faced with a parallel parking situation, she chickened out – especially if there were other cars waiting. But having seen a space so close to Rue Notre Dame, she knew she at least had to try. And she'd surprised herself, thinking through the manoeuvre as carefully as a seventeen-year-old on their test, and somehow recapturing skills that had long lain dormant.

It must be a good sign, she decided.

When Alfie had emailed the group asking if they could meet in a café instead of at his home – 'my mum's a bit poorly today' – she'd been a little relieved. It meant that wine would be off the menu, and coffee (and hopefully some sort of cake) would be on. She'd enjoyed the wine last time, but hadn't wanted to ask Nathan to come to pick her up after the group had finished.

Not that anything was awry with her and Nathan. After their potato argument, he'd returned and apologised. 'I just... it felt a bit like a slap in the face,' he'd said and she'd accepted his apology. She hadn't admonished him for roaring off in the car, or for the four hours he'd spent incommunicado. She was just relieved he was OK.

At least she'd been able to distract herself by racing through the last of *Wuthering Heights*, sitting in the garden and enjoying the spring sunshine while he'd been out. She'd just been turning the final couple of pages as the car had crawled guiltily back into its usual place on their drive, so when Nathan had seen her, had been wiping a couple of tears away.

'Oh, love,' he'd said, wrongly assuming she was crying with relief at his return. 'I'm sorry.'

She hadn't corrected him.

They'd settled back into their usual groove. Nathan had even sheepishly given her a gift – a bag of potatoes from the market. And she'd used the surplus eggs they still had from previous collections to make the frittatas after all (much to Scarlett's horror: 'Eggs! Again! Why can't we eat something normal?').

Still, despite the fact she'd cleared up the actual broken eggs, she felt a little as if she was walking on eggshells around Nathan. She didn't want to upset him again if he was feeling vulnerable, and this meant she was barely able to talk about the garden, vegetables or even the chickens (sadly their three main topics of conversation these days) without carefully considering what she said and whether it was appropriate to make a joke. And she hadn't been able to raise the subject of his frequent, fragrant trips out.

She wasn't quite sure how she felt about being kept at arms' length like this. It was healthy, though, wasn't it, to spend a bit of time apart? She just wished he could do it without exuding that weird air of mystery.

'You would tell me, wouldn't you, if there was anything wrong?' she'd asked him a couple of days ago when he'd appeared in a crisp, white shirt, smelling of soap and aftershave. And he'd laughed and told her this was what came of reading too many romance novels.

She hadn't the energy to explain that *Wuthering Heights* was a complex love story – a classic! But she'd felt a little offended that he'd mocked her new hobby.

Perhaps this latest novel was her equivalent of freshly pulled potato crop – jokes about her reading felt too close to home.

Wuthering Heights reminds me of a freshly pulled but ultimately disappointing potato crop, she imagined saying to Grace, and smiled to herself. Perhaps not.

Now, as she locked the car and began to walk towards the road where Alfie's chosen café was situated, she tried to banish thoughts of her marriage and the latest disagreement with her teenage daughter (who'd asked to have her phone with her at night and was outraged at being denied) from her mind.

Despite living on the outskirts of one of the most beautiful cities in France, she didn't make it into the centre as often as she ought to. She'd been along Rue Notre Dame before once or twice, when they'd first arrived and been exploring, but now any shopping expeditions she made were purposeful – she'd seek out large chain stores or out of town shopping areas rather than strolling through the older quarters, taking the time to appreciate the architecture and history.

Perhaps Nathan was right. Perhaps she ought to do this more often too.

Because it was truly beautiful. She took her time, allowing the April sun to caress her skin, and smiling at passers-by as they made their way past, holding bags inscribed with shop insignia, or clutching cameras, or camera phones, and snapping pictures of some of the quirkier shops or of the church that rose majestically above all of them.

The cafés and restaurants had set tables outside and most of them were taken, the punters making the most of the weather. There was a buzz of conversation in the air – she caught snippets of French words she recognised, the odd sentence in English spoken in an American or British accent. And she felt energy course through her as she breathed in the city at its best.

One of the reasons they'd moved close to Bordeaux had been her love for the city she'd first visited in her teens. How ridiculous that the place was practically on her doorstep, she rarely visited in a meaningful way. Life had become hectic, but when she looked at it objectively, perhaps she had made it that way. It would be easy to carve out time – Saturday mornings, Tuesday afternoons, maybe the odd evening – to spend properly soaking up the sights and sounds and atmosphere. Especially now Scarlett was older and would be more than happy to be left home alone. *And there was always Gollum to ward off any would-be intruders*, Leah thought to herself with a smile.

She was so deep in thought that she missed Alfie's chosen venue altogether, emerging from the end of Notre Dame and finding herself in an unfamiliar street which was peppered with graffiti. She turned and made her way back, searching properly this time, until she found it: *L'intemiporal* – meaning timeless. She wondered whether Alfie had chosen the café for its name or whether it was just one he knew or was fond of.

She pushed open the door, walked in and was instantly bathed in the scent of fresh coffee. The space was light and bright, with an eclectic mix of round and rectangular tables, dotted with seats in a range of different designs. The walls were painted a bright cream and there were several large watercolours showing local scenes. The whole place was buzzing with life and she felt herself react to the bustling energy in the air – it was infectious, somehow, and made her feel more positive almost immediately.

The group was easy to spot – they'd pushed two round tables

together, making an awkward figure eight, and had clearly stolen chairs from one of the other tables, which sat empty of customer seating. Alfie looked up and gave her a smile, before saying something to the group who all looked up in turn. The table was a mess of books and coffee cups and Leah had to check her watch to make sure she wasn't terribly late.

'Sorry,' she said, as she approached, noting to her relief that most of the cups were full.

'No problem m'dear,' Grace said, pushing out the spare chair for her to sit on. 'We've only just got here. And poor Monica had to rescue George on the way – he was at the café three doors down!'

George grinned. 'Got a bit lost and panicked,' he admitted. 'Seriously, there are about five cafés on this one street!'

'You know you're in France, right?' Leah joked, putting her bag down on the floor beside the chair and slipping gratefully in it. 'It's obligatory to be in easy reach of a café at all times.'

They exchanged small talk for a few minutes – Leah ordering a coffee and buying Alfie another orange juice. George had been working on fitting a stained-glass window in the property he was renovating. 'My mate designed it himself,' he said proudly, passing around a phone. 'Beautiful, ain't it.'

Monica looked much happier than when they'd last seen her. Peter was apparently back on a fortnight's leave and had taken Bella last night so that she could finally get some sleep. 'Honestly,' she said. 'I can't believe that a couple of years ago, I used to pull all-nighters. Now my favourite pastime is literally passing out.'

'It'll pass,' said Grace, unintentionally creating a bit of word-play that made them all groan. 'Well?' she said, clearly not having thought about what she'd said. 'It will!'

'If you need a hand, anytime, you can always ask,' Leah found herself saying. 'I know we don't know each other that well, but I'd love to help if you need it.' It would be nice, she thought, to spend time with Bella – a little girl who almost certainly wouldn't scowl at her every word.

Grace opened her mouth as if to echo Leah's offer, but closed it again.

Monica flushed a little. 'Thank you,' she said to Leah. 'That means a lot.'

'And if you want to get out *sans bébé*, then pop over to mine for a coffee anytime,' Grace added at last.

Grace then regaled them with a tale from art club about a session where they'd elected to draw a pet. 'I invited them to mine, of course. But do you think Hector would play ball? Damn cat sits perfectly still most of the time, so I thought he'd be ideal. But no. Suddenly, he is the most playful, bouncy pussycat you've ever seen. We had to abandon it entirely!'

When asked how things were in her world, Leah decided to simply say they'd been fine and 'working on the garden'. She realised that, other than the potato argument, they hadn't had anything interesting happen to them this month. Was that a good thing? Interesting times, anecdote-generating moments, were often the most difficult ones. Perhaps things were just ticking along fine, and that was why she had nothing to report. But it felt a little odd, just to nod and say, 'Yeah, not bad thanks,' when asked about her month.

Finally, they got onto the matter in hand. 'So,' said Grace, taking charge, 'what did we all make of the wonderful *Wuthering Heights*?'

'Oh, I loved it,' Monica began. 'The gorgeous descriptions – the undying love. And Heathcliff,' she rolled her eyes in a mock-swoon. 'It's all just so romantic! That level of love, passion. It's just...'

'But it's not really a love story, is it?' Alfie piped up. They all looked at him.

'Surely it's the *definitive* love story?' Grace said. 'The sense of eternal longing between Cathy and Heathcliff. Yes, it's not a happy ending; but surely the love is there?'

'It's just...' Alfie said. 'I was expecting... Everyone says it's a love story, don't they? Everyone says Heathcliff is this romantic character. But, well, does anyone else feel he's a bit of an arsehole?' He blushed, looking at Grace. 'Sorry,' he said. 'A—hole.'

'Heathcliff is the epitome of a romantic lead!' Grace cried, almost as if mortally offended by his words. 'He embodies that raw passion, the wildness of the moors, the natural...'

'But he's a bully,' Alfie said, simply. 'He's a bully and he's an abuser – and I know he's had a pretty awful childhood, but that doesn't excuse how he behaves later on.'

Grace shook her head, almost fondly, at Alfie. 'But surely it's his love for Cathy that drives him? And yes, he's a bit... well, violent-tempered, I'll give you that. But it's the violence of love that compels him! He doesn't give up when the going gets tough.'

'Violence of love?' George interjected, his tone scoffing.

They looked at him.

'Sorry,' he said, going red, 'didn't mean it to sound that way. It's just... well, I agree with Alfie that this Heathcliff bloke is a bully. You know, you read stuff in the papers. About abusers and that. And there's always, like, an excuse – like he was "so in love", or "driven by passion", or whatever. But that ain't an excuse now and it shouldn't have been then.'

Leah nodded. 'I sort of agree,' she said, looking sideways at Grace. 'I know, I loved Heathcliff when I read it the first time. But this time, being a bit older... I *hated* him. The way he treats poor Isabella! Throwing that knife at her. Oh, and her poor dog!'

'I know what you mean,' Monica said. 'But there's something about him, don't you think?'

'I suppose women always like a bad boy,' quipped Grace.

'Yeah, but there's a bad boy and there's Heathcliff,' said George. 'He's not some rebel on a motorbike. He's evil, if you ask me. Poor kid had a tough start in life. So, I suppose it's not his fault, or whatever, completely. But he's... Put it this way, if he walked into this café, I'd give him a piece of my mind.'

It was such an absurd comment that Leah laughed. George looked up, caught her eye and joined in. 'Sorry,' he said. 'I realise that's pretty unlikely.'

'Because he's fictional?' Leah said.

'Fictional and dead.'

'Yeah, makes it a pretty empty threat.'

They all laughed.

'Still, what is it that women see in a bad guy?' George continued. 'In real life, I mean. Like, my last girlfriend left me, and said it was because I was "too nice". That's one of the reasons I came out here actually, to forget about all of it. But it keeps coming back – like, how can someone be *too nice*?'

Everyone was quiet for a moment.

'Sorry,' he added. 'Bit off topic there.'

'It's OK,' Alfie said. 'I get what you mean. Nice guys finish last, they say, don't they?' He pushed his glasses up his nose and gave George a slight nod of solidarity, nice guy to nice guy.

'Well, more fool the women who fall for men like Heathcliff, I suppose,' Grace said. 'Myself included. But then I always did have the most appalling taste in men. My ex-husband was a case in point. Perhaps I need to re-read the book with new eyes.'

Another silence.

'Mind you, you can see why people single Heathcliff out as the romantic lead. The other male characters aren't exactly inspiring,' Leah said, supportively. 'I mean, they're not cruel bullies. But they're... well, pretty unappealing, all said. No real "book boyfriend" potential.'

'But, like, there has to be a middle-ground between weak blokes like Edgar and bastards like Heathcliff, right?' George questioned, thoughtfully.

'Well,' Monica said, 'Someone with Heathcliff's looks and passion but Edgar's kindness. I'd probably date him!'

They all laughed.

'What about the women in the book, though?' Leah said. 'I know they're all kind of trapped by the expectations of society at the time. Cathy can't marry Heathcliff because she needs to find someone with the right status for example. But at the same time, I think the women have sort of power over the men, don't you?'

'Agreed,' Grace said. 'Kind of a manipulative power – but maybe that's all that was available to them in those times.'

They broke off as a waiter came to offer another round of coffees.

'Didn't half have a hangover after the last meet,' George admitted. 'I had to plaster a wall the next day and it weren't my best work, to say the least.'

'Still, it was nice,' Leah said, loyally, nodding at Grace. 'Such gorgeous wine.'

'Oh, yeah,' George said. 'Brilliant. Great choice.' Clearly, he was beginning to learn how to handle things with Grace.

'Yeah, sorry about not having any this time,' Alfie said. 'You know I wanted to have it at mine. It's just my mum...'

'Oh, I'm sure no criticism was intended!' Grace assured him. 'This is lovely. I don't actually visit the city often enough!'

'And there'll be plenty of wine at my place next time,' Monica added with a smile. 'Coffee too,' she added hurriedly.

'Maybe we ought to get back to the book?' Grace said, seeming more like herself again. 'What about the moors – all that delicious symbolism. The beautiful description, their wildness.'

'Yes, I love the wildness of them,' Monica said. 'The way they make Wuthering Heights – the house, that is – seem dangerous and ghostly from the start. It makes me shiver.'

'Reminded me a bit of this place,' George said, and they all looked at him slightly askance. He laughed. 'Sorry I don't mean Bordeaux, obviously. But the place I'm working on, it's kind of set back in the countryside, on its own. It's not a grand house or anything – just an ordinary farmhouse. But it's that feeling of being isolated. You don't get that in England, not that I've found anyway. Everything's more spaced out here, isn't it? You can feel properly alone here.'

Grace was nodding, looking at him with interest. 'Are you staying in the property?' she asked. 'It can be hard to be away from... well, humans, even with all their flaws.'

He shook his head. 'Nah,' he said. 'I thought I would at first – it was September when I came and I'd been living in Manchester and it was like, wow – peace and quiet, and sunshine and everything looked amazing. But then the winter...' He shuddered. 'It was bloody – sorry Grace – blummin' freezing. And it gave me the creeps being there. A couple of the other lads are still staying there, but I'm renting somewhere in town. Might go back in the summer.'

Leah nodded. 'Sounds like you made a good decision.'

'Not that I was doing a Heathcliff or anything and losing my mind,' he said. 'And so far no ghosts knocking at the windows, so...' he lifted both hands slightly so they could see his crossed fingers and they all laughed.

Grace smiled. 'Doing a Heathcliff,' she said. 'I love it.' She meant it too – George might not have the turn of phrase of a literary critic – but he was insightful to say the least. She thought about Stephen, how he'd turned his nose up at anything new, never wanted to join in with her interests. It was nice to see a guy like George get stuck into a text, however out of his depth he claimed to feel.

'I think we've all done a Heathcliff from time to time,' Leah said. 'I mean, not at his extreme, but... well, losing the plot a bit.'

There was an awkward silence.

'Maybe just me then?' Leah joked, and they all laughed.

'I couldn't help think about the loneliness in the book,' Monica said quietly. 'Like, with Heathcliff, he has people around him. But the only person he wants is Cathy – it doesn't even matter to him whether it's her ghost. He just wants to be near her. I get that. The idea of feeling alone, you know, despite everything. I guess it shows that loneliness can come from within.' She trailed off.

Leah looked at her. 'Are you OK?' she said.

Monica flushed. 'Yeah. Sorry,' she said. 'Just tired – despite the extra sleep. And Peter's doing a three-weeker next time. Not looking forward to that.'

They all made sympathetic noises. 'But don't worry!' she said brightly, 'no ghostly hands through the window yet for me either.'

'It's weird,' Alfie said, out of nowhere. They all swivelled to look at him and he flushed. 'Sorry,' he said. 'I didn't mean... not you Monica or anything. I was just thinking how this book was written – what – two hundred years ago? Well, almost. And it's about this orphan and his adoptive sister kind of falling in love. Which is pretty, well, unusual. And the property, and the things that happen – Heathcliff going mad. All of that.'

'Yes?' Monica prompted gently.

'It's just...' he looked at Grace. 'Like you said about classic books being relevant now and I didn't know what you meant, but I suppose we've all found something in *Wuthering Heights* that, like, spoke to us. A bit anyway.' He took a sip of his orange juice and sat back, exhausted, seemingly, from the enormous input.

Leah nodded. 'Yeah,' she said. 'It is weird.'

They all murmured. 'Well, talking of classics,' Grace said, 'I think it's Leah's turn to choose the next book, am I right?'

They all looked at Leah expectantly. She coloured – she'd been set to mention a contemporary book about a midlife woman having a 'hilarious' (according to the critics) breakdown. But with all the talk of classics, she suddenly felt inadequate. 'Um...' she said hesitantly.

Alfie's phone, placed in front of him on the table, began to buzz excitedly. He picked it up. 'Yeah?' he said. 'Oh, hi Mum...'

Grace looked at Leah and raised an eyebrow.

'Yeah, no, don't worry. No, I'll come home now. Yeah, sorry,' he glanced at his watch, 'I didn't realise. Yeah, I reckon about twenty minutes. No... yeah. OK, love you.' He hung up and looked at the group. 'I've got to go,' he said, standing up. 'That was my mum, so...'

'Of course,' Grace said generously, officially releasing him from any obligation. 'I'll email you details of the next book.'

'Yeah, mate. Say hi to Mummy for me,' George said, with a wicked grin.

Alfie went red.

'Ignore him,' Leah said. 'I think it's sweet.'

This didn't seem to make Alfie feel any better. 'You know...' he began, taking a step forward, then, 'Never mind.'

'See you next time, Alfie,' Monica said.

He nodded, once, to affirm and then turned and walked quickly out of the café. Once on the street, he started to run.

12

They sat in silence for a minute, the dynamic slightly broken by Alfie's hasty exit. 'Shall we grab another coffee?' Grace said. 'Or do you have to get off too?'

Leah checked her watch. It was only half past six. It was nice to have arranged the group for an afternoon instead of an evening for once – it gave them more flexibility on time. 'I think I could manage another,' she said. The rest of them agreed and Grace duly got up, taking their empties on a tray.

'That kid,' George said, sitting forward slightly in his chair. 'You know, he seems so... but the minute his mum calls, he's like...'

'I know,' said Leah. 'You do wonder whether... I suppose when British kids are brought up somewhere else, without wider family, well, maybe he's been a bit cut off. Maybe he's a bit... reliant on his mum?'

'Yeah, or she's reliant on him,' George suggested. 'Either way, you've got to worry if it's healthy.'

'How old do you think he is?' Leah mused.

'Nineteen, twenty, maybe?'

'Yeah, I think so too. He seems a bit... I mean, I love that he's joined us, and he really seems to enjoy the books. But you have to wonder...'

'Why he wants to hang out with us oldies?' George said, with a grin. 'Yeah, I thought that. I asked him, actually.'

'You didn't!'

'Yeah, guilty! Just a bit of bantz though, not... I wasn't horrible to the kid or anything. I just said – we were having a piss... sorry... pee, and I said I was surprised he wanted to come and spend time with a load of middle-aged bores.'

'Speak for yourself!' Leah said, in a tone of mock-offense.

George laughed.

'What did he say?' Monica asked, leaning forward in her chair.

'He said it was his mum's idea,' George said.

It was hard not to laugh. 'Oh, bless him,' Leah said. 'Still, there's nothing wrong with being a mummy's boy, I suppose.' She thought about Scarlett. How would her own daughter react if Leah suggested something? Or if Leah phoned out of the blue and asked her to come home? She was pretty sure Scarlett would ignore her completely on both counts.

Scarlett seemed to prefer spending time with anyone other than Leah these days. It was probably considered healthy and natural, this breaking away from her adult influences and finding her own identity and all of the other things the parenting books said. But it would still be nice to feel as if she mattered. Leah would see her daughter, sometimes, with a couple of friends, laughing away and wonder why the smiles always seemed to disappear whenever she appeared.

Grace returned with a tray of wobbling coffees. 'Hope it's not too late for all this caffeine,' she said. 'I probably should be on tea really.'

'Ah, you'll be alright,' George said, reaching for his latte. 'When in France and all that.'

They lapsed into silence as each of them personalised their drinks with sugar, stirred, sat back in the comfy chairs that surrounded the low table and sipped.

'So, what brought you to France?' George said to the group. 'Like, I know why Monica's here – with Peter being a pilot and that. But what about you, Grace?' he said, sitting forward and smiling at her with genuine interest.

Grace flushed slightly – a startlingly rare occurrence – and cleared her throat. 'I suppose I have to say my errant husband,' she said. 'Long divorced now.' She looked at her hand as if to confirm the absence of a wedding ring. 'But it feels sort of disingenuous to say that, really.'

'How so?'

'Well,' she said. 'Not disingenuous to *him*. Disingenuous to France, well, and to myself, I suppose. It was his idea to come, but he never really settled. And, yes, I... perhaps initially, I stayed to prove him wrong. To show him that I could make a good life here.' She shrugged, clearly a bit uncomfortable. 'But I've come to love the place. So, I suppose I feel that yes, I came here for him. But I *stayed* for me – nothing to do with him at all. No credit to Stephen.' She lifted her coffee as if in a toast.

Leah nodded, reaching out a hand and giving her friend's arm a small squeeze. 'Well, you've certainly showed him,' she said. 'You have such a full life here.'

George was silent for a minute, his eyes fixed on Grace. 'Alright George?' Leah asked him, and watched him jump slightly as if startled.

Grace shifted slightly in her chair. 'And, of course, Leah's here to live the good life!' she said, deflecting everyone's attention onto her friend.

Now it was Leah's turn to feel a little uncomfortable. 'Not exactly "the good life",' she said. 'Just... a better one. I mean, a better one for *us*,' she added in case anyone thought she'd had some sort of religious conversion or had become a missionary or something. 'We were slaves to our mortgage and jobs over there and we wanted... I suppose we wanted to try something different.'

George was nodding. 'I get that,' he said.

'Only now,' Leah said, with a half-smile, 'it's not quite working out the way I'd hoped.'

'Trouble in paradise?' Grace quipped, looking at her much more pointedly than was comfortable.

Leah felt flustered. 'Not paradise, exactly,' she said. 'At least Adam and Eve managed to grow an apple. We can't even manage a serving of potatoes.'

They laughed and made sympathetic noises as she told them about their latest crop, leaving out the argument attached to it. 'And until we manage to grow serious amounts, I'm stuck doing copywriting shifts three or four days a week. It's better than our life in the UK, but I feel... it's like I'm not fully *here*.'

'So, you regret it?' George said. 'Grass wasn't greener in the end.'

'Oh, no, I don't regret coming!' Leah said, shaking her head emphatically. 'Not moving here. Definitely not. Maybe I regret being a bit unrealistic about what growing our own stuff and being self-sufficient might mean, though. There are only so many ways you can create an egg-based meal!'

'Have you told Nathan this?' Grace asked her.

'No. He's... well, he's a bit sensitive about it all. Like, *his garden*. And he wants it all to work so badly, I just can't,' she admitted. 'No. We'll find a way to get things established,' she added, picking up her coffee and sipping as if to end the subject. 'How's Bella?' she asked Monica once she'd swallowed.

'Oh great, thanks,' Monica said. 'Smiling and laughing all the time now.'

'That's so sweet.'

There was silence for a minute. Grace placed her cup back on its saucer with a clink. 'Oh of course!' she said, changing the subject. 'We were just about to hear about next month's book.' She looked at Leah expectantly.

'Oh yes...' Leah thought again of the brand-new hardback that had arrived yesterday. The delicious smell of new pages, the idea of diving into something she really fancied reading. But then they'd all been talking about classics, and now she was here, it seemed a bit odd to foist something blatantly aimed at midlife women onto Alfie. 'I thought maybe... *Pride and Prejudice*. You know, to continue our theme of "classics",' she added hurriedly, choosing a failsafe she knew would at least please Grace.

Grace nodded. 'You didn't fancy something more... modern in the end?' she asked, recalling something Leah had said to her recently about ordering a new book.

'Well, I did,' she said. 'But then I thought, well, *Pride and Prejudice* is one of the books that sort of inspired me to come to France.' They were all silent in their confusion. 'I know,' she said, 'a book about quintessential British society inspiring a move to the continent. But it was the pace of life, the countryside. The idea of having land, space. I wanted that. A simpler existence. Strolling in the gardens...'

'And the possibility of a half-naked man in a clingy white shirt swimming in a lake?' George said, with a grin.

'Well, a girl's gotta dream,' she quipped in return.

They all laughed.

'OK, *Pride and Prejudice* it is,' Grace said. 'I'll let Alfie know.'

'And can you check he's OK, too?' Monica said. 'He looked a bit... odd when he left.'

'Probably just embarrassed,' said Grace. 'The last thing you want as a young bloke is a call from your mum.'

'Then they pass, and it's all you want,' George said, looking suddenly melancholy. 'Sorry,' he said, seeing their eyes on him. 'Mum died last year. Ah, she was old, it was time. All the things. But you know.'

They nodded. They knew.

Minutes later, they exited the café with its low conversation and the sounds of clinking and hissing from behind the counter, and emerged into the early-evening air. It was bright but had an edge of coolness to it, reminding them that summer was still a distant dream. Leah pulled her cardigan on and grinned at them all. 'Good group,' she said.

'Yes, good group,' Monica echoed. 'Really enjoyed it.'

'See you all next time?'

They nodded.

Monica said her goodbyes and crossed the road, disappearing down the alleyway that led to the next street, and Leah turned to make her way back to her expertly parked car. 'Bye,' she called to George and Grace, who remained standing together, talking about one of the other groups Grace ran.

'It's gardening, mostly,' Grace was saying, 'but they're a lovely bunch of people...'

Leah wondered whether George's comments about being alone had activated Grace's tendency to get involved. George would probably find himself signed up for a week's worth of events if he wasn't careful. She smiled, shaking her head gently to herself. Grace's heart was more or less in the right place, but she was definitely 'A Lot' sometimes.

Moments later, Leah reached the curve in the road just a few metres from where her car was parked and looked back along the street, with its vintage shops and buzzing atmosphere.

By the café, she could just about make out George and Grace, half-hidden by tourists and local shoppers, still talking animatedly.

13

To: Grace, George, Leah, Monica
From: Alfie
Subject: Sorry

Hi Everyone,

Sorry I had to rush off last night. Bit of a crisis at home, but all's good now! Hope the rest of the group went well. Let me know the next book and I'll get it ordered. Looking forward to seeing you all next month. Alfie.

To: Alfie
From: Grace
Subject: Re: Sorry

Hello Alfie,

Nice to hear from you. Don't worry about rushing off. Hope everything is OK.

Leah has chosen *Pride and Prejudice* for the next meeting. Don't forget to think about your own book choice in a couple of months! I've got a spare copy of the text if you want it? Let me know.

Monica's hosting – she'll send the address through to you soon.

Best,
Grace

To: Alfie
From: George
Subject: Re: Sorry

No worries, mate.
See you next time.

To: Alfie
From: Leah
Subject: Re: Sorry

Hi Alfie,
No probs. Hope your mum's OK?
Leah. x

To: Alfie
From: Monica
Subject: Re: Sorry

Hi Alfie,
Don't worry at all. It was great hearing your thoughts on *Wuthering Heights*. You really made me think!
Lots of love,
Monica

Monica sat back in her chair and took a sip of decaf. Outside the enormous, ornate window of the apartment building, she could hear the buzz of the city as it came to life: voices and car engines, the occasional sound as someone leant on their horn. When Peter had said they were moving to Bordeaux, she'd told him straight-away that she wanted to be right in the heart of things. Having lived in London all her life, she had grown up feeling she was at the centre of the world. She wanted theatres, shops, restaurants, parks and more than anything else: people. She'd loved seeing Grace's house – it was pretty, and not particularly cut off. But she'd have hated the evenings, the nights in that location. Too much silence had always made her feel uncomfortable.

She set down her cup on its delicate saucer and looked around the immaculate kitchen. 'It's perfect,' Peter had said when he'd told her he'd found an apartment for them. 'Old, historical Bordeaux on the outside, all the mod-cons on the inside.' When he'd shown her the pictures, she'd squealed.

Despite the building being a couple of hundred years old, inside it was newly renovated to what the estate agent had called a 'high spec' – polished, wooden floors, bright-white walls. White, gloss kitchen cupboards that reflected the light. Counter tops made of white marble, with a patina that sparkled like diamonds. 'We'll start off renting,' Peter had enthused, 'get settled. But the landlord's up for an offer if we decide to buy.'

As usual, she'd trusted him. Had relied on the photos he'd shown her on his phone. And, just as he'd hoped, she'd absolutely loved the place when they'd first arrived – that feeling of being in the centre, yet in their own private enclave all at once. The bath, which bubbled and frothed on demand and was so big, she could almost have swum in it. The balcony, with its polished tile and teak table that looked over the street, was both private and in the heart of things at once.

Three bedrooms – one, the master, with fitted wardrobes and en suite, another, smaller room with a double bed where friends could stay. And the final one, a smaller room, still with the same wooden floor and white walls, where the cot would go.

'It's beautiful,' she'd said, and she'd meant it too. And she'd put her hand to her stomach and felt Bella somersault and kick her approval.

They'd barely brought a thing over with them. Peter's contract was for three years initially, then they'd decide on whether to stay or go. The flat in London was sitting empty, full of the debris of their old life. The clutter that Monica had longed to clear out but never had the energy for; the souvenirs and trinkets they'd acquired from when they'd gone travelling a decade ago. A lifetime ago. It would be silly to bring it with them and clutter their perfect new life with relics from the past.

This would be the new her, she'd thought, when they'd arrived and she'd felt the space around her, the cool, calmness of the newly renovated apartment that made her feel peaceful. Throwing open the shutters and stepping onto the balcony, despite the cold, she'd imagined the spring to come when she'd have a baby in her arms and would feel part of the community that thronged below.

Monica wished she could recapture that feeling now. Next to her, the baby monitor lit up slightly as Bella stirred, but settled again. Later, they could go for a walk, she decided. It would be nice to pass people who smiled and said *bonjour*, to sit in a café and sip a cool glass of juice with her baby at her side.

At least, they'd probably go. She looked down at herself and her new uniform of jogging bottoms and baggy T-shirt. Somehow, the immaculate apartment made her feel even more unkempt and shabby. Her old clothes didn't fit, and she hadn't the energy to order new ones or even make an effort. She didn't recognise who she had become.

Sometimes Monica would think back to the woman she was before they'd tried to conceive – so certain about her desire for motherhood, so sure that she'd be a pro at it. Now, when she looked at Bella's trusting little face, she sometimes wanted to cry. Because she simply wasn't up to the job. She loved her baby, but at times, she felt a resentment building inside. There wasn't a moment's peace: a moment to herself. She missed the woman she'd used to be, but couldn't see a way back. And no matter how hard Monica tried, she never felt as if she was doing a good enough job for her daughter.

Right now, too, she was painfully aware of being alone. She'd already spoken to Peter on the phone today, and Mum. She'd sent her emails, scrolled through social media. She'd connected with the people she had in her life. And in Bordeaux, she only had the group – but she just didn't feel she knew them well enough yet to call any of them or ask to meet up.

She stood up, stretching, walked to the floor-length windows and opened them wide, then carefully pinned them back, before looking out over the sun-drenched street below.

Suddenly, she was no longer alone. There were people moving purposefully or meandering along. Mothers with pushchairs, couples hand-in-hand, important-looking men and women dressed in office clothes. Tourists taking photos of the architecture. She sometimes wondered if she appeared in any of these photos – a little stranger on a balcony, a faceless figure in the background of people's holiday snaps.

Moving back to the kitchen table, she sat again at her laptop and tapped her fingers briefly on the table's marbled surface, before typing in the name of a bookstore and ordering a copy of *Pride and Prejudice*. She'd never read it, but had watched the film a couple of times. Maybe the book would be different, more engaging. It had always seemed a little odd for her why people romanticised it – all those women pursuing men for their money: their only option to better themselves. To her, it just made her feel frustrated that the women had had to marry well or be damned.

Of course, she had married well, she reflected. Peter came from a family with money – had had the kind of childhood she couldn't imagine, where everything was paid for and nobody worried whether they'd be able to pay the electricity bill.

But it had been Peter's easy charm, his sense of humour and the way he loved her so completely that had drawn her in. Not the money.

Her own childhood had been fine – her parents both had jobs with the council and she'd never wanted for anything. But when she spoke to Peter about the house she'd used to live in, the perfectly good state school she'd attended, and the fact that she'd had a paper round when she was thirteen, it was as if to him she'd lived some sort of Dickensian, deprived existence. 'Well,' he'd said when they'd been together a few weeks, 'you'll never have to worry about money again.'

She never really had. Money had been tight on occasion but had always come along.

She'd left home at twenty-one and secured a good job as a trainee in an accountancy firm, drawing a good salary and renting an apartment in Brixton with friends. 'You live above a shop?' Peter had said when she'd first taken him home. He was incredulous. 'How do you manage?'

His own apartment, when she'd made it back there a couple of days later, was breathtaking. The sort of place that exuded luxury, with lifts and polished marble halls and security cameras. 'It's not much,' Peter had said, 'but it's home.'

She'd never been sure whether he'd been joking.

She'd been pregnant when Peter had landed the job last summer – 'it's based at Bordeaux airport,' he'd told her. 'Obviously,

I could commute from almost anywhere – no harm having to travel a bit for work. But wouldn't it be exciting to live there for a bit, bring this little one up in style?'

She'd known his new position would involve some time away – Peter was often away in his current role with a London-based airline. But she had just assumed that she'd manage as well as she did in London. She was used to being alone, enjoyed it to a certain extent. And it kept their relationship fresh – that first reunion after a three-week stint felt magical every time.

The first time he'd gone away after they'd moved, she'd spent time wandering the shops, picking up baby clothes and things for the nursery. Her mother had come to stay, fussing over her bump and making her put her feet up. The time had flown by.

The second – just a month before her due date – had felt a little fraught. Mum had been busy at home and planning to come after the baby was born. And Monica had realised as if for the first time that although she was at the heart of things location-wise, she didn't yet know anyone in the city. She'd crammed a bit of rudimentary tourist French, could handle herself in a café or restaurant, but had no idea how to make connections with the couple who lived on the ground floor of their building, or the old lady who lived on the floor below. They were all smiles and *bonjours* and friendly greetings – often enquiring about her baby and its due date. But nothing further – how could there be, when they could only really communicate in a combination of mime, smiles, gestures and broken English?

After Bella had arrived, life had filled up. But now Peter was away – this time for four weeks – she felt the emptiness of the apartment settle around her again. The white cupboards, the white walls, the whiteness of everything made the place feel like a hotel. And opening the windows and looking at the scurrying life below didn't mitigate the feeling of loneliness, as she'd hoped, but exacerbated it. She was watching life throng below her, but was cut off from it entirely.

She hadn't yet told Peter how she felt. Didn't know how to.

'He's working so hard,' she'd say to her mum on the phone. 'And it's only a few years! And my French is getting better.'

'But I worry about you, love,' her mum had said. 'All your friends are here. Your sister, our family.'

'I know, Mum,' she'd said, trying not to let the fact she was crying show in her voice. 'But its only for a few years. And if we stay, well, I'll be settled in by then. And I have Bella,' she'd added.

Friends had come and stayed – for long weekends or, in one case, a fortnight. Together, they'd done the tourist things – looked around the cathedral, wandered the boutiques. Each time, she'd felt like a salesperson, showing the best of her life, without admitting the worst. They'd gasp at the apartment, express jealousy at her balcony view, enthuse about the cafés and architecture and coo over Bella. And for a little while, she'd bask in it – feel happy, tell herself that they were right; that she was indeed, living the dream.

And then they'd go, and it would be her, her baby and the white walls again.

She'd started to seek out other English speakers and, when Peter had sent her the ad for the book group, had decided to give it a go – hoped perhaps it would be the answer. But, so far, she'd felt a little out of place in the group – she wasn't sure whether Grace liked her, she always seemed a little closed off. Leah seemed OK, as did George. And Alfie was sweet. But none of them were real friends, not yet.

She'd come to realise that the life that had felt so simple in London had also come about slowly. She'd moved there knowing only two people, but she'd been in her twenties then – that time of life where everyone goes out, everyone wants to meet others. There had been endless possibilities to find new friends, join new groups.

Not in the forced way she had to now, but naturally. People would stick to each other like sprinkles on ice-cream as they bowled along enjoying the ride. They'd go to clubs, bars, concerts, festivals. Their group had grown as more and more acquaintances joined in or popped round to the flat. Then Peter, the wedding – she'd felt absolutely surrounded by love in the midst of their 200 guests.

Then suddenly, it seemed, she was here. And starting again. But this time, she was in a different phase of life – the kind where you have children and meet up with others who have kids. Or maybe chat to other mums in the park. You find your tribe.

Only she'd left her potential tribe behind in London.

Bella stirred again, breaking Monica's train of thought. She picked up the baby monitor and moved towards the nursery.

It was for the best. It wouldn't do her any good at all to wallow. Besides, Peter would be back in a short while and, when he next left, she'd have hosting the group to look forward to. She'd already bought the wine – Peter had advised her on that – and the bottles were set into the ornate rack between the built-in cupboards. She knew already that everyone would exclaim over the flat – everyone always did.

But she felt no real sense of ownership, of pride at having a beautiful home. She'd loved Grace's house – the way it was filled with Grace, somehow. Her personality shining out from each and every painting, every colour choice, every ornament. But at the back of her mind, she'd known what Peter would think of it. He liked clean lines, modern fittings. Hated mess. Would have been appalled to learn that Hector slept on Grace's bed. Monica smiled; she loved Peter and would laugh at his obsession with cleanliness. She wondered how obsessive he'd be about it if he actually had to do any cleaning himself. Growing up, his family had had a housekeeper. She'd laughed out loud when he'd told

her, assuming he was joking, then stopping as she saw his face
register confusion.

In some ways, she envied Peter's upbringing – saw how the
money had smoothed his passage, insulated him from difficulties.
But sometimes she wondered whether having money insulated
you from life too. Stopped you from understanding other people as
much as you might. She remembered Peter's face when he'd first
seen her childhood home. How out of place he'd looked in the red-
brick semi.

But he couldn't see the life that had happened in those relatively modest rooms – the memories of family sing-songs at Christmas, of she and her sister dancing around in their night-dresses
before going to bed. He couldn't appreciate the times when she'd
sat up late with her Dad as he explained her homework to her
patiently, until she'd understood. The photos of their holidays to
Dorset and Cornwall didn't do the memories justice – she'd seen
his expression as he'd taken in her windswept, messy hair and ice-
cream-covered face in the album. But he couldn't feel the whip of
salty air on skin, the sand-between-the-toes gloriousness of a
family holiday that might not have all the mod-cons but was absolutely perfect in its own way.

She peeped into the nursery, almost hoping that Bella would
be awake. But her baby lay, still sleeping.

Moving back to the table with her open laptop, she sat, pulled
up a website of her favourite clothing brand and idly clicked. The
white jeans and flimsy summer tops she'd used to favour felt a
world away from what she wore now. She'd lost most of the baby
weight, but her body had changed – her hips were wider, her waist
wasn't as defined. She'd have to visit a store to try things on. But
everything was too difficult at the moment with Bella. Even getting
her ready to go out was a nightmare. She couldn't imagine trying to
do anything other than wander with the little girl squalling in her

pram. Besides, the thought of standing in a brightly lit changing room and having to disrobe in front of an unforgiving mirror was more than a little off-putting.

Before she could browse any further, Bella's hungry cries pierced the air and she went to switch on the bottle warmer.

She looked at the clock. It was still only seven in the morning. The day stretched away in a way that should have been luxurious. But to her, time had become a menace – something standing in between her and Peter, her and her next interaction. Her and the next group meeting, with the closest thing she had to friends.

She picked up the lukewarm bottle and made her way to the nursery. 'Shh, Bella. Mummy's coming.' Her little girl continued to wail, but stopped when Monica leaned over her cot. She set the milk down and reached for the warm, wriggling body – surprised, as she seemed to be each time – at Bella's lightness, her fragility. The baby clung to her and she felt a shiver of recognition. Setting her baby into the crook of her arm, Monica lowered herself into the leather nursing chair and manoeuvred the teat into her baby's desperate mouth. Then she sank back as Bella slurped and gasped, listening to her baby's tiny noises and, from the open kitchen window, the muffled sounds of life passing by below.

'I'm sorry, chick,' she said to her tiny, pink bundle. 'I'll try to be a better mum. I promise.'

14

Leah knocked cautiously on Scarlett's bedroom door.

She'd put off this moment for an hour, telling herself she ought to keep reading in order to get through the rest of *Pride and Prejudice* by the end of the week. It was the middle of April and May's meet-up was just around the corner. A meeting per month, a book per month, had seemed eminently doable when they'd arranged it, but it was odd how quickly the meetings seemed to come around.

Then again, if she was honest, she had also been pleased to delay having to knock on Scarlett's door.

The problem was not knowing exactly which Scarlett would lie on the other side. The pleasant version (almost the Scarlett she'd used to be during childhood) or the other version (a hardened teenager looking at her with disdain). The two personalities could switch in a heartbeat.

Leah ought to be above all of this, of course, she thought to herself. Whatever she was experiencing on the outside must pale in comparison to what Scarlett was going through with her ups and downs and mood swings. She'd read enough books now to know that Scarlett's brain wasn't fully developed, that she'd think about things differently from Leah, that it was natural for her to want to 'break away' from her mother. She'd even read that she should take it as a compliment that she was the one who was often the target of her outbursts. Apparently, this meant Leah was Scarlett's 'trusted person': Scarlett knew Leah loved her unconditionally and felt safe being... well, *mean* to her.

Whenever she finished a chapter of yet another parenting book, or reflected on what she'd read, or sat in the evening half-watching TV and thought about the day just passed, she felt a well of sympathy for her daughter and would resolve to take it on the chin and see it for what it was.

Yet whenever she approached her daughter's room, she felt trepidation – a bit like she'd felt at school when approaching a group of more popular girls. A little bit sick, a little bit cowed and – occasionally – scared.

She shook herself. It really was time to grow up.

'What?' came the response from the other side.

She peered around the gap. 'I was just wondering if you could give me a hand,' she said. 'I wanted to sow some broccoli while your dad's out. Surprise him.'

'With broccoli?' Scarlett was incredulous.

'Just getting it done for him,' Leah said. 'So when he comes home, he doesn't have to work for once.'

'Where is he anyway?'

Now it was Leah's turn to snap. 'He's just out for... well, he's gone out for a bit to clear his head. And I thought we could...'

'Nah. I don't feel like it.' Scarlett remained on the bed, phone in hand, her eyes on the screen as if her life depended on it.

'Scarlett! Nobody feels like it. But sometimes you have to get on and do it anyway!' she said. 'It's a lovely day; it'll do you good to get some fresh air.' She felt the echo of her mother in her own voice – was she really that person now?

'Maybe in a bit,' her daughter said, still looking at the phone.

'But Dad's out *now*,' she said, trying to keep as much frustration out of her voice as possible. 'And I just thought it might cheer him up to find we'd done something for him. I think he's getting a bit frustrated with the garden. Things aren't... well...'

Scarlett tore her eyes away from the phone and fixed them on her mother. 'Why don't you just get the stuff from the shop like normal people then?' she asked.

Leah felt her body prickle with heat. She tried to keep her temper in check. She was being tested, but she was the adult here. She ought to be setting a good example. 'Because, growing vegetables – our own stuff – is healthier,' she said. 'And we're eventually going to sell them. Money doesn't grow on trees, you know.' There she was again, her own mother channelling the old adages through her.

'Money doesn't grow in our garden either,' Scarlett said, looking back at the phone.

Leah didn't know whether to be proud of the clever comeback, annoyed at the insult, or irritated that her daughter had pretty much hit the nail on the head. Surely, by now, they ought to be harvesting crops to sell at the markets as they'd planned? She thought of their shrinking bank balance. Well, giving up simply wasn't an option. This was Nathan's dream – just seeing how dispirited he was whenever a crop failed should be enough to drive her forward.

Don't lose it her mind urged. *She doesn't mean it.* 'Scarlett, for heaven's sake, put the phone down and look at me.'

Her daughter slowly lowered the phone to the side of her and fixed her eyes on her mother. Leah regretted asking for what turned out to be a death stare that seemed to penetrate her very core. *She's just a fourteen-year-old girl,* she told herself, *pull yourself together*.

It was something about loving her so much, she thought. Something about still seeing the little girl inside who'd used to leap into her arms and demand cuddles, for whom the prospect of spending a day with Leah would be enough to make her squeal with delight. She'd known Scarlett would grow up, but hadn't expected her to push her away so much.

'Yes?' Scarlett prompted.

'It doesn't matter what you think about our vegetable garden or whether you think we're on a highway to nothing,' she said firmly. 'I've asked you for some help. It's Saturday. You're sitting on your bed. You have the time. Just do it, will you?'

Her daughter rolled her eyes and swung her legs around. 'I don't even like broccoli,' she said.

'That's not the point! That...' Leah took a breath. 'Well, never mind,' she said in a calmer, more cheery voice. 'It's good for you – for us all – and I just want to do something nice for your Dad. He seems a bit—'

'Absent?' Scarlett suggested, meanly.

'Scarlett! Not absent. I was going to say, "down in the dumps",' she said.

'Depressed.'

'No, not depressed. Look, I didn't come for medical advice on your dad. I just want you to help me with this planting,' she said, folding her arms. Was Nathan depressed? She wondered. How were you supposed to tell? He seemed OK most of the time. She was pretty sure he was just common – or garden – 'fed up', rather than anything more serious.

'Er, are you coming then?' Suddenly, Scarlett had teleported to Leah's side.

Leah jumped. She'd been lost for a moment in thought. 'Oh,' she said, surprised that she'd actually succeeded and trying not to show it. 'Yes. Good.'

Outside, the morning still had the edge of freshness that
seemed to herald each April day. The prepared beds stretched
before them in neat runnels. Leah set her fork in the earth then
bent down to the little seedlings nestling in their individual plastic
squares. 'You need to plant them quite a distance apart,' she said.
'Twelve to eighteen inches, apparently.' She hoped the plants
would make the most of the space and actually produce
something.

Scarlett was looking out over the fields, lost in thought. Or
ignoring her. It was hard to tell.

'Scarlett!' she said abruptly, and her daughter jumped. She felt
a swell of guilt at the sharpness of her tone. Her daughter had
simply been taking in the view – and it was nice to see her appreciate the beauty of where they lived. 'Sorry, but you didn't seem to
be listening,' she added.

'Just thinking,' her daughter said. The edge of malice had gone
from her voice and suddenly, it was as if the younger version of
Scarlett was there with her, having broken through the surly teen
and fought off whatever hormones had her in their grasp.

It was weird, but in these moments where she saw glimpses of
Scarlett inside the teenager, Leah hardly dared breathe. She
wanted her to stay. Connect with her. Be her daughter again. 'What
about?' she said, trying to keep her tone light. She snapped off one
of the little pots of seedlings and passed it to her daughter, then
began to dig a small hole the plant could be slipped into.

'Dad.'

Leah paused. 'Dad? What about him?' Something inside her
seemed to sink.

'Well, where does he keep going?' her daughter said.

Leah relaxed back on her haunches. 'He's just taking a bit more
time out. A bit of time for himself. I think the gardening, being at
the house all the time... It's taking its toll, and he's kind of – you

know – getting a bit of headspace,' she said, trying to sound confident and convinced.

'Really?' Scarlett's fingers worried the side of the plastic pot. 'Because it just seems...'

'Seems what?' It was getting harder not to snap and Leah felt something rise up inside her. A kind of sick feeling, although she wasn't going to vomit. Just the cold, clammy dread that sometimes comes before you are sick, but without the churning in her stomach to back it up.

'Well,' Scarlett cracked the side of the pot, and held the little plant in her hands. She made no move to bend and put it in the hole that Leah had now dug for it. 'Doesn't he want to take time out with *us*?'

'No!' Leah snapped. Then, 'No, I think he needs to... well, a bit of time out of all of it,' she said, hearing the words and feeling a little bit worse. 'It's just... I think he feels like a bit of a failure,' she admitted.

'Because of the carrots?' Scarlett said, looking at her.

Leah couldn't help but smile. 'Not just the carrots. Maybe all of it. That's why I want to do this for him. Because we're a team. And I want him to remember that.' Out of the corner of her eye, she eyed the chicken coop. Several of the birds were scratching around, pecking at the earth. Gollum stood close to the hexagonal wire, looking at her. She ought to collect the eggs, really. Maybe later, though.

Scarlett scuffed the earth with her trainer.

'Careful!' Leah said, noticing their bright whiteness for the first time. 'You should be wearing your boots really, Scarlett. Those will get ruined.'

Her daughter ignored her. 'Mum' she said. 'Do you ever think about the other week.'

'The other week?'

'Yeah, you know. Dad with that woman. Did you ask him about it?'

'Scarlett!' Leah said, trying to laugh. 'That was ages ago! And it wasn't even him... we don't think. Besides, he is allowed to talk to women, you know.'

Her daughter was silent. 'OK,' she said. She bent down and put the plant slightly lopsidedly into the hole in the earth.

Leah decided not to criticise the half-hearted planting and instead slightly righted the little seeding as she packed the edges with compost. 'Why?' she pressed, unable to help herself. 'Are you worried, love?'

Scarlett shrugged. 'Not really.'

'Because your Dad loves us.'

'Yeah, I know.'

'And he'd never do... anything like that,' Leah said, wishing she felt more certain. Yet again, this morning, Nathan had disappeared. Yet again, he'd smelled of aftershave. Yet again, he'd said he'd rather be alone. Should she be pushing him more – asking exactly where he was going? But, no. He was entitled to a bit of privacy and she had no real reason to doubt him. Not really.

'Yeah,' said Scarlett, picking up another plant and watching Leah as she dug another hole.

'Do you want to do some digging too?' Leah said, holding out another trowel. 'It'll take us ages like this.'

Her daughter bristled at the criticism. 'Alright!' she said. 'You don't need to go on about it.' And in that moment, the recognisable, original Scarlett who'd appeared inside the new teen version seemed to vanish. 'Maybe that's why Dad goes out all the time,' she said, hacking at the earth with her trowel. 'You're always moaning at him too.'

'Scarlett!' Leah felt her face go red. 'I am not always moaning at your dad.'

Scarlett shrugged. Leah wondered if there were websites out there that advised teenagers how to really hit the mark with their snarky comments. Was she always moaning at Nathan? She didn't think so. She'd ask him about the garden, help him with things. Remind him about jobs. Practical stuff.

'Whatever,' her daughter said, driving the point home as she squashed another seeding into its freshly dug grave.

'Scarlett! Careful with those!'

'See!' her daughter stood up, all self-righteous anger. 'You ask me to come and help but it's never good enough, is it.'

'I just don't want you to...' Leah gestured at the poor, squashed seedling, its tiny leaves practically reduced to nothing.

'Yeah, but it's not all about what you want, Mum!' Scarlett declared.

Leah wanted to say that she didn't make the bloody rules when it came to gardening, she just googled them and followed the instructions. But she managed to keep the words in. 'It's not what I want,' she said. 'It's just... well, you've squashed the poor thing, is all.'

'Oh, sorry to squash your precious plant.'

'You know that's not what I mean. I just want them to grow.'

'Yeah, well, maybe if you worried less about pathetic plants and more about your husband, he'd be here instead of going off all the time,' Scarlett said.

'Scarlett!'

'What? It's true! You're so boring, Mum. You're either moaning about the garden, or you're reading books. You never notice me, or Dad. We're just... You don't care about us!'

'That is so unfair.'

'Is it?' Scarlett said, her face flushed. 'Well, maybe I don't want to stand around here and be moaned at all the time.'

'Oh, come on, I only said...'

But Scarlett had now reached peak self-righteousness. 'Forget it!' she said, flinging down her trowel and stomping back into the house.

Leah was left in the early-morning sun, with a bed stretching away and an enormous number of seedlings yet to be planted. She could do it herself. It might even be more pleasant just to work quietly.

But her mind was chattering. Did Scarlett really think Nathan might be tired of her? That Leah ignored them both? Or was she just finding weapons she knew would hurt Leah the most?

Was Scarlett hurting? Did she need her mum more? Was Leah being distant with her daughter? She thought about her reluctance to knock on Scarlett's bedroom door. Had she been avoiding her?

Or had Scarlett simply managed to manipulate the situation so that she got what she wanted – a morning sitting on her bed while Leah worked alone in the garden?

Either way, the argument had stirred something in Leah. Something she'd been half-ignoring. Where was Nathan going? And why was he being so evasive about it all?

15

The café was bustling with life, despite the fact it was a weekday morning. Leah felt it wash over her as she was absorbed into the interior. Thoughts of Scarlett and Nathan seemed to melt away as she walked across the tiled floor towards her friend in the corner.

She'd surprised herself by calling Grace, suggesting they meet up for a coffee. She was almost always the invitee, rather than the inviter, when it came to their friendship. Mainly because she sometimes found her friend a bit exhausting. Yet when she'd needed to get out, Grace had agreed immediately.

Leah had made an effort today – swapping her usual jeans for a smarter pair of linen trousers and a white, sleeveless top. She'd kept her hair loose and it fell to her shoulders in gentle waves – she could smell the ghost of her shampoo when she moved her head. She'd forgotten what it was to feel beautiful, but today, she realised she must look better than usual – one or two men glanced at her as she walked towards the back table, their glances appreciative. She hated that kind of attention ordinarily, but it was nice to know that despite hitting her forties, she could still turn the occasional head.

Grace was already there, sitting with a copy of *Pride and Preju-*

dice open in front of her. Next to her was a tiny coffee cup and the wrapper of a square of dark chocolate. She'd clearly been here a while.

'Hello!' Leah said, pulling out a chair and sinking into it. 'Am I late?'

Grace looked up, smiled and marked her page with an ornate, silver bookmark. 'Not at all,' she said. 'I couldn't sleep so thought I'd come in early and use the opportunity to read.'

'Sounds blissful, actually,' Leah said.

'It was,' Grace said, 'although I think I've probably had one too many espressos.'

They laughed. Grace was dressed in a fitted blouse and jeans, her hair neatly straightened into submission around her face. Leah got to her feet. 'Shall I get you another?' she said, 'or maybe something else?'

'Mint tea?'

'Sounds like a plan.'

'Thanks for meeting up,' Leah said when she'd returned with their drinks. 'I just needed to get out.'

'No problem, we should do it more often,' said Grace.

'It feels a bit like we're cheating on the rest of the group!' Leah quipped, eyeing the book on the table.

'If you don't tell, I won't,' Grace said with a grin.

They really should do this more often, Leah thought as she sipped her coffee. It seemed odd, she thought, that she and Nathan were officially 'masters of their own time' and yet to have none left over for fun. Perhaps Nathan was right, making this sort of stand – taking himself off to Bordeaux to wander around and get a bit of headspace and perspective.

As usual, thoughts of Nathan's disappearances made her heart lurch a little. Was she being paranoid? Had Scarlett's words hit a nerve? She and Nathan had been married for fifteen years – they'd had difficult times before where they'd seemed to pull away from each other, or life had got in the way. But they'd remained faithful, loyal. Why should now be any different? It wasn't as if he was disappearing overnight and returning with lipstick on his collar, or any of the clichés you'd expect. 'Leah – everything OK?' Grace interrupted her reverie, her face concerned. 'You look miles away.'

'Yes, fine,' she said, decisively. 'Anyway, tell me about you. How's the gardening group going?'

Grace shook her head slightly, 'Yes, fine. Well, unless you bring up the subject of lawns.'

'Lawns?' Leah asked, head askance.

'Yes. People seem determined to create perfect English lawns out here, have you noticed? And of course, the climate's different, the soil's different. They spend half their time weedkilling and seed-sowing, the rest mowing. And it still looks ghastly. But don't you dare suggest they plant clover or give up on the idea of an orderly lawn,' she said. 'Honestly, it's exhausting.'

Leah laughed. 'Well, at least that's something I'm not guilty of. Not a blade of grass in sight at ours.' She thought again about the rows of fresh earth. How Nathan had thanked her for planting the broccoli on Saturday when he'd returned, but only in an abstract, disinterested way. She'd hoped more for fireworks, or at least an enormous smile. Instead, he'd seemed distracted. Asked her if she thought his hair needed a cut.

Then later, she'd wondered at herself – since when did she need a 'well done' for planting a few seedlings?

'Earth to Leah!' Grace quipped.

'Sorry,' she said. 'Just thinking.'

Grace nodded, brought her cup to her lips then lowered it. 'Look, I hope you don't mind me saying,' she said. 'But you know, you can trust me.'

'Of course!' Leah said, feeling her cheeks flush a little.

'I can be a bit... well, I'm talkative, I know,' Grace said, almost sadly. 'But I don't talk about people behind their backs. Divulge secrets, that sort of thing.'

Leah's face was now on fire. 'Of course,' she said again, weakly.

A few times in the past, Leah had wondered whether Grace might be a little psychic. Her ability to read Leah's mind – or at least sense when something was up – was astonishing at times. 'Everything's fine, honestly,' she said. But she felt her lip give a tell-tale wobble. 'At least, I think it is,' she admitted, feeling her mask fall as a tear began to well in her eye.

She hadn't come out to talk about Nathan – she'd wanted to forget about her worries for a couple of hours.

But the truth had decided to out itself, and there seemed to be nothing she could do about it. Grace reached a hand over and covered hers, saying nothing.

Leah dabbed her eye with a napkin to soak up the pesky tear and took a deep breath. 'You'll think I'm being silly,' she said. 'It's just...' And she told Grace about the last couple of months, how Nathan had been disappearing. Not only that, but the strange distance she could feel between them. The way he never seemed completely open about where he'd been or when he'd next be popping out. The fact he showered and dressed up before leaving the house – a real red flag in Nathan's case; since they'd been in France, his 'good clothes' had hung neglected in his wardrobe almost every day, in favour of his tracksuit bottoms and holey jumpers.

She finished and looked at Grace hopefully. This was when a friend might say something like, *It sounds like you're just tired*, or, *Is that all?* The sort of phrase that would make her feel she was just being paranoid – that would shine a light on her suspicions and show them to be unfounded.

Only Grace was looking at her quite seriously. 'It sounds,' she said... 'a bit like...'

'Ello, ello, ello!' said a voice, making them both jump. They looked up to see George, dressed in an old shirt and paint-splattered jeans. He was clutching a takeaway cup of coffee. 'Didn't expect to see you two in here,' he said, pulling out a chair without being asked. 'I was just grabbing a caffeine fix before heading out to the site.'

Grace flushed in surprise and checked her watch. 'It's eleven o'clock,' she said. 'Bit late to be clocking on?' Unlike Leah, she seemed quite at ease with their new tablemate. Probably because she wasn't waiting in suspense for a verdict, Leah thought.

'Ah, had a bit of a session with the lads last night,' George admitted. 'We gave ourselves a morning off. What's the point of working for yourself if you can't have a bit of fun?'

They both nodded. 'So,' Leah said, a little pointedly. 'You're heading off now, then?'

But George had removed the lid from his takeaway cup and was stirring in an extra sugar. 'No rush,' he said, blowing the heat from the top and taking a sip. 'What are you girls up to?' He spied the copy of *Pride and Prejudice*. 'Not discussing the book in advance, I hope?' he said with a grin.

Leah felt she might burst with impatience. Ordinarily, she'd have been pleased to see George – he was a nice bloke and always made her laugh – but for him to interrupt just as Grace was giving her verdict was almost too much to bear.

But Grace seemed unfazed. 'We wouldn't dream of it,' she said. 'We were just having a bit of a heart-to-heart.'

Hopefully, Leah thought, that would alert George to the fact that this was a private moment.

But, 'Oh aye?' he said, raising an eyebrow, as if expressing an interest. 'Everything alright?'

'Well,' said Grace.

Leah felt herself stiffen in horror. Surely she wasn't going to tell George about Nathan? She realised that it was private between them, didn't she? She tried to catch Grace's eye, but her friend was looking at George.

'We have a mutual friend,' Grace said carefully. 'And she's worried her husband might be having an affair. He keeps disappearing – all dressed up. And his stories aren't quite adding up. That sort of thing. We're just talking about what she should do.'

Leah felt a flood of relief.

'Sounds suspicious,' said George, clearly enjoying the conversation and not realising he was in the company of 'The Friend'.

'Not necessarily,' Leah said. 'I mean, this husband... our friend's husband. He's a good bloke. He's not the sort of person who does this kind of thing.'

'Riiight,' said George.

'What? He's not!'

'It's just...' he said, leaning forward rather conspiratorially, 'no-one is that sort of person... until they are. You know, if he's met someone. It can change a person.'

It was hard not to react as each word pierced her heart, but she did her best. George was just speculating on a story he'd barely heard. She'd probably have done the same, Leah thought.

'I was about to say,' Grace said, 'I think our friend should do what she can to alleviate her suspicions. Ask him directly. Bite the bullet.'

But George was shaking his head. 'She can't do that!' he said.

'Whyever not?' Grace looked affronted at her idea being shot down.

'Because if he's not doing anything wrong, he's going to feel really shit, I mean, awful about that,' George said. 'Maybe annoyed that she don't trust him.'

'Well,' said Grace, 'maybe she *doesn't* trust him!'

I do! Leah wanted to say. *I really do. At least, I think I do.*

'Yeah, but if he knows that... and he's, like, not doing anything wrong... it could make things worse between them,' George said. 'I know that if someone accused me of cheating, I'd wonder what they thought of me.' He shrugged a shoulder. 'Mind you, I've never done that to anyone, so...'

They were all silent for a moment. Leah felt the truth in George's words. If she did confront Nathan with her suspicions, it could drive a wedge between them.

'Well, what should she – our friend – do?' Leah asked George, who was clearly now fully invested in the situation. 'Because she's tried all the more subtle ways – she's tried to get him to chat about what he's been up to. But he's being cagey about it, won't say anything.'

'Well,' he said, 'what I'd do, if it was my... husband, is find out what he's up to for myself.'

'Well, yes,' said Grace. 'That was the idea of speaking to him.' She took a sip of her mint tea.

George leaned forward, as if imparting a secret. 'Yeah, but I'd do it more subtly. Like, so he won't know she's suspicious,' he said, tapping the side of his nose conspiratorially.

'Well,' said Leah, trying to keep the impatience from her voice. 'How exactly would you achieve that?'

George scratched his chin. 'Well, do you think she might be up for... following him? Next time he goes out and starts acting suspiciously?'

'Following him!' Leah said. 'No, that would be awful.'

'But it's a way of finding out where he's going at least,' George said, with a single shoulder shrug. 'And if she does it well, he won't ever know. And she'll know whether to confront him or not.'

Leah looked at Grace, expecting to see her friend's disbelief at

George's suggestion. But to her surprise, Grace was looking thoughtful. As if she was seriously considering his idea.

'Anyway, what do I know?' said George, refitting the lid to his cup and standing up. 'I'm just a chronically single bloke who's late for work.'

They smiled. 'Nothing wrong with being single,' Grace said. 'All the best people are, you know!'

George looked at her and grinned. 'Ah, but not for long, I'll bet,' he said. 'You're not the type to be left on the shelf.'

'Nothing wrong with being late, either,' Leah added. 'Master of your own time, remember?'

George grinned. 'Good point.'

'So, have fun at work.' Leah said, now eager for him to leave so they could discuss 'their friend' more openly.

'Always. See you at the meet-up,' he said. 'Nearly finished the book!'

'Well, done. And I'll call you later about the... the gardening thing we were talking about,' Grace said, stumbling slightly over her words.

'Look forward to it,' he said, giving a wink. Then turned and strode confidently out of the café.

'Great timing,' Leah said, rolling her eyes.

'The best,' her friend smiled. Had Grace missed the sarcasm in her tone? It was hard to say. 'So, what do you think?'

'Well, you were going to tell me what you thought about Nathan. You know, before George turned up,' Leah prompted.

'Yes,' said Grace, thoughtfully. 'But George could be right. If you speak to Nathan directly, it could damage things between you. If he's innocent.'

'Which he probably is,' added Leah.

'Quite. I rather like George's idea.'

Leah nearly spat out a mouthful of her coffee. 'Seriously?' she said. 'What? Dress up in beige macs and cut holes in newspapers to spy on him through? Follow his footprints with a magnifying glass? Come on, Grace, that's the sort of thing people do in films. Bad films. Not real life.'

'Still, it could be a way of finding out some answers,' Grace said. 'And he'd never have to know. Not if we were subtle about it.'

'You're serious, aren't you?' Leah said, incredulously.

'Deadly serious, darling,' Grace said, with a wicked grin. 'Come on, you and me. We can do anything we put our minds to. Let's follow him and find out once and for all whether you've got anything to worry about.'

It was the last sentence that hooked Leah. Because if she was honest, the worry about it all was eating her up. The fear of where he was going and who he might be meeting was driving her to distraction, however much she tried to pretend to Scarlett – and herself – that it wasn't.

'But do you really think we can do it?' she said. 'Without Nathan knowing?'

'If we're careful,' Grace said. 'It's always busy here; there are plenty of people around to hide behind. And maybe if he does see us, we could pretend we were just off to a café or something – that's not out of the question, is it?' she said, looking around her pointedly. 'We do *do* that, once in a while.' She smiled.

And Leah found herself smiling back. Perhaps they could really do this. Really put the whole worry in its place, before it grew out of control.

Perhaps George was right.

Perhaps they ought to follow Nathan.

16

Alfie quietly moved across the room, not wanting to wake his mum up. He knew the pattern of floorboards by now, the uneven one that sometimes tripped him, the board that creaked no matter how gently you stood on it. He set the water down on her bedside table, then quietly opened the window a crack, reaching for the shutters and releasing the catch just enough to allow a small strip of daylight into the room. He left the windows open; the fresh air would do her good.

He hated first thing in the morning. Waking up. Because sometimes when he was asleep, he'd forget. Even dream, sometimes, of how things had been – his strong, vibrant mother picking him up from school, or playing football in the garden, laughing when the ball missed the net by a mile. The mum who'd driven him to high school every day because the bus left too early, and anyway meandered around the various districts before heading to its destination, wasting half an hour and making him feel sick in one fell swoop.

He hadn't appreciated her back then. Well, he had, he just hadn't known it, hadn't felt it like he did now. He hadn't thanked her, other than the odd grunt as he'd exited the car. He hated his younger self for not wanting to cuddle her when she'd reached for him, complaining if she dared to ruffle his hair.

He'd spent some time being angry at her too, in the early years when he'd been brought to this unfamiliar place and dropped into a school where people spoke a language he didn't understand. He'd told her he wanted to go back to England. Told her he hated her more than once. He simply hadn't understood what she was doing for him.

Alfie looked at his mum, turned on her side in bed, the duvet barely raised by her tiny body, and felt a rush of love and guilt. 'I love you, Mum,' he whispered. But she didn't stir.

17

Grace seemed almost too delighted when Leah rang the following week to say that Nathan was going out shortly and that Mission: Follow Your Husband was on. 'At last!' she said. 'I even bought trainers! Don't want to be held back by heels at the crucial moment!'

Leah wondered whether her friend had forgotten what they were actually going to follow Nathan for and what it might mean. It might be an adventure for Grace, but it was a deadly mission for Leah.

'What shall I do? Where shall we meet? Should I call you?'

'Don't worry,' Grace said. 'Follow him from a distance, park up when he parks up and then call me. I'll be there in a split second, I promise.'

It was ridiculous.

It was terrifying.

It was the end of April and the temperature had risen to a comfortable but warm twenty-six degrees; everything still felt fresh and brand new. She wanted to look forward to the endless evenings, the barbecues and drinks on the terrace she associated with summer. Scarlett had about ten weeks left of school before she'd be on holiday, and Leah had been considering booking something up – a late-deal holiday; probably expensive, but it would do them good to get away, if they could get someone to feed the chickens, collect the eggs and water everything in their absence. But until she knew, until she felt safe, she wasn't sure she could move on with anything.

Leah already felt as if Nathan suspected something. 'Why are you looking at me like that?' he'd said earlier when he'd finished breakfast and grabbed a fresh towel for the shower.

'I just thought we were weeding this morning?' she'd said, trying to sound nonchalant. 'Normally, you don't get spruced up to crouch in the mud.'

'It's a bit... well, I thought we might do it this afternoon?' he'd said. 'It's... the weather's lovely and I thought I might just, well, see if I can find a few bits for the kitchen this morning. In, um, well, in town. There's a couple of antique places I've had my eye on...'

Leah wondered whether her husband could hear her heart thump as she asked him, 'That sounds fun. Should I come? It does look lovely out there.'

She'd felt a frisson of hope when he'd paused, looking at her. And for a moment, she'd thought he might say yes. That the trips out would become *their* trips out – and she wouldn't have to worry about it all any more.

Then the familiar, 'Honestly, don't worry. It'll probably be pretty boring. You just put your feet up. And no touching those weeds – we'll do them together afterwards!'

She wanted to say, *Actually, I love antiques stores*, or, *Seriously, why can't I come?* But she knew she had to let him go unquestioned if she wanted to finally play detective and find out what was up.

Since her meeting with Grace a week ago, she'd hoped that her husband's strange and sudden exits might simply stop. That she could laugh about them and say, *I must have been imagining it!* but Nathan had continued to slip out under various excuses. Occasionally, she'd see him texting furiously on his phone beforehand.

Of course, it wasn't as if he'd never left the house before all this started. He'd often used to shoot out to the bricolage for something else they'd needed and overlooked (they weren't natural gardeners, it had to be said). She didn't keep him prisoner or want to be glued to his side at all times. But something was different when it came to these disappearances and she had to know what it was.

Scarlett had left for school an hour ago; it was still early. But Grace had said 'anytime', hadn't she? So as soon as the water started to run, Leah had dialled her friend.

'OK,' she said now. 'Keep your mobile by your side and I'll call you as soon as I can.'

'Will do, captain!' Grace quipped. 'How exciting!'

'Grace!' she said, careful to keep her voice low. 'It's not exciting for me! It's… well, I feel awful about the whole thing.'

'Of course you do, of course you do,' Grace said, her voice much more sober. 'I just… I suppose it's thrilling to follow someone, isn't it? And it'll be nice for you to find out the truth.'

'I…'

'I'm sure it will all be perfectly innocent,' Grace said firmly.

'Well, I hope so,' Leah said. 'I guess we're going to find out.'

'Ooh. I'll get my hat. Great excuse to wear it!'

Ten minutes later, Leah was in the Clio, wondering how she'd be able to follow Nathan without him seeing her in the rear-view mirror. He'd left the drive and turned left moments before. As she bumped onto the road, she saw him disappear around the corner.

It was half past eight and traffic was building up; she was grateful for the two cars that stood between her and their Scenic ahead. Hopefully, it would be enough. If not, she'd just tell Nathan that she'd raced after him for some spurious reason. To remind him about something. She wracked her brain desperately. She really should have got her ducks in a row before setting off.

She'd just have to be careful, she thought, five minutes later after the two cars she'd kept between them turned off and she watched him turn decisively left, heading towards the centre. He slowed, and she hung back for a moment, trying to move quickly enough to avoid having the driver behind sound his horn, but without catching Nathan up or – even worse – having to pass him.

At the turn, he signalled again then out of nowhere, slid into a space. She quickly turned right into a little side road as he straightened up, and managed to wedge the Clio between a badly parked people carrier and a motorbike which took up a disproportionate amount of space. She could still just about see him through the window and held her breath as she watched him looking around for a meter to pay for his parking. She prayed he didn't make use of the one close to her turning. But luckily, he found another and began to type his information in on the electronic screen.

Then, glancing around almost furtively, he began to walk down the street. She was going to lose him! She slipped out of the Clio, feeling like a criminal already for failing to pay for a ticket. But there was no time. Hopefully, she'd get away with it just this once.

She walked a distance behind him, on the opposite side, making sure to stop whenever he did and annoying a couple of pedestrians who almost bumped into her when she halted abruptly, then slipped into the crowd on the pavement, keeping to the side furthest from the edge of the roadway where she hoped he wouldn't spot her.

It didn't take long for her spying mission to come to its conclusion. He turned into a café and stood, nonchalantly, in the queue, checking his phone and waiting to be served.

A café! She didn't know whether this was a good sign or a bad one. It could be a quick espresso before going to the antiques stores he'd mentioned. It could be the meeting point for an illicit liaison. Either way, he'd be there for at least ten minutes, she reasoned, watching the person in front of him point at the menu impatiently. She turned and rushed back to her car – thankfully un-ticketed – slipped back into the driver's side and called Grace.

'Grace,' she hissed, although really, why was she whispering? It wasn't as if Nathan could hear her. It just felt somehow to suit the mood. 'He's in a café, on Cr Victor Hugo. He'll probably be there for a bit.' She very nearly said 'over' but stopped herself just in time.

'Is he... is anyone with him?'

'No, thank God! He's on his own. Shall I come and pick you up?'

'God no,' said Grace, and Leah could hear the purr of an engine. 'It'll take far too long. I'm about ten minutes away. I'll head over now.'

'You're already on the move?'

'I simply couldn't help myself,' her friend said. 'When you said he was heading to central Bordeaux, I thought it would be helpful for me to be a little closer.'

Grace seemed to be at pains to keep her voice neutral, but it sounded to Leah as if her friend was still excited by the whole mission. She felt a little anger bubble up, but forced it back down. She was lucky to have someone willing to do this with her – now wasn't the time to argue with her friend.

She exited the car again and managed somehow to pay for her parking, despite the fact that half of the buttons on the meter closest to her car seemed to be broken through overuse. Then she stood, not quite knowing what to do.

Should she go to the road outside the café in case Nathan made a move? But what would she do if he did? Plus, what if he'd chosen a window seat and saw her? Perhaps she should wait here for Grace. And then what?

In the end, she simply couldn't help herself. Carefully, she pulled a cap from the glovebox of her car, walked around the corner and along the road opposite the café again. Nathan was no longer in the queue, but she couldn't see him at any of the outdoor tables, or at the ones visible from the window. He might have left! He might have bought a takeaway coffee and left! And if so, what would she do?

She tried to calm her breathing. She'd go home. She'd try again. She'd remind herself that this was probably just overblown paranoia and that he was simply spending a bit of time in the city.

Her phone beeped.

Here.

Grace had made good time. Leah texted her new location and within moments, Grace turned the corner, sporting fitted jeans, a light, striped jacket, trainers, an enormous pair of sunglasses and a floppy sunhat which seemed a little extreme for the season.

Leah had never seen a more welcome sight.

She practically flung herself into Grace's arms, glad now that she hadn't had words with her friend – because she was here. And there was no way Leah could have coped with this alone. 'Thank you, for coming. For helping!' she said, realising her eyes were filling with tears. 'I have no idea what I'm doing.'

'Nice hat,' Grace commented.

'You too,' Leah said more doubtfully, looking at the large, floppy sunhat.

'Disguise,' Grace said, and moved her head as if she might be winking, but without her eyes visible, it was impossible to tell.

Leah felt her mouth wobble slightly. 'Grace, I'm terrified.'

'Now come on,' Grace said firmly, holding her by the shoulders. 'Remember, you are just doing this to reassure yourself. Probably. And if not, well, we'll cross that bridge when we come to it. Now where is the blighter?'

'Blighter' wasn't a term Leah had heard often in the last two decades, and it was hard not to smile, despite her racing heart. 'Well, he was in that café, but I'm not sure whether he's left or not. I had to pay for parking and...'

'So, let's assume he's still there for now,' Grace said decisively. 'We'll watch the doors for a bit, and if he doesn't emerge, how about I treat you to a croissant and we rearrange this for another day?'

Leah had never wanted a croissant quite so much.

They made their way to the pavement opposite the café, making sure to keep back against the buildings to ensure lots of pedestrians walked between them and the edge of the street. Leah tried to concentrate on both looking innocent and watching the café door like a hawk. It was a difficult manoeuvre to pull off successfully.

In the end, they found themselves standing close to an ATM as if waiting to withdraw money, waving others in front of them whenever they reached the front of the tiny queue. It was one of the few places they could loiter without looking too ridiculous.

But it was ridiculous. The more she stood there, the more Leah felt the absurdity of her situation. Here she was with some sort of detective version of Grace – honestly, all she needed was an enormous magnifying glass to complete the ensemble – and for what? To watch her husband visit antiques stores? The more she thought about Nathan, the kind of man he was, the man he'd been over their fifteen years of marriage, the more she suddenly realised how unnecessary this was. Nathan would never cheat on her! He'd never shown any signs of dissatisfaction with their relationship, not really. Sure, they were going through a bit of a rough patch, but they were still strong.

'What's up?' Grace said.

'What?' she asked, still watching the doors.

'You're smiling.'

Leah snorted slightly. 'Sorry, I'm just kind of looking at myself from the outside. Seeing... it's like we're in a film or something, isn't it.'

Grace nodded. 'I was thinking more of a cartoon,' she admitted. 'I'm kind of regretting the sunglasses.'

'Yeah, and I'm not so sure about the hat,' Leah said, touching the brim uncertainly. 'I mean, it hides my face but...'

'We're not exactly subtle.'

'We are definitely not subtle,' she said, catching her friend's eye.

And Leah felt giggles bubble deliciously inside her as she waved another punter in front of them in the ATM queue.

Grace, seeing the expression on her friend's face, caught the mood and began giggling too. To her knowledge, Leah had never seen Grace giggle before. Smile, yes. Laugh, definitely. But giggle a little like a young girl? Never. Watching Grace's shoulders rock in their neat, striped jacket set her off even more. 'What are we doing?' she said.

'I'm not...' Grace began, then her hand suddenly clamped onto Leah's shoulder. 'Oh,' she said, her face changing abruptly to a look of concern.

'What?' Leah followed her gaze. And there was Nathan, standing smiling in the street just outside the café, looking directly ahead of him at a woman, dressed smartly with neat, blonde hair, who seemed to be approaching him.

As they watched, Nathan leaned forward and kissed the woman on each cheek. They smiled at each other before the woman gestured and they both began to walk purposefully along the road, arms linked.

'Oh my God, oh my God,' Leah began.

'No time,' Grace said. 'Follow the bastard!'

She grabbed Leah's hand and half walked, half dragged her along the pavement in the same direction. Only to round a corner and see the woman climb a small set of steps at the bottom of an old building, repurposed into apartments. She took a key from her bag, and with Nathan standing close behind, opened the front door before the pair of them disappeared inside.

18

MAY

It was still bright – the sky white but with no hint of rain. Ordinarily, this kind of evening – springlike but with a promise of summer – would have lifted Leah's mood. But tonight, she barely noticed.

Wondering whether she'd cope, Leah stood outside Monica's apartment building as Grace leaned forward and pressed the buzzer. The intercom crackled, then Monica's voice came on. 'Come on up!' she said, sounding cheerful.

Leah almost hadn't come to the meeting at all. In the six days since they'd seen Nathan disappear with that – beautiful, it had to be said – woman, she'd lived a kind of half-life. Not knowing what to do with the information, scared to confront her husband. 'It might not be what it looked like,' she'd said to Grace after the pair had disappeared into the building together. 'There could still be an innocent explanation.' She'd heard the desperation in her own voice. The residential building. The kiss. The linked arms. The looks exchanged as the woman had turned the key.

Together, she and Grace had tried to come up with possibilities. Maybe she was just a friend – an antiques expert he'd paired up with. It wasn't completely left-field for a French woman to greet someone with kisses! Perhaps she was a dealer and had had an antique at her apartment she'd wanted to show him. However, instead of reassuring herself with the speculation, Leah had become surer by the minute that what she'd seen simply couldn't have been innocent.

But when she was at home with Nathan seeming his usual affable and loving self, she'd found she couldn't bring herself to shatter what they had by calling it into question. She was worse off than she had been before!

On the day, Grace had wanted to wait it out – to confront Nathan on his exit. But Leah simply couldn't bear to. Either to admit she'd been following him, been suspicious, or to hear the words that she'd been dreading: that he was, after all, having an affair and that he wanted to leave.

Instead, they'd decamped to a café where she'd sat, holding in tears that were waiting to burst out while trying to nurse a cup of coffee. She'd realised she never should have involved Grace – now that Grace knew, she'd push her into doing something. And she hadn't been sure she was ready or able to face up to this.

She'd called Grace earlier today asking her to pass her apologies to Monica. 'I just can't talk about books when all this is happening,' she'd said, despite Grace's protestations. So she'd been surprised when Grace had turned up at her house to drag her to the group anyway. 'I'm just not in the mood,' she'd protested, gesturing at her soiled clothes and messy hair.

'You can never,' Grace had replied, steadfast, 'not be in the mood for *Pride and Prejudice* – it's a simple fact.' And she'd strode into the house, given Nathan a frosty greeting and insisted that Leah get herself ready.

Admittedly, now she was here gazing up at a beautiful apartment block, Leah did feel a little better. Just getting away from the possibility of talking to Nathan seemed to help.

'Thanks,' she said to Grace now as they made their way up the wooden staircase.

Until recently, she'd thought of Grace as well-meaning but a little annoying, perhaps too interfering. But the comfort she'd given her during this strange time had been nothing short of amazing. Her willingness to support Leah, to find the truth, and now, to try to help her even when she wasn't sure what she needed herself; Grace really was a true friend.

'Anytime.'

After several flights of stairs, they arrived on Monica's floor a little on the sweaty side. The front door was ajar and they pushed it open. 'Cooee!' said Grace.

Did anyone else in the world say 'cooee' any more? Leah wondered fondly.

'Come in!' called Monica. 'We're in the sitting room.'

It was hard not to gasp as they entered the apartment. The shock of the modern, sleek, and expensive fittings, after the old-world charm of the staircase and hallway, made for a dramatic contrast.

'Wow,' said Leah quietly to her friend. 'I'm guessing piloting pays better than I thought.'

They moved in the direction of Monica's voice and found themselves in an airy room with impossibly high ceilings, in which almost everything was white – the sofas, the rug on the floor, the walls and the windows which were flung open to reveal a generous balcony.

George was already there, sitting rather awkwardly on the white sofa, and still wearing what were clearly his work boots. He stood up when they entered. 'Hello ladies,' he said. 'Sorry about the state of me. Work's gone mental and I didn't have time...' he gestured at his jeans. Then, 'Are you sure it's OK for me to...?' he asked Monica, pointing at the sofa.

'Don't worry about it,' Monica said. 'Honestly.' She indicated her own, slightly baggy jeans. 'I'm covered in baby sick half the time anyway.'

George sank back down, still looking rather uncertain. Leah saw Grace's eyes flit to the tiny crumbs of dried mud he'd already shed and look just as doubtful. But she remained silent.

Leah took a place on the other sofa with Monica, and Grace sat on the opposite end of George's sofa. 'No Alfie tonight?' Grace asked.

'He's on his way, apparently,' Monica said. 'Bringing a friend, too. His girlfriend, apparently.'

'Oh!' Grace said, looking a little perplexed. Leah wondered whether Alfie ought to have cleared it with Grace first. Although the group was 'their' group, it had been Grace who'd started it, and she was a person who liked to know exactly what was going on.

'Wine?' Monica asked, making her way to an ornate sideboard, again white, on which sat a tray of glasses and two bottles of red wine.

George looked anxious. 'You haven't got any white?' he asked, the end of the sentence coming out in a bit of a squeak.

Monica laughed – she seemed a little more relaxed than when Leah had seen her before. Perhaps it was to do with her being in her own space. She was wearing an off-white, short sleeved blouse, that looked at odds with her un-ironed jeans. Her skin, smooth and nut brown, looked almost luminous, and her hair hung, glossy and perfectly well behaved, to her shoulders.

'I'm so sorry,' she said. 'I was going to go out and get some white. Some beer too. But...' she trailed off, a shadow flitting across her face. 'It's just hard with Bella. And...' she trailed off.

'I'm sure red will be delicious!' said Grace, loudly, making Monica jump slightly.

'Oh, yeah,' George said. 'It's not that. Just... clumsy.'

'It doesn't matter,' Monica said. 'Everything's new. I'm not attached to any of it.' She shrugged as if it simply wouldn't matter if they sprayed wine across the whole of the flat.

George baulked a little. 'Well, just a smidge for me,' he said, holding up his finger and thumb about an inch apart. 'Just in case.'

Monica poured the wine into a large, crystal glass and handed it to him. He held it nervously, taking a tentative sip. 'Wow,' he said. 'Nice.'

'You think?' she said. 'Peter's favourite.'

'It's lovely,' George confirmed with a nod.

'And he is where?' Grace asked, accepting her own glass.

'Working,' Monica said with a slight eyeroll. 'He took on an extra shift so is out for a week longer than planned. I'm beginning to forget what he looks like!' she gave a grin, but it didn't reach her eyes.

'Hello?' a voice called nervously.

'Come in!' Monica called. 'We're all here – shut the front door behind you.'

Then Alfie was in the room, in baggy jeans and a hoodie, his hair in disarray. Behind him stood a beautiful woman, her veneer of perfection throwing his scruffiness into even stronger relief. She was dressed in a pair of tight, white jeans teamed with a blue top; her glossy, dark-brown hair was tied in a ponytail and her face was make-up free because why would you need it if you looked like that? Leah thought.

'Hi,' he said, smiling slightly awkwardly. 'This is Camille.'

'Hi,' they all said, almost transfixed by the contrast between Alfie and his girlfriend. His messy, awkward style next to her beauty and apparent confidence. His Ed Sheeran to her Beyoncé.

'Hello,' she said, in a heavy French accent. 'I hope you do not mind me joining you? I am trying to improve my English and I read the latest book. And Alfie, he say that you are very kind.'

They all nodded and murmured their welcome and accepted the compliment. Alfie and Camille sat down on separate chairs, brought into the living room for the occasion. Camille reached into a tiny handbag and pulled out a copy of *Pride and Prejudice* – it was a bit like watching Mary Poppins pull a lamp out of her bag, thought Leah. The neat, leather handbag looked far too small to have contained a book, and yet here it was.

Once they were all settled and armed with half-filled glasses, it was Grace who started them off. 'Ah, *Pride and Prejudice*,' she said, with a little glance at Camille. 'Our archetypal English novel. Probably most people's favourite Austen. So, what did we think?'

George sat forward. 'I liked it,' he said carefully, 'but I dunno. I kind of felt sorry for Mrs Bennet.'

Leah looked at him in surprise: Mrs Bennet, the mother of the young women in the book, behaves in both a comedic and ridiculous way for most of the story. If anything, Leah found her borderline annoying – definitely not sympathetic.

'But she's dreadful!' Grace said. 'Her hysterics! The way she is so determined to micro-manage her girls' lives. And she even gets what she wants in the end – two married off very well.'

'She's even quite pleased about Lydia's wedding, in the end, despite the scandal,' added Leah.

'True. Yes, see?' Grace said. 'She's not worried about her daughters' happiness, just their station in life. Bit selfish and money-grabbing, in all honesty.'

'I guess she must feel a bit desperate though,' George said. 'She's just trying to make sure her daughters are OK. It must be difficult knowing that Mr Bennet isn't allowed to pass the house on to a female heir in his will, so she and the girls are basically screwed... um, in trouble, when he dies. Enough to make anyone desperate. Especially in those days.'

Leah had never looked at Mrs Bennet with anything other than humour or exasperation. But she could see it – the lack of choice in society that had led to Mrs Bennet becoming the extreme meddler she was. 'I suppose you're right,' she said. 'And as a character, too, she's great fun. When you step away from the... position she's in and just look at her actions. She's such a quirky character – I bet Austen enjoyed writing her.'

'I find the book very strange,' Camille admitted, flicking her hair back over her shoulder and sitting forward. 'Because it is strange to me that all the girls they want to marry for money and not for love. Even Elizabeth, the love she get from Mr Darcy, it is strange. He say he love her, and he do things... but I cannot imagine how they would live together! After the wedding, what do they say to one another? Are they happy? I cannot see it.'

Leah thought about Mr Darcy – his frosty manner, his stiff haughtiness. Yes, he let his guard down later in the book. But he would hardly be a relaxing companion. 'No fun at parties,' she said, nodding her agreement.

'Still, they've got the ten thousand a year to keep them occupied,' Monica said.

'What would that be in today's money?' Grace speculated.

'At least a million,' Monica said. 'I looked it up. Some people reckon it's more like £450,000 and some estimate it as up to £8 million. But in any case, that would just have been a return on his investments – he'd have had loads more. And he's got the estate at Pemberley too – that sounds, well, pretty good.'

'Yes,' said Camille. 'But that is not love. That is money.'

'Sometimes they come hand in hand,' Monica said.

Camille shook her head. 'But this is rare. And I think for Elizabeth, she like the money a lot. Because she say to her sister, Jane, that she fall in love when she see Monsieur Darcy's estate at Pemberley. So, maybe it is the money, for her too.'

Grace shook her head. 'No, I don't see it that way. I think she's joking there with Jane – in the way sisters do. I think she does start to soften at Pemberley but it's when she sees the other side of Darcy – maybe he's more comfortable on his home soil, so to speak. She can see that he's more than this dark, brooding man who seems so awkward and judgemental.'

'Maybe,' Leah said. 'And there's the letter, isn't there. Where he explains things more. And I wonder whether she can see through his kind of awkward mannerisms once she's read it?'

Camille shrugged. 'To me, this is not love. It is making a life and having money and perhaps it is the only choice they have. But this book is not about passion, *l'amour*. It is more like getting a job.'

Alfie laughed and leaned slightly against her. 'Always the romantic,' he said.

Camille looked at him, her eyes lighting up. 'At least with us, we know that it is not about money, eh.'

Alfie blushed. 'Sadly not,' he said. 'No, not *sadly*... what I mean is, it would be nice to have both. A bit of money too.'

'Amen to that,' said Monica.

They all murmured. George sipped his wine. 'What do you think of Lydia?' he said, one eyebrow raised.

'She's certainly a fun character. Always giggling, seeing the funny side,' Leah said. 'And I feel a bit sorry for her – she's only a kid and gets totally led astray by Mr Wickham.'

'I feel sorry for her,' said Monica. 'I know she causes problems for the family when she elopes, but looking at it with modern eyes... For goodness' sake, she's fifteen! This man – he's definitely quite a bit older than her – persuades her. And she's... well, vulnerable and susceptible. And has everything to lose.'

'Yes,' Camille said. 'It would be quite a scandal, yes, for her. But for him, he can get away with it.'

'Not much different to nowadays,' Monica said. 'Obviously, you wouldn't be ruined for sleeping with someone. But it's still much more men who get the high five and women who get talked about behind their backs.'

'Not if she was fifteen though,' George said. 'He'd be thrown in prison.'

'Hopefully,' Grace said.

'You do wonder,' said Leah, 'about their lives together after the wedding – whether they could really be happy. I mean, Wickham's more or less forced into marriage by Darcy; it's not something he's naturally wanted to do. And he and Darcy are no great fans of each other. I'm guessing things might not be that happy behind the scenes.'

'Were they for any of them, though?' Monica said, shaking her head. 'Like, with such a, well, shallow pool of suitable suitors, it's not likely any of them found anything really meaningful. The kind of relationship that can stand the test of time. The ups and downs.'

They were all quiet for a moment.

'Shallow pool?' Camille ventured.

'As in, there aren't many of them. Not much water in the lake,' Grace explained.

'Ah yes! Like the fish in the sea. There are not enough,' Camille said, nodding.

'I think Bingley and Jane are probably alright,' said Leah. 'He seems like quite a fun guy, they've got £5,000 and Jane seems smitten. Perhaps they're the real winners here?'

George set his empty glass on the coffee table, making sure there was a coaster underneath it first. Monica leant forward and refilled it and a look of horror flickered across his face. 'Sorry?' she said. 'Are you driving?'

'No, it's great,' he said, picking up the glass and eyeing it, clearly just terrified to spill red on all the endless white.

'What about poor Charlotte?' said Monica. 'You know, Elizabeth's friend. She's the one I feel most sorry for. The most desperate of the lot! Mr Collins sounds dreadful! She makes no secret of the fact that she just marries him because she's out of options,' she shuddered.

'At least she knew what she was getting into, though,' Alfie said. 'The way I see it, she treats it more like a business transaction. She wants a secure future and it's the only decision she can make. We kind of feel sorry for her, but maybe she's the one who actually gets it. The rest of them think they're in love, and that's the real problem. She's literally making the best of a bad situation.'

'Gawd, that's a depressing view!' Grace said. 'Surely there's a little romance here too? Not for Charlotte obviously. But at least, I think Austen wants us to believe that Elizabeth and Darcy are a good match.'

'Yes, I think so,' said Leah. 'Perhaps our definition of what a happy ending means has changed, in modern times.'

'You have to have hope,' Grace said. 'You have to hope that there's happiness, love, moments of joy for them all.'

Leah looked at Grace's earnest face. 'Definitely,' she said. It was curious hearing Grace talk that way – she had never presented herself as anything but single and happily so – not someone who yearned for romance, but someone in love instead with her own company, her own carefully crafted life.

'Yes, there must be love, of course. But for Charlotte, not with her twenty-seven years,' said Camille sadly. 'She is too old for the happiness by now, eh?' She smiled and they all laughed in acknowledgement.

'Horrible to be considered an old maid at twenty-seven! Wonder what that would make me!' said Grace.

'I don't know,' George said. 'Never too old.' He gave Grace a look and Leah noticed her friend's face flush slightly.

'But then, life expectancy was so low in those days,' Leah ventured. 'I googled it – women only lived to about forty-nine years! Obviously, the figure's a bit skewed by infant mortality rates and there would have probably been a big divide between rich and poor, but still. Twenty-seven would have been beyond middle-aged.'

'I sometimes wonder how anyone achieved anything in those times,' George said. 'I only just got myself figured out by that age. I feel like I'm just starting out sometimes.'

'Ah, but we are lucky now, of course,' Camille said, laughing. 'Now we can make love at any age and it is good.'

'*Fall in* love,' Alfie corrected.

She looked at him. 'It is wrong, making love? It is not what you say?'

'Well, we do say it,' said Alfie, getting redder by the second. 'But we... it's what we say for sex, not falling in love, relationships, that sort of thing.'

Camille shrugged. 'It is all one, no? We fall in love, we make love... and we are never too old to make love.' She seemed completely unembarrassed. They all studiously sipped their wine. 'Perhaps Mr Collins, later, he take a lover. And Charlotte, she take a lover too. And they are all happy,' said Camille.

'What? Cheating on each other!' Grace spluttered, taking a sideways glance at Leah. 'But that's not... marriage is...'

Camille shrugged. 'But if she does not want the sex with him, perhaps he find it somewhere else.'

It was getting too close to the bone. Leah found herself thinking of Nathan. Their life that had fallen into a monotonous pattern. They still had sex, occasionally. But were often too tired from the manual labour, or too stressed, or just... It was as if sometimes they forgot to make the time, make the effort. She'd thought it was a mutual thing. Perhaps it was normal for the sex part to peter out a bit after a decade and a half? Suddenly, she wondered if the petering out had all been one-sided.

'Leah!' The voice was sharp, brought her back into the room. 'Watch out!'

It was too late; her hand had relaxed and the glass she'd been cradling had spilled its contents generously onto the white sofa, the rug and Monica's perfect, expensive, white trainers.

19

It wasn't like her to cry.

Monica had been more than understanding – even blasé – about the spillage. 'Honestly,' she said. 'Bella will be crawling soon and we'll have to change the décor anyway.'

'But this all looks so expensive,' Leah had said, wiping her eyes. 'And it's ruined!'

'It'll be fine; nothing that can't be cleaned,' Monica seemed almost nonchalant about it, as if she didn't much care for the beautiful apartment at all. Leah hoped she wasn't just a great actor.

Once things were mopped up as much as they could be, and Leah was given a fresh glass of the wine (and a side table to place it on), they tried to resume.

'So Leah,' Grace said, clearly trying to distract her and bring her back to the book, 'you mentioned that *Pride and Prejudice* was one of the reasons you moved here. Remind us why?'

Grace was being kind, moving the conversation on. Keeping Leah occupied, she realised.

Leah sniffed and looked around the room. Everyone's eyes were fixed on her. She took a deep breath. 'It obviously... I suppose it was a weird comment, wasn't it! I realise that a typically English book wouldn't normally get someone dreaming of France. And it wasn't France, per se. But I used to fantasise about having loads of space – land, I suppose. They're always walking and riding and taking turns about the garden – and I used to imagine what it'd be like to have a garden that wasn't the size of a postage stamp.' She gave a watery grin. 'I suppose now I know. And it's no picnic.'

'Well, they didn't actually do anything on the land, did they?' Grace said. 'No labouring. Obviously, they had people for that. You needed to have a lot of money to enjoy the land without all the hard work that comes with it.'

'Yes,' nodded Leah. 'And you don't really see any of their servants, do you? The people who are actually slaving away and making it all possible. The maids and the cooks and the gardeners, they're sort of invisible in the background. But they must be there.'

'It's true,' Grace said, thoughtfully. 'It would be nice to read a story re-written from their perspective – what they thought of Darcy, and Elizabeth and, well, all of them.'

'Someone wrote one a few years back I think,' said Monica, turning her book over in her hands as if it might contain the pertinent details.

'I bet they had a few choice words to say about Mrs Bennet,' said George.

'Maybe a future pick for the club?' said Grace, thoughtfully.

They lapsed into silence for a moment.

'I still think it's a great love story though,' Monica said. 'And I defy any woman to read it without falling in love a little with Darcy.'

'Really?' Alfie interjected. 'Is Darcy any better than Heathcliff?'

There was a collective pause as they all wondered whether Alfie was going to shatter their illusions yet again about another romantic hero.

'Well, of course he is!' Grace said, rather defensively. 'For starters, he's a gentleman. He rescues Lydia from the scandal with Wickham. He also changes during the text – he shows that he's capable of being thoughtful and learns from his mistakes.'

'True,' Alfie nodded. 'But still... it's all on his terms, isn't it?'

'Not when he proposed to Elizabeth. And she turned him down.'

Alfie nodded. 'Yes, that's true. Must have been a shock to him after a life when everyone probably always just agrees with everything he says.'

'So maybe he's not perfect, but at least *Pride and Prejudice* has a happier ending than *Wuthering Heights*,' Monica said. 'Elizabeth and Darcy are both alive, for starters.'

'Setting the bar low,' quipped George and she grinned at him.

'I suppose it's what you want from a marriage that matters,' she said. 'I know I complain a bit about Peter being away – but it can be nice sometimes to have a little "me" time. Maybe it's good for a couple. Maybe once they settle into Pemberley, Darcy will be off doing his own thing, she'll be the mistress, running everything from behind the scenes. It's a bit like working together. So they'd have time together, but not be in each other's pockets.'

'So basically, his marriage proposal is more of a job offer?' George said.

'I've had worse jobs,' Monica found herself saying, before feeling her face get hot. 'You know what I mean,' she said.

'I think it's hard, after all the adaptations on TV, to really see the story the way Austen intended it any more,' said Leah. 'I can't read the book without seeing Colin Firth.'

'Yes, he's the classic Darcy,' Grace agreed. 'Brooding and handsome.'

'And the lake scene!' Monica interjected. 'I could watch that for hours!'

'Oh, me too!' joked George and they all laughed.

Alfie's phone rang and he leapt up and disappeared out of the door.

'This really is lovely wine, Monica,' Grace said generously.

'Thanks. Peter's quite the wine enthusiast,' she said.

There was a noise on the baby monitor and Monica stared at it for a moment, before the little cry became a snuffle, then went silent once more.

'How's Bella?' Leah asked.

'Fine. Keeps me sane,' Monica said with a small smile.

'And Peter's back...?'

'Soon.'

They all nodded.

'You must have so much to keep you busy,' Grace said. 'This gorgeous apartment, right in the centre. Bella. It must be wonderful.'

Monica shrugged. 'It's alright.' A look crossed her face and she opened her mouth as if to say something more, but closed it again.

'Are you...' Leah began, but was interrupted by the door opening again.

Alfie stood there, already in his jacket. 'Sorry,' he said. 'Gotta go. That was my mum; she needs a hand with something.' He looked at Camille. 'Do you want to come? Or stay? I don't mind.'

'I will stay, I think,' she said, getting up and kissing him on the mouth, as if to remove any doubt that she was his girlfriend rather than just a beautiful friend he'd set his hopes on. 'But I will come to you later, yes?'

'OK.' Alfie said. 'Bye all. And, well... sorry.'

'No problem,' said Grace, as if it was her apartment Alfie was leaving. 'See you again soon.'

The door slammed behind him, and they could hear his foot-steps as he practically ran down the stairs. The room fell silent for a moment, and Leah picked up her wine and took a generous gulp. Grace was driving her home tonight and she may as well make the most of it. Putting the wine back down on the table, she smiled at the rest of the group.

'Wasn't it Alfie's turn to choose the next book?' she said. 'I meant to ask him. I can probably email...'

'Ah, I know which book he choose,' Camille said. 'At first, he cannot decide between a book about a man who live in an old people home, and another about a woman who is not happy in her marriage. But then I say that perhaps it is good that you read a French book. Not in French of course,' she said, acknowledging all of their language-related inadequacy with sympathy, 'but one that is translated. *Madame Bovary* – you know this?'

'Perfect!' Grace clapped her hands together. 'Another great classic!'

'Never heard of it,' George said.

'Oh, I think you'll like it,' Grace told him. 'I've got it at home actually, if you'd like to borrow a copy?'

'Yeah, thanks. Maybe I can pick it up when I pop in tomorrow?' he said.

Grace coloured. 'Yes, um, if you happen to be passing,' she said. 'If you need to be in the area for... something else, perhaps?'

'Yeah, sure,' he said.

Grace cleared her throat. 'Anyway, well, that seems like a good choice, Camille. As long as Alfie is OK with it.'

'*Oui*, yes. Of course.'

Grace shook her head. 'That boy is full of surprises,' she said. 'Goes to show you can't judge someone on their appearance. I didn't think Alfie would even come back after our first session. And when I imagined what book he'd choose, I thought he'd go down the horror route, or something. Yet here we are.'

'Yes, indeed,' Camille smiled.

'More to the boy than meets the eye,' Grace said, thoughtfully. 'Although he does seem to be...'

'A bit of a mummy's boy?' George suggested.

'What is this "mummy boy"?' Camille asked, confused. She crossed one endless leg over the other. 'That he love his mother?'

'I was going to say, he's a bit at her beck and call,' Grace said. 'But yes, I suppose so.'

'Well, he's still young,' Leah said. 'Still plenty of time to fly the nest.'

'Still,' Monica said, leaning forward as if imparting a secret. 'It's a bit... well... it's not ideal at his age. Doesn't necessarily bode well for the future.' She suddenly seemed to remember Camille was Alfie's girlfriend and blushed a deep shade of red. 'Sorry,' she said.

Leah found herself looking at Camille. Obviously, it hadn't put her off to have a boyfriend who spent more time on the phone to his mum than with her. She was sitting back, quite relaxed, legs still crossed, observing them from over her glass.

'It is OK,' Camille said, moving forward. 'I think that it is very attractive to have a man who care for his mother. It show that he care for people, *non*? And that he has a good heart.' She patted her own chest as if to confirm this was where such a heart might be located.

'Sorry,' Leah said, blushing. 'And I mean, you're right really. I don't know why people would describe being a "mummy's boy" as a bad thing.' She thought of Scarlett and couldn't imagine a circumstance when a call from Leah would have her rushing away from a social occasion. Maybe if she was on the brink of death? But perhaps not even then.

'Besides, he is not – how you say – a mummy's boy,' Camille added. 'Yes, he help her a lot. But he is not over-attached to her? He love her, and he help her. He share with her some of the books from the group. But it is not normal for him right now, of course.'

There was a silence as they all wrestled to find meaning in the words. 'Sorry, you've lost me,' George said at last. 'What is not normal?'

'Well, he is very close to his mother now, yes. Because his mother need him more.'

'Oh.'

A look flitted across Camille's face. 'Oh, but you do not know!' she said.

'Know what?'

Camille looked at them. 'Perhaps I should not say this,' she said. 'Because he hasn't told you himself. But perhaps it is important for you to know. Alfie's mum, she is not well.'

'Oh no,' Leah said, feeling her heart sink.

'They think that she is dying.'

20

As Monica got up to see Camille and George off, Grace leaned over to Leah. 'Do you mind,' she said, 'if we stay to help her clear up? She's got a lot on her plate.'

'Of course,' Leah said, eyeing the rug again. She felt guilty about having ruined her host's décor, no matter what Monica said. She wondered if she should find out where Monica got the rug from, see if she could replace it. But had a sneaking suspicion it would be way out of her price range.

'Poor Alfie,' Grace added.

Leah nodded, not quite sure what to say.

After Camille's bombshell, she'd explained that Alfie's mum had cancer, that the latest treatment hadn't worked as well as it should. 'It make her very ill,' she said, 'but the cancer, it stays. Now she is very tired and they are losing hope.'

'Oh no,' Leah said, lifting her hand to her mouth. 'And his dad isn't around?'

'No. Alfie, he doesn't know his father in England. It has always just been them. And his mother, she brought him to France for a better life. To spend more time with him. And to get away from the place where they live, which was not nice I think.' Camille said.

'Do they know,' Leah asked cautiously, 'how long?'

Camille shrugged. 'I think not long. But there is a new treatment to try – it is a trial, though.'

They'd fallen silent, thinking of Alfie – his running off, the air of sadness he sometimes carried. Even his joining the group to please his mum. It all made sense now.

'Poor Alfie,' Monica said. 'You won't tell him what we said, will you?'

Camille smiled. 'No, but I think even if I do, he understand. He is sad but he still can – how you say? – take the joke.'

They'd wound the conversation up soon after that. They had already exhausted their thoughts on *Pride and Prejudice*, and it would have seemed odd to talk about it any further without Alfie. Monica offered everyone coffee, but George and Camille both said they needed to get going.

'Give Alfie our love,' Leah had said as Camille left the room.

Monica reappeared now in the doorway. 'Do you...' she began.

'We thought we'd stay and help you with the mess,' Grace said. 'You've got enough on your plate.'

'Honestly, it's...' Monica began. But then the baby monitor burst into life as Bella finally realised her tummy was empty. 'Actually, thanks,' she said, disappearing for a moment, then reappearing with a sniffing baby on her shoulder.

It was the first time they'd seen Bella outside of the photos and Leah had a sudden urge to reach out and touch the little girl's hand. She was astonishingly small, in a white, fluffy onesie that dwarfed her tiny frame. 'Oh, she's beautiful,' she said.

'Do you want to hold her?'

'I'd love to,' Leah found herself saying. 'If you don't mind.'

'Not at all, gives me a rest,' Monica said, passing the tiny bundle to Leah. Leah gathered the little girl against herself and felt the warm fragility of her tiny body beneath the onesie.

'Oh,' she sighed, as Bella snuggled her head into her shoulder. 'Oh, she's just lovely.'

A memory came to her: Scarlett snuggling on her like this at the hospital. All the times Leah had held her during childhood: at bedtime, when she was hurt, when she was scared, or happy. Or sometimes 'just because.' When had the last time been? If she'd known it would be the last hug she'd have with her daughter, she'd have held on forever, she thought. Or at least committed every moment to memory.

She felt the tears coming but managed to choke them back before anything was noticed. 'Why don't you sit down with the baby, and Monica and I can wash up?' Grace suggested.

'That'd be great, if you don't mind,' Monica said. 'I can warm up her bottle. But not if you don't want to, of course...'

'I'd love to,' Leah said, firmly. She wasn't about to let this little bundle go – at least not for now.

'I know you're meant to breastfeed, and I did try but...' Monica began.

'Don't worry,' Grace said. 'Honestly.'

Leah remembered feeling similarly when she hadn't been able to feed Scarlett. That feeling of having fallen at the first hurdle. 'I couldn't either,' she said. 'And honestly, you can only do your best.' She couldn't help but hear herself, her voice confident in the quiet room. She couldn't let on to Monica especially how lost she was right now as a mother, how she'd swap her current concerns for worries about feeding and nappies in a heartbeat. The first few months of motherhood had felt out of control, but back then, she hadn't any idea of what would happen later.

Monica smiled tightly and went into the kitchen, with Grace following. Leah sat, feeling the delicate lightness of Bella in her arms, her senses tingling with longing and love for the tiny girl whom she didn't know. Fourteen years ago, her arms had held another bundle and she remembered thinking how the bond between her and Scarlett would never be broken.

And it still isn't, she reminded herself. It was just stretched and twisted and sometimes put under pressure. But the bond was still there. It had to be. Scarlett would come back to her once she'd grown up a little more. Still, as she looked at Bella's tiny, squalling face, Leah wondered whether she'd completely messed up this motherhood thing.

When Monica came back in with a bottle, Leah kept her face focused on Bella so that her friend wouldn't see the tears that had pooled in her eyes.

'Sure you're OK to do this?' Monica said, uncertainly. 'I'm happy to...'

'No, it's fine. More than fine,' Leah reassured her. 'I'd love to.' She turned her face to Monica with a smile that she hoped looked relaxed and genuine. Hoped that her eyes weren't shining too much.

'Everything alright?' Monica asked.

'Yes,' she said. 'Ignore me. Just babies... I mean, she's gorgeous.'

'Thanks,' she said.

Monica disappeared to the kitchen, picking up a couple of bowls of half-eaten nuts from the coffee table as she did so. And Leah was left to sit and hold Bella and dream about a time that wasn't so very long ago, but seemed a million years away.

By the time Monica entered her kitchen, Grace had the washing up well underway.

'Oh, we have a dishwasher!' Monica said, as she saw Grace dunk a wine glass into a sink full of suds. 'You can...'

'Don't worry, I've started now,' Grace said with a smile. 'And I do always think it's better to wash glasses in the sink. Too much tarnishing in the dishwasher.'

Monica nodded. 'I suppose I'm just a bit lazy when it comes it that sort of thing,' she admitted.

Grace gave her a quick look. 'Well, you've got a lot on your plate,' she said, then nodded at the pile of side plates next to the sink. 'Literally and metaphorically' she quipped.

Monica laughed, the kind of laugh that was almost a cry. 'True,' she said. 'Well, sort of.' Her voice broke slightly and Grace gave her another look.

'Here,' she said, picking up a tea towel. 'How about I wash and you dry?'

Monica caught the towel as Grace gently threw it to her, then went to stand at Grace's side, lifting a glass from the drying rack and beginning to wipe the water and remaining suds away.

'So how is it going?' Grace asked softly, her eyes still fixed on the sink of suds, sponge soaping away a red wine stain.

'Yeah, fine,' Monica said.

Grace turned her knowing eyes towards her friend. 'Are you sure?' she said. 'Because it can be tough with a new baby. I know I don't have any children... I never...' she said. 'But my sister, my friends. I've seen how difficult it can be. No matter how gorgeous and sweet they are.'

Monica's lip wobbled slightly. 'It's nothing really,' she said. 'No idea why I'm upset... it's just I'm very tired, I suppose. And she doesn't sleep. Not really. Not as much as...'

Grace nodded. 'Sleep deprivation is tough,' she said. 'When I went through menopause, I was up at three every morning for a while. I know it's not the same, but...' she smiled at Monica sympathetically.

'And I just...' Monica added. 'I feel as if I'm getting it all wrong. Just... I get so frustrated. So – well, sometimes I get a bit bored with nappies and bottles and things like that too.' She said. 'And I suppose I don't know quite who I am as a mother, yet. I feel a bit lost.' It was the most she'd confessed about the way she felt to anyone. Even her friends. Even her own mother. Part of her longed to step back a little in time and keep her mouth shut. Because now it was out there: the evidence that she simply wasn't cut out for this.

Grace handed her another glass and she began to dry it. 'What about Peter?' she asked.

'Well, he's great. When he's here,' Monica said. 'It's just... he's really busy at the moment. Holiday season. And he's covering other pilots too, and he's just away so much more than I imagined he might be,' she said. She took a breath, unsure whether she was going to say the next bit. But she was here now; she'd gone this far. And Grace was kind, listening, attentive. 'I'm not sure whether it's me,' she said. 'Maybe he doesn't want to spend time with me.'

'Why would you say that?'

'I don't know,' Monica admitted. 'Just... well, nothing's quite the same as before I was pregnant,' she said, patting a stomach that, to Grace at least, looked impossibly flat. 'And I wonder whether he might have gone off me.'

'I'm sure that's not true,' Grace said. 'You're annoyingly gorgeous.'

Monica grinned. 'Thanks,' she said.

'Oh, believe me,' Grace said. 'You are.' She passed another glass to Monica.

'Obviously, part of me knows I'm being OTT. It's just... I suppose all my life, I've been defined by my looks. And now I can see a time... well, things are starting to slip. I don't feel as confident in myself. In Peter.'

'Ah, the privilege of ageing,' said Grace. 'Happens to us all. Or at least the lucky ones.'

'I suppose you're right. I suppose it is a privilege,' Monica said thoughtfully.

'But let's face it, it comes with a side order of yuck,' said Grace, making Monica chuckle. 'You have to reframe it, is all. Of course, none of us likes what happens to our bodies, our faces as we get older. But what's the alternative? I'm as vain as the next person. But I've come to accept that physically, I'm past my prime. And you know what? Mentally, I'm stronger than ever. As long as I avoid looking in the mirror too often!'

Monica laughed. 'Grace, you are gorgeous,' she said, patting her friend's arm. 'In every way.'

'That's one of the first things to go,' Grace said, darkly.

'What?'

'The eyesight,' Grace quipped, grinning.

Monica snorted and shook her head. They lapsed into silence, the clink of glasses in water, the screech of a sponge against a smooth surface the only noise. Then, 'I think I'm probably just being silly,' Monica added. 'I just... I'm not feeling myself. And with Peter not around, I'm feeling a bit lost out here, you know? It's just me and Bella all the time, and it's hard to go out with a baby – kind of overwhelming. So I'm here, and I suppose I need Peter here more to sort of, balance things out.'

Grace was silent for a moment. 'I understand that,' she said. 'I felt that way when...' she trailed off, not finishing the sentence. 'Keeping busy helps,' she said.

Monica nodded, setting the last glass back on its shelf and reaching for one of the bowls. The tea towel was sodden and barely took the water off. She dropped it, and reached in a drawer for another.

'It's odd,' Monica said. 'I guess most of my twenties were spent dreaming of the kind of life I have now. Perfect husband, gorgeous baby, beautiful home. I live right in the centre of Bordeaux, for

God's sake! I get annoyed at myself sometimes that I'm not feeling happier.'

'I know how that feels,' Grace said, soaping up the last bowl. 'Sometimes it can be hard getting what you want.'

Monica laughed. 'Definitely,' she said. Then, 'Oh ignore me. I'm just tired, like you say. I do know how lucky I am.'

'Yes,' Grace said, 'but it's OK to feel down about things too. Even lucky people are allowed to be human.'

'Thanks.'

'But do you mind,' Grace said, emptying the washing up bowl and drying her hands on a fluffy, white hand-towel that hung close to the sink on a chrome ring, 'if I say something... well, personal?'

Monica felt herself stiffen, a kind of defence mechanism. 'Sure,' she said.

'It's just... and I had to learn this for myself. I understand that you want Peter around more at the moment. It makes absolute sense, what with Bella being so tiny. But long term, you can't rely on a man to complete you. They are, after all, only human.'

'But...'

Grace held up a hand. 'I'm not saying Peter isn't a wonderful husband, who loves you enormously. But if his being away is leaving this sort of gap in you, then maybe you need to learn to fill it with yourself.'

'Sorry?' said Monica, not quite understanding.

'Well, when I ended up here alone...'Grace said, brushing over the details, 'I had two choices. Wither away or seize life. And I chose to seize,' she said. 'And I realised that although it was nice to have a husband, I didn't need anyone else to complete me. I was... am, already complete.'

Monica nodded. 'That's amazing. And I agree, in theory. It's just... I've kind of lost sight of who I am.'

Grace put a hand on her shoulder. 'We all do,' she said. 'And it wasn't easy getting to where I am now – within myself. We all lose ourselves, adapt to others. Forget who we are because of jobs, circumstances, babies... And, well you already know, life changes us. Changes how we see ourselves. Changes how others see us.'

Monica nodded, a hand hovering close to her face, ready to swipe away a tear.

'But that's why it's important to have a good relationship with yourself. To be your own champion, cheerleader. To be the person who forces you to get up, to go out and try something new. And it's hard. But over time, you can build something... well, wonderful.'

Monica nodded again, silent.

'I'm not saying my life is perfect,' Grace said, 'far from it. And I'm not saying that I don't sometimes miss... well, having someone special in my life. But the point is that I know now that I can survive – thrive – on my own. That I can depend on myself. That I've got my own back. If someone comes along, it would be lovely. But if they leave, or never arrive at all... that I will be perfectly OK, content.'

Monica smiled. 'That does sound good,' she said.

'You were saying about not recognising yourself,' Grace said, taking the obsolete tea towel from her friend's hands and folding it neatly over a chair back to dry. 'And I understand. But darling, that would have happened anyway. We change, we evolve, not always for the better. I sometimes look in the mirror and think to myself, who is that old hag?'

Monica laughed. 'But you're beautiful, Grace. Surely you must know that?'

Grace kept her eyes on the tea towel, slightly uncomfortable. 'Well you make the best of what you've got,' Grace said. 'But you have to be realistic. Nobody wants to die young, but if you want a long life, then you have to accept that ageing, changing is going to be involved. And it's liberating in a way. All the sagging and wrinkling and becoming invisible.'

'How so?'

'You get seen as a person. Not just as an attractive woman, but a person first and foremost. It's strange at first, but then it's kind of amazing. Because you realise people are finally seeing *you*,' she said. 'Seeing *who* you are, not *what* you are.'

Monica nodded. 'Oh,' she said. 'When you put it like that...'

'So you need to decide,' Grace said, 'who Monica is as a person. What do you want? Need? What things make you happy? And don't wait for someone else to bring those to you. Build them for yourself. You love Peter, and he loves you, and that's wonderful. But it has to be the icing on the cake, not the cake itself.'

21

Leah drove the fork into the earth, watching it crumble beneath the metal spikes. She patted at a clump and it broke down in submission. Then she stopped, breathing heavily.

She should have said something before, she thought. She should have confronted Nathan way back when she'd seen him with that woman. She'd come back from following him with Grace determined to have it out with him. But she'd held back. And then, it had seemed as if the meetings might have stopped. Nathan hadn't gone AWOL for a week.

But today, he'd come downstairs looking dapper and her heart had sunk. 'All dressed up?' she'd asked pointedly.

'I thought I'd just...' he'd said, rattling off some excuse about clearing his head, and looking at veg prices on the Saturday market before disappearing in the car.

Now, she was here, digging over a bed close to the house – one they'd used for radishes in the past but that she wanted to grow mixed lettuce leaves on – alone. Her arms were aching, her legs were sore. But the most pain she experienced was in her chest: her heart.

When she'd heard the word 'heartache' before, she hadn't thought it was literal thing. More a description of feeling blue. But she felt it now – a continuous hum in her chest. Because suddenly, she couldn't even deny to herself that something was going on.

She stuck the earth with her fork again, this time driving it deeper than before. Only now, she'd gone too far in and couldn't lift the stubborn earth. She leaned against the handle, almost as if it was a lever, trying to push it and lift the soil. But it wouldn't budge. And suddenly, she was crying, kicking at the fork. 'Where is he?' she hissed to the innocent garden tool. 'Where is Nathan?'

She took a breath and sank down onto the soil. The day was warm and she needed a drink. Probably shouldn't be digging anyway in the May sunshine; it was heading towards twenty-eight degrees – better to have left it to the evening. But she'd wanted to do *something*.

She pulled out her phone and checked the time. 11 a.m. Nathan had been out for almost two hours. Then she scrolled through and pulled up Grace's number.

Her friend answered almost immediately. There was a buzz of conversation in the background – wherever she was, Grace was busy.

'Hi,' she said. 'Sorry, I can call back later.'

'No, it's fine,' Grace said. 'I'm at the craft fayre, remember?' The sound behind her stopped abruptly as she exited to somewhere quieter. 'I've been put on teas and coffees,' she said. 'It's good to have an excuse to get a break.'

Leah smiled, then remembered why she was calling. 'I just...' she said. 'Nathan's...'

'Out again?' Grace said, in her forthright way.

'Yes.'

'Oh, Leah.'

Leah waited for the habitual reassurance Grace often doled out. *It's probably nothing*, or *try to think rationally*, but it didn't come.

The realisation that even Grace seemed out of reassurances made the tears come. 'I just...' she said. 'I can't take this, Grace. Why is he doing this to us?' She kicked at the fork, jarring her toe. 'And I'm left doing the bloody garden on my own. And I just can't...'

'Honestly, don't then,' Grace said kindly. 'Give yourself a break.'

'But the lettuce...'

'Forget the lettuce,' Grace said firmly. 'First of all, it'll still grow if you plant it tomorrow. Second of all, I'll buy you a bloody lettuce if it comes to it!'

Leah sighed. 'I suppose I'd better...'

'And don't you dare go into that chicken coop,' Grace warned. 'You don't have to prove anything to me, or yourself. And certainly not to a bunch of blummin' chickens.'

It was hard not to smile. 'Still, it's important that I show them who's boss,' she said.

'Important to whom?'

'Good point.'

'Let Nathan take the brunt when he gets home. Lord knows he deserves it.'

'So, you think...?' Leah said, her voice sounding small in the open air.

'What I think,' Grace said pointedly, 'is that whatever is going on, he is messing you about – being all mysterious – so he deserves a good pecking even if he's literally just trying to get a bit of space. If that's all it is, why all the mystery? Why the aftershave? Who does he think he is? James Bond?'

'I can't see 007 working on an allotment, to be fair.'

'Well, I reckon he'd be bloody good at it.'

Leah couldn't help but laugh. 'He'd be better than I am, that's for sure.' She left the fork where it was and made her way to the bench on the front terrace. From here, she could see the view – the thing that had sold them the house in the first place. The red roofs of houses scattered on green, falling away until all was countryside: peaceful, beautiful and unspoiled. Phone still clamped to her ear, she leaned her head back and let the warmth of the sun play on her skin. It was somehow soothing. She breathed in.

'Still there, love?' Grace interrupted.

'Yeah,' said Leah, feeling calmer. 'Just trying to find my inner Zen.'

'Atta girl, although don't lose that fire in your belly completely, will you?'

'What do you mean?'

Grace was silent for a second. 'It's hard,' she said, 'watching someone else's relationship. Because you can never really "know" another couple fully. Not really. And back when... with Stephen, people, my sister, they'd sometimes say he was a bit selfish. A bit, well, not as nice to me as he could have been. But it would make me angry if anything. I didn't want to see it.'

'OK...?' Leah felt herself stiffen, sensed something coming.

'And I don't want to interfere...'

Leah held back a small smile. Grace was notorious for her interference – but she was beginning to see this tendency differently. As an excess of caring rather than being a busybody or nosy. 'Of course,' she said. 'But go on. I really need someone to talk to about this and... well, you're the only one who knows. Scarlett sees what's going on but she's too young to realise... what it might mean. At least, I think...'

'Well,' said Grace, 'seeing as you pushed me into it, I think it's time to rip off the plaster.'

'The... what?'

'Bite the bullet! Seize the day! Carpe diem!' her friend said.

'In what way exactly?'

'It's time to talk to him, honey.'

Leah felt her shoulders tense. She knew Grace was right. She admonished herself almost daily for not just asking Nathan what was up. He clearly wasn't going to divulge anything without a bit of interrogation. Only, when she ran the scenario through her mind, she always came up short. Because she couldn't see it as a conversation that would end well. She couldn't think of a single innocent explanation for why he'd be meeting an attractive woman, in secret, and lying to her about it. It was textbook affair behaviour, surely?

'I'm... I guess I'm just too scared,' she told her friend. 'Of what he might say. Of... opening Pandora's box.'

'You can't afford to be scared!' Grace said. 'This is tearing you apart and you deserve better. You have to be open – brave.'

Leah felt herself stiffen further. It was all very well telling someone not to be scared, but it didn't do anything to relieve the awful feeling of it. 'It's easy for you to say,' she found herself saying.

'What do you mean?' Grace's tone was guarded. 'I just feel that it's better to be an open book. Not to hide parts of yourself away. Because it's clearly not doing you any good.'

'I mean,' she said, 'that it's easy to give advice, but not quite as easy to apply it to your own life. Of course I'm scared – this is my marriage, my life!'

'But if you don't say anything, you're living a lie.' Grace said.

Leah snorted. 'A lie! What about you?' She could feel heat rise inside her. Beneath, a little voice was telling her to calm down. Not to say what she was about to say. But somehow, she couldn't stop herself.

'Excuse me?'

'Well, no offence, Grace, but you're great at giving us all advice on how we should live our lives. Monica in the kitchen the other day, me... pretty much everyone you know, in fact. And it's great. It's... it's nice, I guess. Look, I know you mean well. Or I think you do. But have you ever thought about *your* life?'

'My life,' affirmed Grace, 'is exactly as I would wish it.'

'Is it?'

'What are you implying?'

'Grace,' Leah said, her voice slightly softer. 'Your life is full and you have so many friends and... and things to do. And you're so... so involved. You involve yourself with everyone. Everything.'

'Which is hardly a crime, as far as I'm aware.'

'But Grace, you never let anyone in. We've known each other for – what – three years, and I've heard you mention Stephen a handful of times at most. I have no idea how you actually felt about him, and what really happened... Whenever I've asked anything, you change the subject.'

'It's in the past. I don't dwell on—'

'But it means I have no idea who you are. Not really. What your interests are, your feelings, your fears. You must have fears, Grace. We all do. You don't let anyone close to you. How can we be friends if I don't really know what's going on with you?'

'I—' Grace began.

'And isn't all that hiding a sign of fear too? Because deep down, I think there's something you're afraid of. And maybe if you stopped telling me to face my fears and faced your own, you'd realise it's not as easy as you make it out to be.'

As soon as she'd hung up, Leah was flooded with regret.

She tried to breathe in through her nose, out through her mouth, as she'd been taught in the yoga classes she'd used to attend. It was meant to help with anxiety, but the feeling of guilt and apprehension still buzzed inside her.

She knew she'd probably hurt her friend, but then Grace had hurt her too – forced her to look something in the face despite the pain it caused. She didn't want to lose Nathan. And, for all of her complaints about allotments and veg and digging and endless egg-related meals and vengeful chickens, she didn't want to lose her life – their life – here either. She loved the buzz of Bordeaux, and the fact that although they lived close, once she was home, she felt removed from the city and out in endless countryside. She loved the house – the biggest she'd ever lived in – for all its faults and cracks and the strange wiring system. She'd loved, until recently at least, watching Scarlett grow up and blossom and – even though things were difficult between them right now – still felt her girl was better off growing up here, where she could have both her parents around most of the time, where she was settled in her school and where she had the opportunity to be truly bilingual – despite her complaints about conjugation and endless grammar.

But she couldn't carry on holding this secret – this suspicion – inside any longer.

There was a creak up above as Scarlett opened her shutters and window, letting air and light into a bedroom stale from this morning's lie-in.

'Morning,' she called, as Scarlett's crumpled, still sleepy face came into view for a moment. 'Sleep well?'

'Yeah, OK,' came the response.

'Fancy coming and helping me?' she said. 'I'm hoping to dig over the beds before your father comes back.'

'He's out again!' Scarlett exclaimed. 'Shouldn't he be helping? I thought he was the chief gardener – that's what he's always saying.'

Strictly speaking, Nathan had never said those exact words. But in fairness, he did drink out of a mug that had that festooned on the side.

'He's not doing it on his own though, is he, Scarlett? He's part of the team. We all are.'

There was a snort.

'What?' Leah said, suddenly angry.

'Nothing.'

'Well,' she said. 'Are you coming down to help?'

'Maybe later,' her daughter said. 'Too tired.'

'Tired!' Leah found herself saying. 'You don't know what tired is! I've been up for, what, four hours!' There it was again: a phrase straight from her mother's playbook.

'Not my fault,' came the response.

'Come on, Scarlett. You could at least come and help.'

But the window closed above her, decisively. She probably ought to run upstairs and assert her authority, force Scarlett downstairs. But she'd realised recently that you only really have authority as a parent if your children go along with it. You can't actually drag a child from her bedroom, put a fork in her hand and force her to dig.

She stood for a minute, looking over the view, feeling the sun play lightly on her skin. She should really call Grace back. But what would she say? She hadn't meant to hurt her, but she stood by what she'd said.

Sighing, she got up and grabbed the fork again. It would be nice to get the bed at least slightly underway before Nathan got back. To show him she was committed to their life here, even if he wasn't. Her copywriting shift started in two hours, but she had time to at least make a bit of an inroad.

She drove the fork into the earth again and tried to put thoughts of errant husbands, hostile daughters, insistent friends and malevolent chickens from her mind. She couldn't solve any of those problems right now, but this... with a bit more effort, she could at least make a difference here.

22

'So, how are my girls?' Peter said, the moment Monica picked up the phone.

'We're OK.'

'You sound a bit...' He paused. 'Is something wrong, Mon?'

She had tried to put on her usual cheery voice – the voice of the person she was trying to be – but he'd detected something in her tone. 'I'm fine,' she began. Then thought better of it. 'It's just, I can't help feeling a bit... lonely sometimes,' Monica tried to keep her voice level as she held a sleeping Bella on her shoulder. Peter was calling her from a hotel in Dubai, somewhere she'd never been. It was hard to picture him there and she was aware – not for the first time – of the distance that stretched between them.

'Come on, Mon!' he said. 'You're in the middle of Bordeaux – all the action happens there! How can you feel lonely!' His joviality sounded slightly forced.

'I'm not sure,' she admitted, patting Bella's back slightly as her child wriggled in her sleep. 'I suppose... I don't have any real friends here, not really. Not yet. And it's the night-times. When she's up, everything's so... well, silent and it's just her and me in the half-light. And I feel kind of...' She searched for a word. 'Some-times it feels as if we're the only people left in the world.'

He was silent for a minute. 'Do you think,' he said, 'you might need to go to the doctor? Are you feeling... it's common isn't it, to feel a bit down after...?'

She shook her head. 'No,' she said. 'It's not like that, I don't think. I think I just miss, well, Mum. Having my friends around. London. Just being in a more familiar place.'

'Poor thing,' he said, 'but sweetheart, it's not forever. Three years and we'll be able to make another move if you want.'

She couldn't tell him that three years, in this situation, living in paradise but somehow feeling on the outside of it all felt too much to bear. It wasn't fair on him. She'd agreed to move – even been excited by it. And he was working his socks off for the airline. 'I know,' she said. 'I just miss you, that's all.'

'Well, I miss you too,' he said, firmly. 'And when I get back, how about we find a babysitter or au pair or something and hit the town. You can show me all the sights of Bordeaux. A proper day out – just you and me.'

'Sounds good,' she said, although she'd only left Bella with a babysitter a few times and never for more than a few hours. She remembered Grace's words. Monica had sensed, without knowing much about Grace's past, that she'd been unlucky in love – and perhaps her view of relationships was tarnished by that. By being hurt.

But still, what she'd said had made a lot of sense. *What do you want? Need? What things make you happy? Don't wait for someone else to bring those to you. Build them for yourself.*

Sure, she barely spoke French, felt lonely living by herself. But Grace was right. There was life out there for her to find, if she pushed herself a little. She remembered those first days in London – knowing barely anyone. The way she'd found things to do, galleries, museums, clubs, and how her life had finally opened up and taken shape. Yes, she was older now, in a country where communication might prove an issue. But she was still the same person. Still someone who knew how to build a life, despite not knowing a soul. And perhaps she oughtn't to put the responsibility for her happiness into Peter's hands. It was a lot for him to carry, for anyone to carry.

It wouldn't hurt, at least, to put some feelers out, she decided, opening her laptop and pulling up Facebook. There, she clicked on a group link to 'English speakers in Bordeaux' and began to type.

23

Alfie put on the bedside light, the one with the bulb that glowed softly – anything too bright would hurt her eyes. In bed, his mum turned and blinked. 'What time is it?' she said.

'Eleven.'

'Oh, God, I'm sorry,' she said.

'Don't be silly. It's good to get rest. It'll do you good,' he said. He gently helped her to sit up, noticing how fragile and almost bird-like she was now. The feeling of ribs against skin – too thin. He didn't let it show in his face, puffing up the pillows instead so she could sink back into a comfortable sitting position.

He sat on the edge of the bed. 'How's the pain?'

'I'll live,' she said.

'Mum?' he prompted. 'Six out of ten? Eight?'

'Something like that,' she said. He passed her the four pills she was required to take each morning and she swallowed them with some difficulty. It was hard to watch her throat constrict and move, as she struggled to wash them down her parched throat with his proffered glass of water.

He put his hand on her arm. 'Well done,' he said.

She looked at him then. 'When did you get so grown up?' she asked. 'I should be taking care of you!'

He shook his head. 'Mum, you've done that for years. It's my turn now. And I want to. I'm happy to.'

'Are you off out today? Any classes?'

'A couple, but look, I don't have to...'

'Nonsense! I've got Margaret coming in this afternoon, and I've always got your number if I need...' she said stubbornly. 'Your degree is important.'

He looked at her. 'Mum?' he said.

'What?'

'Promise you'll call me if you need anything.'

She rolled her eyes, looking a little more like herself. 'Brownie's honour,' she said, holding up three fingers in a salute.

He smiled. He was good now, at putting on a brave face. Although every time he saw her, he experienced a sense of shock – at how thin she looked, how frail, how tired. It seemed that one version of her – the healthy version before she'd got sick – was fixed in his mind, meaning each time he saw the version ravaged by this cruel disease, it was a little like a stab to the heart.

'I've nearly finished *Madame Bovary*,' he told her. 'I'll read a bit to you later, if you like.'

Her eyes were closed, but she smiled slightly and gave an almost imperceptible nod.

Ever since her diagnosis a year ago, he'd been filled with a desire to 'fix things' for her. Somehow make things better, and get her better in the process. He'd started working on the house – as best he could – painting the faded walls, tidying up more than he ever had. Doing the washing – another novelty. He knew it was stupid, misguided, but he couldn't shake off the feeling that if he did enough – if he was enough – somehow, everything would be alright.

Even his attending the reading group had been for her really – at least at first. 'Oh, I wish I could get to that,' she'd said sadly when he'd shown her the flyer. 'Maybe one day.'

'Do you want me to go?' he'd offered.

He wasn't insulted when she'd let out an incredulous laugh. He was hardly an avid reader. But he'd meant it – maybe he could go in her place, talk to her about it afterwards. Make her interested in books and reading and... well, life. If she had enough things going on, maybe it would be enough to make her stay.

He'd read all sorts of articles, done deep dives into various forums. Everywhere you went, people seemed to be touting miracle cures – special diets, hypnotherapy, meditation, homeopathy, positive thinking. He knew he'd never convince her to deviate from the regime the hospital had set her on (and had no desire to; after all, he wasn't a doctor). But the positive thinking angle had caught his attention.

Somehow, he felt, deep inside, her body must know how to heal itself and if she felt enough pleasure, enough of a pull to the land of the living, just maybe something would shift inside her. If not, at least going to the group for her was something he could do. Because he needed to focus this restless, desperate energy somewhere.

So, he'd joined the group, reading the books with her, telling her about the women and George and the thoughts they'd had. Sharing some of her opinions on Heathcliff, on Darcy, with the group and telling her how they'd responded. And she'd smiled and said she was proud of him and that she was so thrilled that he'd rediscovered his love of reading.

The biggest surprise of all was how much he'd begun to look forward to the meetings. Alfie's interests normally lay in all things digital, in gaming and YouTube shorts and all the things his peers raved about. But he'd enjoyed the reading more than he'd thought he would. And the group – the group had become special to him in a way he couldn't fully explain.

He'd realised what little time he'd spent with people of his mum's age over the years. He'd never known his dad – Mum still couldn't be drawn to tell his story and he'd set it aside in recent months. Perhaps there were some things he'd be better off not knowing.

Having the group, though, had made him realise just how few friends his mum had over here. She still knew a couple of the mums she'd bonded with when they first came over – both English. She had a friendly relationship with the neighbours, talking in her careful but adequate French. But she never seemed to get properly close to anyone. Maybe if she got better, he'd help her. Help her back into life.

'I'll call you between classes,' he said to her now. 'Just ring if you need me. Honestly.'

She nodded, shuffling slightly on her pillow. He fetched a jug of water and a glass for her nightstand, as well as some chocolate she probably wouldn't touch, and fluffed the pillows again until she was forced to tell him to 'go or you'll be late!'

Then, with a deep sigh, he shouldered his backpack, opened the door and disappeared into the late-May morning.

24

Leah took a sip of coffee and felt the hot liquid scorch down her throat. She looked out of the window at the garden, bathed in early-summer light. Nathan was diligently hacking his way through the rest of the bed that she'd started yesterday, dressed in his habitual 'work clothes' and definitely – as far as she could tell – not about to slip out into the city centre.

Already today, she'd cleaned almost everything in the kitchen – even getting onto a chair to wipe the dust from the top of the light fitting (which had been filthy), tidying cupboards, mopping the floor. She'd stopped short of collecting the eggs – she wasn't a masochist after all. But despite all her attempts to distract herself, the feeling that had been building up inside her since she'd woken with a start at six this morning had built to an almost explosive level.

She'd finished the last chapter of *Madame Bovary* late last night and had been surprised to find tears running down her face. Perhaps if she'd read it years ago, she'd have sympathised with Madame Bovary herself – the restless, beautiful Emma – someone who was yearning for excitement and passion. But now her heart went out to Charles, her ordinary, cuckold of a husband. Yes, he was a bit dull, but he loved Emma and was steadfast and reliable.

That's when she'd realised. If she was identifying with a dull, nineteenth-century fictional doctor who dies a miserable death, she really had to get a handle on herself.

It was time.

No more being afraid. No more sleepless nights. No more justifying her fears, or writing off his absences as something completely innocent. She had to know the truth, whatever it might be.

'Nathan!' she called, trying to keep her voice light. 'Could you pop in for a minute?'

He looked up. 'I'm just—' he said.

'I know, but have a break, yeah? I've made a coffee. And I need to ask you something.'

Last night, he'd cuddled into her in bed in a way he hadn't done for ages, his arms wrapped around her, body spooning to hers. She'd rubbed his arms and allowed herself to sink into his embrace. It was a relief, this intimacy after a couple of weeks of being too tired, too busy or too stressed. And she'd almost changed her mind about talking to him at all.

But today, she'd woken up with Grace's words echoing in her ears. Whatever Nathan was doing – however innocent – he was doing it under the radar. Creating unnecessary stress for her. 'Think about how you'd feel if the situation were reversed – even if it is completely innocent,' Grace had said. 'You'd hate to think you were hurting Nathan unintentionally, wouldn't you? He owes you an explanation.'

'He owes me an explanation,' she said, quietly to herself as her husband made his way across the uneven earth, which clumped and gathered on the bottom of his boots, his face unreadable.

Nathan sat on the front step and slipped off his boots with a grunt, then stretched and wandered into the kitchen in his grey socks. 'Thanks love,' he said, seeing the large mug of coffee she'd made for him. He stood by the table and took a sip, sighing with pleasure.

'Actually,' she said, her heart thundering almost painfully. 'Nathan, can you sit down?'

'Why?' he asked, almost immediately. Almost too immediately. 'What's wrong?'

'Just...' she said, gesturing to a chair and pulling one out for herself. As she sank into her seat at the table, her eyes wandered over the garden, the countryside, the blue sky with the promise of a perfect day ahead, weather wise. Their life was perfect, simply perfect, she thought. Could she really throw a grenade into it? Was it so bad to feel that her husband had a secret? Did she have to know everything?

He was looking at her now, obediently sitting in the chair she'd pulled out for him, his face serious. 'Love,' he said, reaching out a hand, 'you're scaring me now. What is it? Is it... are you sick? Is it Scarlett?'

'Oh, God, no,' she said. 'Sorry. Nothing like that. I just need to...' she trailed off.

'Then what?' he asked, taking another sip of coffee. 'Spit it out.'

See – it wasn't easy when you were the one in the dark, she thought, looking at his wide eyes. He sensed something was up and was desperate to know – yet couldn't credit her with the same sensibilities when he went on his mysterious trips. The frisson of anger she felt at this realisation gave her the strength she needed to finally say it. 'Nathan, you're keeping something from me,' she said, putting her cup down and looking at him so directly that he looked away.

'What do you mean?' he said, sounding a little like Scarlett had used to, aged eight, when she'd been caught covered in chocolate, or Leah's perfume or other forbidden substances and tried to feign innocence.

'Do you really want me to spell it out?' she said.

'Honestly, love,' he said, putting down his coffee and trying to smile at her. The result was lopsided, unnatural. 'I really don't know what you're on about.'

'OK,' she said, taking a deep breath. 'Nathan, you've been going out, what – twice, three times a week?'

'But I...' he began to protest.

'Let me finish,' she said firmly. 'It's not normal; something's changed. You get dressed up, you put on aftershave, you're mysterious about where you're spending your time. And I never know when you're going to disappear next.'

'I'm just...' he said, spots of colour appearing on his cheeks. 'I suppose I'm a bit sick of feeling scruffy when I go into town, is all. Everyone's so dressed up. I just... want to make an effort.' The lopsided smile returned.

Leah was shaking her head. 'Don't lie, Nathan,' she said.

'This is ridiculous!' he said, his nostrils flaring slightly. 'I'm not lying! What do you think? That I'm meeting some... some woman? Getting dressed up and having an affair?' His tone was clearly meant to sound incredulous, but to Leah, it just sounded guilty. Something like a smile played briefly on his features before he regained control. Was it guilt, she wondered? Awkwardness?

'Nathan, I saw you,' she said. Then, quickly, corrected herself. 'I mean, someone saw you, and told me,' she said, not wanting to fully reveal all of her cards. 'You met a woman.' Her voice broke on the word 'woman'. 'You disappeared into an apartment with her.'

Nathan's brow seemed studiously furrowed. 'When?' he said.

'For God's sake!' she said, her voice coming out louder than she intended. 'Don't play for time. You know it happened, and I know. But what I need to know is have you been seeing someone or not:

having an affair? What's going on, Nathan? What aren't you telling me?'

Her husband's eyes were fixed on the table, and he paused for what seemed like an unbearably long time. 'OK,' he said, at last, raising his face and looking her in the yes. 'OK. Yes, I've been… well, I haven't been completely truthful. But it's not what you think.'

Leah wondered whether hearts could actually leap out of chests. She'd heard the feeling described metaphorically in the books she'd read in the past, but never thought it could be an actual physical phenomenon. Yet her heart was throwing itself against her ribcage so forcefully, she thought it might break through.

'Then what is it, Nathan?' she said, feeling her eyes fill with tears. 'What's going on? And why haven't you told me?'

His gaze fell to the table, hands worrying at the side of his mug, but he remained silent. The silence seemed tangible, to be a thing between them growing and filling the whole of the room. 'Nathan?' she said again.

He looked up. 'OK,' he said. 'OK.'

'What is it?'

'It's not what you think,' he began. 'No, no. I realise that's a cliché. But it really isn't. The thing is – and I haven't wanted to tell you – is that…' he paused unbearably. 'Look, I've been feeling depressed. Well, not clinically… just, well a bit down. A bit lost.' He looked at her, clearly hoping to meet a sympathetic look.

'So, what are you saying? You felt a bit depressed so you had to find someone to cheer you up?' she said. 'Is that what you're telling me?'

He shook his head. 'No! No. Not at all. Well, sort of. But not in the way you think,' he said.

'For God's sake, Nathan,' she said. 'Can you please just tell me what is going on? Please?'

He sighed, deeply. 'She's not. I'm not having an affair,' he said at last. 'I'm seeing a life coach. A counsellor, of sorts.'

'A life coach?'

'I know. It sounds... but she is. I felt like I was falling, Leah. I didn't know... I wasn't sure where to turn. Then I saw an advert in the paper. She's... it's expensive, but I'm finding... She's really helping me, Leah.'

It still didn't feel right. '*Is* she?' Leah heard herself say, icily.

'Look, I'd've got a bloke, a male counsellor or whatever, if I could. But she can speak English, Leah. And I know I'm working on my French. But when you're talking about feelings... It's hard enough to find the words as it is.'

She looked up then, met his eye. 'OK,' she said, slowly. 'Say I believe you. That there's nothing going on – then why the mystery?'

He shrugged, looking for a moment almost exactly like his daughter. 'I was embarrassed, I suppose.'

'Seriously?'

'Yeah. I dunno. It feels... well, pathetic. Needing help like that. It's not very... sexy.'

'Nathan!' she said, reaching out for the first time. Touching his hand, just a fraction. 'It's not pathetic at all. Come on, we've talked about mental health before – we talk about everything. You really couldn't talk to me about that?'

The shrug again. 'It sounds stupid now,' he admitted. 'It's just, you're doing all that work online, and helping with the garden. And what am I doing? Waving a spade around and failing to grow anything. I didn't... I just hoped I could find a solution to it all without causing you any stress. I wanted to find a way forward.'

She snorted. 'Safe to say, you caused more than a little bit of stress.' But she could feel herself relax slightly. It felt true. But if he was depressed, how serious was it? Was he just revealing the edges of something much deeper?

'I didn't want you to know I wasn't happy, after it was me that more or less suggested this,' he said. 'I wanted to find a solution.'

'And have you? I mean, is it helping? The therapy?' she said, cautiously.

He nodded. 'I think so.'

'And you're... you don't think you need to see a doctor?'

He shook his head once, briefly. 'I told Dr Leycure,' he said. 'Told her what I was doing. She offered me some stuff to take, but I haven't yet. She gave me her number in case I'm ever... I ever feel... well...' His cheeks reddened.

It was a lot to take on. And after so much time suspecting, Leah was finding it hard to fully accept his reasoning. 'OK,' she said. 'I mean, that's awful and I'm glad you're getting help. But what I don't... what I don't understand is – why didn't you feel you could talk to me? Seriously?'

He shook his head. 'I'm sorry.'

'So what do we do now?' she said. 'Do you want to sell up? Move back?'

'Well, carry on,' he said. 'I don't want to quit this life. I don't think. I'm just working through – working out why I feel the way I do. It doesn't mean this isn't the right life for me, for us.'

She nodded again. 'OK,' she said uncertainly. Then a thought. 'Hang on,' she added. 'If this woman...'

'Adeline.'

'Adeline,' she said. 'If Adeline is a life coach, then how come you'd always go out so "last minute"? Why didn't you tell me you had an appointment? Why all the rushing off?'

He blushed. 'It wasn't really so last minute. I knew. I just wanted... I guess I didn't want you to insist on coming. If I waited till we both worked, got dirty... I knew I could get a head start and look like I was just rushing out and you wouldn't, couldn't come with me.'

She gave a deep sigh. 'For God's sake, Nathan.'

'I know.'

'You're an idiot, you know that?'

'I think I'm in agreement there.' He said, a half-smile on his lips.

'OK,' she said.

'OK?'

'OK. It makes sense. All of it. I suppose. I'm just a bit hurt you didn't feel you could tell me.'

'Typical man?' he offered.

'I guess so,' she said. She held his hand now, properly. 'But seriously, Nathan, this has to be the end of it. Promise you'll tell me if you feel... well, how you feel from now on?'

He nodded.

They sat in silence for a moment. Then he said, 'One thing I can promise you. I'll never cheat on you.'

'Right.' She still felt uneasy. But she couldn't exactly tell Nathan he couldn't see a counsellor because she was female. She herself was in a book club with two men – obviously neither of them appealed to her romantically, but Nathan wouldn't necessarily know that.

'So we're OK?'

She sighed. 'I don't know. I think so.'

He squeezed her hand. 'I'm such an idiot. How long have you... well, suspected something?'

She shook her head. 'I don't know. A few weeks... longer maybe. Since Scarlett saw you with someone...'

'Scarlett did?' He looked horrified.

'Yeah, or she thought she did. A while ago, we were driving...

Just outside on the street. But she... I could tell she thought something wasn't right.'

'Oh, God. No wonder she's been so off with me.'

Leah caught his eye. 'I think that might have less to do with you and more to do with her life stage,' she said. 'But yes, she said she saw you, and she was so panicked about it, I turned the car around. But then we couldn't see you.'

Nathan shook his head. 'Poor girl.'

They sat in silence for a moment. Outside, a tractor rumbled past. In the distance, a dog was barking and, in the fir trees in the field beyond their land, she could hear the rattling sound of a woodpecker doing what woodpeckers do best.

It was so idyllic, so beautiful. So peaceful. Yet in here, in the home they were building together, everything felt jangled, stressful. She wanted to get up from the table, move outside and let the sun warm her skin. And pretend that everything felt alright, that this life they'd chosen was a good fit. That Nathan was definitely faithful.

But the feeling wouldn't come. She supposed it might, in time.

She set her cup down and looked at him, unwaveringly. 'Look, I know you've reassured me. But... I need to hear it again. Properly. Just promise me you're not having an affair.'

'I swear I'm not.'

'And no more secrets?'

He paused for a moment.

'Nathan?'

'I'd never hurt you,' he said. 'I promise that.'

Later, when she thought back, she wondered at his choice of words. Reassuring but always skating on the edges of a proper promise. She wondered why she hadn't noticed that in the moment. But then, you see what you want to, she'd concluded.

'We'd better have a chat with Scarlett, in that case,' she said. 'She's obviously got to know that nothing is going on.'

'Agreed.'

Leah stood up and moved closer to the door. 'Scarlett! Can you come down here?' she yelled.

'Why?' her daughter's voice called back, muffled by the wooden door, the staircase, the empty hall.

'Because,' Leah said, trying to keep her tone even, 'I asked you to.'

There was a snort of derision, but she heard the bedsprings creak and Scarlett appeared in the kitchen a few moments later, dressed in a black T-shirt and chequered pyjama bottoms. The contrast between the sweet pink of the bottoms and the rebellious defiance of the black top – emblazoned with the word 'whatever' – struck Leah. Somewhere under there, under that attitude, that apparent hatred of her mum (and whatever the books said, it really did feel like Scarlett despised her at times), her little girl was still there. At least, she hoped so.

'What?' Scarlett said again, her expression dark, eyebrows knitted together, hair adorably tousled, although Leah would never dare describe it that way out loud.

It struck Leah then that they ought to have decided exactly what they were going to say. *Daddy's not having an affair* didn't sound quite right. After all, she'd already played down the 'sighting' to her daughter weeks ago. Scarlett probably had zero idea of what her mother had been worried about – and 'reassuring' her now would possibly just freak her out.

'Um...' said Nathan, looking across at Leah, his eyes betraying that he'd come to the same realisation. Or at least, that something wasn't quite right.

'Um,' Leah echoed. Scarlett gave a customary eyeroll but for once, Leah didn't blame her. 'Me and your dad were just talking,' she said, at last, 'and we realised that, um, we perhaps don't talk enough, as a family.'

Scarlett folded her arms and perched on the edge of a bar stool, ready, it seemed to escape at a moment's notice. 'So?' she said.

Nathan, seizing on the change of subject said, 'Yes, so we wanted to ask, is everything OK with you? School OK? Friends?'

Leah thought that anyone who has raised or even met a teenager must know the exact nature of the look this incited in Scarlett. It was chilling. 'Yeah?' she said. 'Is that it?'

But they ought to say something reassuring about Nathan, Leah thought, just in case Scarlett was secretly worried.

Scarlett's stool scraped back. 'Oh!' Leah continued, as if the thought had just struck her. 'Also, you know that woman we saw Dad with the other day? Turns out he's getting life coaching!' she said, trying to keep her voice bright. 'He's trying to... well, work out what he wants to do if the gardening thing doesn't work out.'

Scarlett looked at her. 'You seriously called me down,' she said, 'to tell me Dad's seeing a shrink?'

'No,' Leah said, trying to keep the impatience from her voice. 'We called you down to say that we need to try to reconnect as a family. Dad and I had a chat and we'd had some misunderstandings recently, and we realised that maybe we haven't been... open enough with each other. And – we don't always feel as if we get to talk to you much either!'

Something crossed Scarlett's features. It was fleeting and Leah struggled to capture it exactly. 'Oh, I get it,' she said. 'You asked Dad about that woman we saw him with? And she's his therapist, right? Not his new girlfriend?'

'Life coach.' Leah said, firmly.

Nathan's face was maroon. 'Scarlett,' he said. 'That's completely inappropriate.'

'So is having life lessons from some blonde woman in the street,' she said, giving him a look that would have made many weaker men crumble.

'Well, I think it's great,' Leah said, 'it's not easy, you know. Being in your forties...'

'Yeah, being old,' finished Scarlett.

This wasn't going the way either of them had planned.

'Scarlett...' Nathan said, a warning tone in his voice.

'What?'

Nathan clearly hadn't thought it out. 'Just... stop it.'

'Stop what?'

'Oh just, go to your room,' Leah said, exasperated.

Scarlett, evidently getting what she'd wanted in the first place, said, 'Fine, I'd rather be there than talking to you two weirdos anyway.'

As she walked loudly and purposefully back upstairs, Leah's eyes met Nathan's. 'Well, that went well,' she said.

And they smiled at each other, in the midst of their shared parental frustration. It was interesting, Leah thought, how Scarlett could somehow bind them together, even when her behaviour was rude and erratic.

Leah sat down again, let Nathan's hand cover hers, and allowed herself to smile.

'I love you, you know,' he said.

'You too,' she replied.

And, at that moment, it was enough.

25

JUNE

Bella was asleep in her pram.

Monica rocked her slightly as she sipped her *chocolat-chaud*, marvelling as she always did at the tiny details of her – the eyelashes, the impossibly small fingernails. The little bit of fluffy hair just showing under her bonnet. It was the first of June and although the weather was warm, the mornings were still cool enough to bring Bella out without having to worry about the tiny girl overheating. Today, the sky remained resolutely white, and although heat was promised for later in the day, the freshness of the morning was invigorating.

Monica glanced at the time on her phone. It was still only five minutes to. There was time to disappear if she wanted to. Time to forget it all. And nobody would know.

She'd managed to fit into a pair of navy jeans she'd owned before motherhood – the button undone at the top – and a black, fine-knit jumper. She knew she looked more like her old self – more like the Facebook profile she'd created. But she felt constrained and uncomfortable and wished in some ways she'd stuck to her baggy cast offs.

Perhaps this wasn't a good idea. Perhaps...

'Are you Monica?' a voice said.

Monica looked up to see a woman with brown, curly hair, dressed in a light summer dress and carrying a baby in a sling. She hadn't mastered a sling herself – whenever she'd tried one, it felt awkward and uncomfortable, and she envied the ease at which some women seemed to wear their babies as if they were still an extension of their own bodies.

'Yes,' she said. 'Marie?'

'Yes,' the woman smiled and pulled out a chair, sinking into it with a sigh. 'God, what a relief to have a bit of a cool breeze,' she said. 'I'm roasting in our apartment.'

Monica didn't mention that her own apartment had air-conditioning and was always at an even temperature. 'I know,' she said instead.

They were both silent for a moment and it felt a little like a first date.

'So, you want to start a mothers' group?' said Marie.

'Yeah,' Monica said. 'Just something informal. They run one at the *Salle de Fêtes*, and I tried it a couple of times, but...'

'Too French?' Marie said.

Monica felt herself blush. Although there was no shame in speaking imperfect French, when she'd lived here such a short time. 'Well, that,' she said. 'But more... well, I wanted something more informal. A bit more ad-hoc. For mothers like me, who can't get ourselves organised enough.'

Marie laughed at this.

'And I suppose, yes, for those of us who can't speak perfect French yet,' Monica admitted. 'I know, if we decide to stay longer term, I'll get there. But with Bella already here...'

'You need something now?' Marie nodded. 'Yes, me too. When

I saw your post on the Facebook group, I thought, "YES! Someone on my wavelength."'

They smiled slightly shyly at each other, and Marie tucked some of her curls behind an ear. The clump of tousled hair fell forward again almost immediately. 'Is anyone else coming?' Marie asked.

'There should be one other,' Monica said, feeling a little embarrassed that she'd had so little interest. 'But hopefully more next time.'

'It's great,' Marie said. 'I'm sure more people will come once they hear about it. I've got a friend just outside the city who's got a two-year-old and I'm sure she'd be interested.'

Monica nodded. 'That would be lovely,' she said.

The waiter came over and took Marie's order. Bella, still sleeping in her pram, began making sucking noises and moving her lips back and forth.

'Oh, she's precious!' Marie exclaimed.

'Thank you.'

'Timeo does that,' Marie said, rubbing the lump of baby strapped to her front. 'Honestly, he's a typical man. All he thinks about is food... and boobs.'

They laughed. Monica shifted slightly in her chair.

It would take time, Monica realised, to feel completely at ease. But she was doing it. She was building what she needed into her own life.

Another woman began to wheel a pushchair towards them. 'This'll be Jess,' she said, standing up and waving.

The woman waved back and began to make her way towards their table.

The sky was still white, but the edges of some of the light clouds were beginning to glow, revealing that the sun was just underneath, working its way through to flood the afternoon with sunshine.

26

It was surreal, George thought, listening to Blur – a Britpop favourite from his twenties – while working on a building site in France in his forties. He thought of his younger self, visiting clubs, half-working, half-socialising at college, dreaming of the future and wondered what that version of him would say to see him now, shirt off in the French sun, reconstructing a tumbledown wall.

He liked to think that that version of him wouldn't be too disappointed. Sure, he hadn't got the wife and 2.4 kids he'd assumed he'd have by now, but he was relatively happy. He had some good mates out here on the site, and was spending a year in Bordeaux. It sounded OK when you put it like that.

'Coming for a drink later?' Derek shouted over. 'It's going to be a scorcher this arvo, thought we'd wind up soon.'

The weather hadn't been the best for working outside recently. During the spring, they'd often managed ten-hour days, slogging away and seeing real results. But since the summer had come into itself, the heat had been intense and their energy and impetus had drained. George had suggested they start getting up early to get a decent amount of work done before they were forced to stop and drink beer and take a dip in the local lake. So far, everyone had agreed, but nobody had ever been awake and working when he'd turned up at the house, meaning he was clocking up an hour or so before they even opened their eyes.

'Sorry mate,' Derek had said when he'd found him in the kitchen at nine this morning.

'S'OK,' he'd replied. It was Derek's house, Derek's project, Derek paying his bed and board. If Derek wanted to slack off, there wasn't much he could do about it.

'Yeah, why not?' he said now, standing back to inspect his work.

The house his friend had bought had been a 'steal' at 85,000 euros. But not quite the bargain he'd thought at first. Derek had assumed it would just be the interior that needed work, but investigation had revealed he hadn't done his due diligence. While the structure itself was sound, there were several areas that needed firming up properly before they could start work on the interior. The two others – Scott and Harry – had been staying in the property to save money. But Derek had retreated to a hotel and George to his city centre bedsit.

Blur's 'Country House' started up and he laughed. 'Here you go mate, this one's for you,' he said to Derek.

In all honesty, he couldn't believe that Derek – once a real city boy like himself – was planning to live somewhere so remote. Sure, the property was just forty minutes' drive from Bordeaux, but there was nothing much in the tiny hamlet to entertain a single bloke in his mid-thirties like Derek.

Still, each to their own.

George hadn't thought, when he was in his thirties, that he'd still be single, still unsure of what he was going to do with his life by now. He'd assumed when he'd met Alison back then that they'd settle down, do the family thing. Only she'd upped and left almost without warning and he'd felt cut loose ever since. They'd sold the flat and he probably should have used the chunk of change he'd got as a result as a deposit on a new place. Only he hadn't felt like it.

Instead, he'd invested his money in a long-term bond, quit his job and done temping work around various sites – taking a bit of an ad-hoc approach to work, spending time in new areas to get his head straight. Relationships broke up, sure, but he'd always been led to believe that there'd be warning signs along the way. The way it had happened had shaken his confidence.

What he'd thought would be a year of drifting and 'getting his head straight' had turned into a decade. Now it was a way of life. But although it might not have happened by choice, he was relatively happy. And not sure, after all this time, how to make a change.

Six months ago, Derek had called him up – George had worked with him on a property in Cornwall two years before – and asked how he was fixed. And George had felt that a year in France might just be the thing he needed to finally get himself back on track.

Now he was here, he wasn't so sure.

All the thoughts, feelings he'd been running from, had just seemed to come with him.

It wasn't that he wanted Alison back – she was happy now, had a baby even. He'd seen the news on Facebook. It was just he didn't know what to do with himself now. Meet someone new, but live with that feeling they might suddenly whip out a grenade and blow your present and your future apart? He wasn't sure if he wanted to give another person that kind of power over his life.

Derek was single, the other lads had wives and kids and all that. They'd fly back every couple of weeks to see them. George couldn't understand why they'd want to work so far away from their families, but it wasn't the sort of question you asked, was it?

He stood back again and looked at his work, nodded to himself, and began to clear his materials up.

The sun had broken through now, and he could feel the heat prickle on his skin. It'd be nice to head out for a beer. Maybe he'd see if they'd come into the city rather than grabbing a keg from the supermarket. They could probably all manage to crash at his if they wanted. Just about. And it would mean he could drink instead of worrying how he'd get back to the flat in one piece.

27

'Got everything you need?' Nathan said, poking his head around the kitchen door and smiling at Leah.

It was after six and she had just about an hour before the book group descended on her. She was dreading it and looking forward to it in equal measure. It would be nice to see everyone again, nice to get her literary fix. But looking at the house with new eyes – imagining what she might think of it if she was seeing it for the first time – had made her feel frantic. Nothing would ever be clean enough, tidy enough, tasteful enough to welcome her new guests.

She was nervous, too, of seeing Grace. They'd spoken since the argument – she'd apologised to her friend and Grace had accepted. But she wasn't sure of the damage she might have done, whether their friendship had been harmed. Whether she'd really hurt her. Would things feel different?

She looked up now, holding a plate of *vol-au-vents*. 'Yeah, think so.' Then looked again. 'You off out?' she said, trying to keep her voice light.

Nathan shrugged. 'Thought I'd give you lot a bit of space,' he said. 'I haven't read the book, so it's not like I can contribute anything.'

'Where?'

He had the good sense to blush a bit. 'Well, I thought it might be a good time to make an appointment. Adeline does evenings.'

In the three weeks since their conversation, Nathan had been true to his word. Upfront about the times when he was going to meet his counsellor rather than giving a vague excuse as to why he was popping out yet again.

This was what she'd wanted, wasn't it? It would have been nice if he'd told her sooner what he'd intended, though. She'd hoped he might stay and say hello to everyone.

It was her fault, she thought, pulling the cork out of the wine as his car crunched out of the driveway. She should have said something rather than assuming he'd want to meet them all. He surely would have stayed if she'd asked him.

She took a deep, shuddering breath and poured herself a glass of wine. It made sense to taste it – make sure it was up to the standards set by Grace and Monica, after all. She took a slug and decided that yes, this was definitely going to make the cut.

* * *

An hour later, and two glasses down, she was sitting in her living room, feeling a little embarrassed of her slightly worn leather sofas and the parquet floor that was in need of a good polish. But George had commented on the dresser she'd painstakingly chalk-painted herself – said it looked brilliant. Which had been lovely to hear.

When she and Nathan had chosen the house, she'd told herself she was above 'house envy' and having to have everything perfect. It was all about life, living, trying to be sustainable. And so many people she'd met over here lived in houses where their taste could be described as 'eclectic' if you were being kind, and 'chaotic' if you were being realistic. It didn't seem to matter in the same way.

Yet somehow, she'd managed to befriend Grace – queen of the perfect paint job and tasteful décor – and now Monica, who lived in an apartment that felt like the floor of an expensive hotel. Alfie's place – well, they hadn't seen that. And she wasn't sure what George was going to do when it was his turn to host. But, as they'd entered, she'd felt the difference between her place and the others they'd been to keenly.

The antique refectory table with its long, smooth benches either side was practical and in-keeping with the house, but hardly a match for Monica's designer cream furnishings or Grace's tastefully upholstered chairs. The enamel stove – her pride and joy – looked rather old fashioned suddenly. Was it all a bit too rustic?

She'd decided to host in the living room, but there, too, things seemed a little down at heel. The vintage sofas they'd sourced from a *brocante*, and the *chaise-longue* she'd been unable to resist at a local auction looked mismatched. She'd dragged a coffee table into the centre and half pulled the curtains so that the bright sunlight wouldn't highlight the dancing dust particles that seemed to endure, no matter what. It would have to do.

'Sorry it's a bit of a mess,' she'd said, as George had leaned down to kiss her cheek hello on his arrival.

'Don't be daft,' he'd said. 'I love these old, stone houses.'

She'd said something similar to Monica, who'd smiled and said it was beautiful, but who was dressed more smartly than usual in linen trousers and a silk top, and looked quite out-of-place on the tired sofa.

Grace had arrived five minutes late – so unlike her – but had otherwise seemed to all intents and purposes her usual self, handing Leah a box of chocolates and giving her a kiss on the cheek.

'Sorry again,' Leah found herself saying.

'It's fine,' Grace had waved her hand dismissively.

Alfie had yet to arrive.

She'd poured wine for them all and set out a range of nibbles on the coffee table. Earlier, she'd asked Scarlett if she might come down and say hello, but had received the kind of look she'd thought she might – a kind of amused, pitying, incredulous one. Still, she'd tried.

'No Nathan tonight?' Grace said now.

Leah wasn't sure if she was being pointed. Everything seemed pointed at the moment.

'No, he's out,' she said with a smile to show that this was fine with her. 'Thought he'd make himself scarce.'

'And you found a babysitter in the end?' Grace remarked to Monica.

'Yes. She was free after all. Thank goodness!' She smiled.

'You'd have been welcome to bring Bella, if not,' Leah reminded her. 'I'd love to see her again. I'm sure we all would.'

She was yet to tell Grace that she'd finally confronted Nathan. Even though it had been a few days ago, she hadn't been able to face up to uttering the words. It was odd – because the mystery, such as it was, had been solved. And everything was fine. She just didn't feel like talking about it.

She took another sip of wine.

'Shall we start?' she said, looking at the group. 'I've sent Alfie a text but nothing yet. He'll probably be along but...'

The rest of them murmured their agreement.

'Well,' said Grace, leaning forward slightly, her enormous, beaded necklace swinging precariously close to the glass of wine she'd set on the coffee table. 'I did enjoy reading it again. But I just wish things had ended better for the poor love.'

'Poor love being...?'

'Emma, of course. All the girl is doing is looking for happiness. Instead, she's trapped in a marriage with boring Charles – when she wants something... well, more than that.'

They nodded.

'Yeah but,' George said, clearing his throat. 'The guy didn't do anything wrong, did he? He couldn't help being a bit boring.'

'Well, perhaps he should have chosen a boring wife?' Grace said, raising a challenging eyebrow. 'Emma needs more than Charles can give her. It's no wonder she went looking for someone else to fill that void. He shouldn't have been so greedy.'

'Touché,' George said with a smile. 'I get what you're saying. And I know things were different back then. Women didn't have so many... options. But he was never – he never pretended to be anything he wasn't. She got what it said on the tin. An unambitious doctor.'

'A girl could do worse,' Monica quipped. 'Obviously, I get that she wanted *more*, but it was all a bit of a fantasy, wasn't it? Too many romance novels, not enough real life.'

'Yes, we don't want her fragile, female brain getting over-loaded, now, do we?' Grace said. 'Poor woman. No wonder she wanted to break free from the kind of life she was expected to lead!'

'I can't believe people thought romance novels would pollute women's brains back then,' Monica giggled. 'What a weird time to be alive.' She took a sip of wine and shook her head. 'Glad I was born in a more modern era.'

'Mind you, they still call a lot of books in this genre, women's fiction,' said Grace. 'There's still that insinuation that men wouldn't be interested in women's little stories.'

'Yeah, that seems old-fashioned,' George said, brow furrowed. 'One of the lads saw my book and took the... laughed at me. Because it had a painting on the cover. He said it was girly. And maybe I'd've thought that too before this group, you know? But I'm really getting to like reading this stuff.'

'Me too,' said Monica.

They all agreed that romance books definitely had more to them than many people thought.

'Maybe you're right about Charles,' Leah said to Grace. 'I mean, he's an OK bloke. He loves her. He proposed. But she didn't say yes for the right reasons. Maybe if she had, he'd have found someone equally... equally...'

'Dull?'

'Ha. Yes. So maybe he's a victim of the times they lived in too – she didn't have choices open to her, so married someone who couldn't make her happy. And if she'd had more choices, maybe they'd both have been happier.'

'I feel sorry for their daughter,' Monica said. 'She's a doctor's daughter and she ends up... practically destitute once both her parents die. It's like nobody thought about her at all.'

There was a knock on the door. 'Hang on,' Leah said, standing up to get it. She realised she felt a little unsteady – *no more wine*, she thought to herself firmly.

Alfie stood on the doorstep, dressed in shorts and a crumpled T-shirt. 'Sorry we're late,' he said. He clutched a dog-eared copy of *Madame Bovary*. Camille stood next to him, her arm linked in his.

'Everything alright?' Grace asked as they entered.

'Yeah,' Alfie said.

'We were just helping his mother with some food,' Camille said.

The others made space on the sofa and Leah brought another chair in from the kitchen for Camille. She poured both the newcomers a glass of wine and they sat for a moment in silence, the conversation yet to resume.

'We were just talking,' Leah said, taking a sip of her wine

before remembering she'd vowed not to do that, 'about Charles and how he's kind of a victim too in the novel.'

Alfie nodded. 'I get that. He can't help being boring.'

Camille laughed. 'It sound like you think you are boring, Alfie,' she said affectionately.

He grinned, slightly self-conscious. 'Well, if the cap fits.'

'*Mais non!*' she exclaimed. 'You are a very interesting man. You must not talk yourself down like this.'

'Amen to that,' George said, his voice coming out more loudly than even he expected. 'Sorry,' he added, with a grin. 'Anyway, boring is underrated if you ask me.'

Monica snorted. 'You think?'

'Yeah,' George shifted slightly in his chair. 'I get that books need interesting characters. But in real life, I mean. There's nothing wrong with being... well, stable at least.'

There was murmured agreement.

'Obviously, Heathcliff's... well, far from stable. But even in *Pride and Prejudice*, there's Darcy, right. He's a bit... well, stand-offish, and you never really know whether he loves Elizabeth properly or... I don't know. He doesn't treat her well at first, does he? And he's only kind at the end to her sisters and that's to get what he wants. Calculating rather than steady.'

'George!' Monica said. 'Poor Darcy!'

'At least he's better than Heathcliff,' George continued, clearly getting into his stride. 'A bully, misogynist, self-centred... it still makes me mad that he's considered a romantic hero.'

'But let's concentrate on Charles,' Grace said, laying a hand on his arm. 'Charles isn't like either of them.'

'But that's my point,' George said. 'People laugh at him – call him a cuckold or whatever. And he's oblivious to what's going on. And even when he finds out about Emma, he kind of... thinks of an excuse for her affairs – forgives her. And I know in lots of people's eyes that makes him an idiot. Stupid even. But it makes me wonder...'

'Wonder what?'

'Well, what women want?' George said, with a frustrated smile.

They all laughed. 'You and Freud, then,' Grace told him. 'He said something like that on his deathbed.'

'Well, clearly I'm in good company,' he said raising his glass. 'But seriously, Charles is steadfast, he loves her, he provides for her, he forgives her. And yet it's Heathcliff who gets the "romantic hero award".'

They laughed. 'Good point,' Leah said. 'Perhaps we should read a modern love story next and see how the women compare. Maybe modern heroines make better life choices.'

'Maybe the blokes have got their act together more too?' George countered.

'Maybe unlike women in the past, they have a choice?' Grace suggested.

'And men aren't being chased for the wrong reasons?' suggested Monica. 'Works both ways.'

They all laughed.

George nodded. 'I'm not totally serious, obviously,' he said. 'I get it. Charles is... well, he's a drag, ain't he? And he's too trusting – if your spouse was disappearing mysteriously and coming back, well, all flustered or whatever. You'd be stupid to think it was something innocent.'

Leah could feel Grace's eyes on her suddenly and felt herself flush. 'Or maybe if you trust someone, you think they're worthy of that trust?' she said, hearing her tone and regretting it. 'Sorry, I mean, maybe Charles was too trusting – but that's hardly a crime, is it?'

George nodded. 'Yeah, you're right. I just feel sorry for the poor guy. Dumped for being too nice. Too ordinary. Too... well, too stable,' he took a gulp of wine and looked into the middle distance.

It was the first time that George had drunk from his glass, Leah realised. He was driving and was sticking to a few drops. This couldn't be the wine talking then, she realised. It must be from the heart.

'When you get dumped or cheated on, it makes you question everything,' George said wistfully. 'No wonder Charles Bovary just gave up and died.'

They all looked at him. He smiled. 'I'm kidding,' he said. 'But it's like Alfie said. Nice guys finish last.'

'Not always,' said Grace, firmly.

'Obviously, I've never had the chance to be married, so I'm not sure what kind of husband I'd be. Maybe I'd be boring like Charles Bovary. But I'm like... I like to think I'd be good at taking care of someone. Loving them. Doing the little things. Cup of tea in bed of a morning. Taking them out for a meal. Making a nice home for them. Getting involved in the things they liked, learning about them. Making them laugh, giving them a cuddle when they cry. Providing – as much as I can. Working hard for it, at least. And I'm not the sort of bloke who flies off the handle or gets angry and throws things. I don't storm out. I stick it out and talk. And, well, I don't think I'm that bad to look at, right?'

They all murmured that he was fine, and great, and there was nothing wrong with him.

He coloured. 'Sorry,' he said. 'It's just... well, you live alone in a city that people think is romantic, you see couples. It makes you feel more single, you know? And you think – what have those people got that I ain't? You see couples fighting sometimes in the bar or restaurant. Arguing, I mean. And you see ugly blokes – even uglier than me – on the arm of someone beautiful. And you see people kissing and cuddling and on first dates, or anniversary dates, and walking along arm in arm, or talking together, or you hear people talking on the phone and saying they love each other. And I probably have too much time to think. But I can't help but wonder why that can't happen for me. Is it really possible to be too nice? Does that mean boring? Do I need to be more Heathcliff to be worthy of love? Because I haven't got that in me.'

'That's... of course not,' Leah said softly.

'I don't mean... Obviously, I don't think that men need to be mean or whatever. And the blokes I see who seem to have it all in the bag – they don't look or seem any different to me. But I think I'd make a good husband, a good partner. I think I'd be there for someone through thick and thin. And I'd stick around. And I think maybe men like me – the dull ones, the 'nice' ones – don't always get enough credit for that.'

He stopped.

They were all silent, looking at him.

Grace reached over and touched his arm. 'That was beautiful,' she said, softly.

He looked at her and put his hand on hers. 'Sorry,' he said. 'Got a bit carried away there.'

'It's fine,' Monica said. 'We're all friends, right? We're friends now. You can say what you need to say.'

It was true, Leah thought. They were friends. Her friendship with Grace had preceded the group. But the rest of them – they'd only seen each other once a month since the group was formed. Yet they'd bonded. She smiled. 'Monica's right,' she said. 'We're all friends here.'

There was a silence again as they all wondered how to follow George's heartfelt speech.

'So,' Alfie said, coming to their rescue. 'Emma Bovary – what do we think then? Trapped in a loveless marriage and trying to find a way out. Or... cheating woman doing wrong?'

'Perhaps she's both,' Monica said. 'Perhaps she could be both.'

'I think she is quite exciting,' said Camille. 'Yes, perhaps she is not a nice person. But it would be a very dull book without her!'

'That's true,' Grace said. 'If he had married someone dull, there wouldn't be a story at all.'

'It was interesting to me how Emma was portrayed. Because obviously, this book was written by a man, and maybe he couldn't appreciate how her mind might have been working. Not in the way that Austen could with her women. It's the same with Dickens – if you think to the women in *Great Expectations* – you've got Pip's bitter and twisted sister, then the madness of Miss Havisham, and finally Estella, who is cold and hard to like. It's not a great representation of womanhood, is it?' said Leah.

'There's Biddy too,' Alfie said. 'She's... I guess she's the one who got away for Pip. Maybe without the money, he'd have stayed local and married her. Been happy.'

'True,' Leah said. 'But we never really see much of her. She's there really as a prop rather than a person. And compare those women to Jane Austen and her portrayal of the Bennet sisters – she sees them much more as they are – as people rather than things. People with needs and personalities. Some of the writing about Emma in *Madame Bovary* is sympathetic. But then you have her hysterical overreaction to things...'

'Such as?' Grace said.

'Well, when she gets dumped by her lover and she's in bed with 'brain fever' for a month for a start,' Leah said. 'I mean, brain fever? What even is that?'

'It's classic though, isn't it?' Grace said. 'Women in these books always seem to be so feeble, taking to their beds at the slightest thing.'

Alfie got up abruptly and left the room. Probably to go to the loo, they seemed to collectively decide. Nobody reacted.

'I know. But then you've got Jane in *Pride and Prejudice* – she gets a bit wet and becomes ill almost immediately!' Grace said. 'And Austen wrote that.'

'Good point.'

'Maybe we don't play the damsel in distress card enough these days?' joked Leah. 'I could actually do with a few days in bed, being waited on.'

They all laughed.

'This wine is delicious,' Grace said, looking at Leah with approval. 'Couldn't have chosen better myself.'

Leah smiled. 'Nathan picked it up for us – I'll tell him.'

'I will bring some wine perhaps myself next time,' said Camille. 'I know a farmer, he make his own. And it is *incroyable!*'

'That sounds marvellous,' Grace replied, smiling. 'I hope – the reading, is it OK for you? I wish my French was good enough to read a novel in another language. Perhaps one day.'

'Yes, and I will help you if you need,' said Camille.

'Thank you.' Grace turned to Leah. 'But yes, do tell Nathan bravo on the wine front! Unless... is he going to be home soon?' she said, somewhat pointedly.

'No idea,' Leah said, a little tersely. The words seemed to hang in the air between her and Grace. Nobody else felt the import of them.

The silence between them all was broken by Alfie coming back in the room. In the midsummer light, it was clear to see that his face was blotchy and red.

'Mate, what's up?' George said.

Alfie sat heavily in his chair. 'Nothing,' he said. 'Just being pathetic, is all.'

'Alfie... do you know that Camille told us your mum isn't well?' Monica said, softly.

He nodded. 'Yeah. I know. Sorry I didn't say myself. It's just... sometimes it's nice to kind of... forget it a bit.'

They murmured and nodded their understanding.

'It was just the brain fever thing; the idea of a woman taking to her bed,' he said, looking at them all, unashamed now that his eyes were glittering with moisture. 'Sounds stupid, doesn't it? Mum doesn't have... what even is brain fever? But... I dunno. Seeing her in bed every day. And not feeling...' His voice seemed to falter. 'Just feeling...' He leaned forward and suddenly, Leah could see that his back was shaking with the force of the sobs that were trying to push their way out of his body. 'They reckon she's going to die,' he managed to say at last, his voice muffled behind his hands and sounding tiny and boyish and scared. 'And if she does, I'm finished.'

28

Leah stirred Alfie's tea, added sugar, then carefully brought it to him in the living room, aware all the time of the very British reaction she'd had to his breakdown. But honestly, was there anything more reassuring than a cup of tea? She wondered, briefly, what French people traditionally consumed in these situations. Coffee seemed too stimulating. Perhaps they bypassed beverages altogether and went straight for the macrons. No, the mac-A-rons, she thought, as she entered the room, thinking of her recent faux pas.

The window Into the living room was still flung wide, but the air had become cooler in the time they'd spent talking as a group. Once in a while, a gentle gust would move the air, replacing the sticky heat of the day with something more comfortable and pleasant. It was nine o'clock, and although darkness was still a while away, the colour of the light had changed from white to golden – an altogether kinder light that bathed everything in a warm glow.

Alfie was still in his chair, but the rest of them had moved. Monica's chair had been dragged next to Alfie's and she was sitting with her arm around him. George and Grace hovered in front of him, Grace was bending slightly towards him, saying something.

Camille's arms were wrapped around him, her head lying gently on his shoulder. Alfie looked so small, so crumpled in his chair. It was as if he was a balloon, Leah thought, and someone had suddenly let the air out. His defence had been breached and they were suddenly seeing how he must have felt all along. Utterly bereft, scared and alone.

'Anyway, they're putting her on a drug trial,' he was saying. 'But that's a last-ditch attempt, isn't it? What if it doesn't work?' He wiped a hand across his face. 'And I know we're meant to try to be positive. And I do try. I try all the time.' His voice cracked a little. 'I can't let her see me like this – I wouldn't. But sometimes, well, trying is too much.'

'Shh, shh,' Monica said, rubbing his back as if he were a much younger child. 'It's OK, Alfie. You don't have to pretend with us.'

He looked at her and gave a small, watery smile.

Leah hovered with the tea until Alfie noticed her and reached up gratefully. 'Thanks,' he said. 'Look, I'm sorry. I've ruined the evening.'

'Don't be ridiculous,' she said. 'It's not important. Really.'

He took a sip of tea then set it down on the small nest of tables next to his chair. Drawing in a shuddering breath, he seemed to somehow reinflate a little. 'I know, people die all the time. And well, parents... you always know it's going to happen one day,' he said. 'It's just... Mum's all I've got. All the family I've got. And if she... I don't know what I'll do. What am I going to do?' The last words came out in a kind of small, desperate cry. He covered his eyes.

'You're wrong,' Grace said, her voice sounding loud in the hushed atmosphere of the room.

They all looked at her.

'What do you mean?' Alfie said, in a small voice, looking up at her, his eyes somehow enormous. Leah was reminded of Scarlett, aged five or six, how she'd somehow ask the most grown-up, unfathomable questions about the universe, or time, or death and heaven and angels and ghosts and how she'd look at Leah with her eyes bright and full of confidence that her mum would be able to provide the answers.

And although, like all humans, Leah hadn't had all of the answers to the questions, it had been nice to feel that she had the power to reassure Scarlett. To feel that Scarlett's confidence and belief in her was unwavering.

It was natural that it had changed as Scarlett had grown. She'd expected scepticism. Arguments. Battles as her daughter turned from child to adult. But not this. This utter rejection. The looks of disdain that had replaced those enormous, adoring eyes.

'Your mum, God bless her, let's pray she pulls through,' Grace said. 'But she isn't all you have. You have us.' She walked forward and crouched in front of his chair, taking his hand. 'Alfie, we're your family now, too. We are.'

* * *

In the end, Monica offered to drive Alfie and Camille home. By then, he'd seemed brighter, and Grace had promised to ring in the morning. 'I can pop round, too, if you like?' she'd said. 'If your mum wouldn't mind?'

'You can go too, if you want. It's fine,' Leah said to Grace and George, looking at the scattered glasses and plates. 'I've got this. It's not a lot.'

'You know me,' Grace said. 'I can't leave a mess in my wake.' She smiled and mimed rolling up her sleeves. 'Come on, let's get this lot to the kitchen. George is fine to wait.'

'Shall I help?' George said, gesturing at the mess vaguely. 'Or do you—?'

Leah was just about to ask him what he meant, when Grace answered for them. 'You wait there,' she said. 'You've been working all day. Put your feet up.'

He nodded, 'Yes, boss,' he said, with a grin.

The pair had arrived together, with George abstaining from all but a few sips of wine in order to give Grace the lift home she needed. 'I told him it was out of his way, but he insisted,' she'd told Leah, who'd raised an eyebrow.

'You really don't have to,' Leah said as Grace began running water in the sink.

'I do though,' Grace said. 'It's an illness really. But I find washing up puts the world to rights.'

'We have a...'

Grace added a drop of washing-up-liquid and swished her hand in the water to make bubbles. 'Dishwasher? Don't believe in them,' she said, simply.

'Really, because it's right there!' Leah quipped, pointing at the unused dishwasher.

'You know,' Grace said, thoughtfully, only half acknowledging the joke, 'my parents used to wash up after each meal. Every single time. One washing, one drying.' She looked out of the window in front of the sink over the vegetable plots beyond. 'I always wondered, well... if it bound them together somehow.'

'Really?' Leah heard the incredulity in her own voice a little too late.

'Oh, not the actual washing and drying,' Grace said, starting to gently apply a sponge to the first wine glass. 'But the forced proximity – standing together, doing something methodical. Talking. They always talked when they did it. I think about that quite often,' she said, with a shrug.

'I see what you mean,' said Leah. She thought about how she and Nathan loaded the dishwasher together. But it wasn't the same.

He had his method, she had hers. They often sniped over the placement of a bowl or plate.

'I sometimes think,' Grace said, setting the first glass on the draining board for Leah to dry, 'well, if Stephen and I hadn't got a dishwasher, perhaps we'd have talked more. Perhaps it wouldn't have got to... well, that stage.'

'Oh, Grace.'

'Anyway,' Grace said, visibly straightening and shaking off the melancholy subject. 'All a long time ago now. And things are good.' She didn't elaborate as she picked up the next glass. 'I just thought, well, maybe you and I could do with a good... natter.' She looked at Leah, her intelligent eyes fixed on her friend's face. 'We haven't spoken about things for a while.'

'No,' said Leah, slowly drying a glass. 'No, we haven't.'

There was silence for a minute, the clinking of crockery as it was picked up and set down the only sound.

'Poor Alfie,' Leah said.

'I know,' Grace replied. 'Just a kid really.'

'It was lovely, what you said. About being his family.'

Grace nodded. 'Thank you,' she said. 'And I really believe it. Families come in all sorts of forms. Not always the ones you think. Plus, I feel fond of the kid. He needs people around. Perhaps we can be those people for him.'

'I am sorry, you know,' Leah said, softly.

Grace nodded, once. 'Yes,' she said. She was silent for a moment, then inhaled – a huge, shuddering breath. 'But you were right, of course.'

'Right?'

'Well, I'm set in my ways, I suppose. I've got used to not talking. Maybe not trusting people.' She looked at Leah, her eyes shining. 'It takes a true friend to point that out.'

'Oh, Grace.'

'No,' she said. 'Please. It's good. There've been some things I've been hiding from, I suppose. And things that I've been keeping to myself. You were right. It's time.'

'But it's OK to be private,' Leah said. 'I didn't mean to pry.'

'Yes, of course,' Grace said. 'But like you told me – if I want people to know me. If I want... real friends, maybe a relationship. I can't... I have to let go of some of these barriers.'

Leah put her hand out and touched Grace's shoulder gently. 'Still, I could have...'

'Nonsense!' said Grace, sounding more like her usual self. 'Thank you. For being you. For being my friend.'

Leah felt an unexpected moisture in her eyes. 'Sorry,' she said. 'I think I'm going soft in my old age.'

Grace scoffed. 'If you're old, I must be virtually prehistoric!' she said.

They laughed. 'OK, my midlife,' Leah said.

'That's the spirit.'

They resumed their task of washing and drying. Leah wondered if Grace was going to tell her anything more. But the silence bloomed around them. Perhaps it wasn't the right time. Instead: 'I spoke to him,' Leah said at last, trying to force a smile. 'I spoke to Nathan.'

'You did?'

'I'm sorry. I should have told you, after involving you in it all. Turns out it's all completely innocent!'

'Yes?' Grace said. 'Well, that's good.'

'Yes,' Leah agreed. 'He's... well, basically he was a bit lost... maybe depressed? And he wanted to sort it out. Didn't want to bother me. Found a life coach, of all things. Adeline.'

'The woman?'

'The woman.'

'He didn't tell me because of some sort of need to protect me,'

Leah said. 'Didn't want me to think he was weak. He's with her tonight, actually.' She glanced at the clock. It was half-past nine. He'd gone out at six. How long had his appointment been?

Grace looked at her.

'Oh, God,' Leah said.

'What is it, love?' Grace's voice was soft.

'Hearing it out loud,' she said. 'It's not real, is it? I mean, it's not... plausible.'

'Well...' Grace said. 'It's... it could be true.'

'I'm such an idiot!' Leah flung the towel against the kitchen counter. 'What am I doing, endorsing my husband meeting up with a young, gorgeous woman? Waving him off with my blessing. He's having an affair, isn't he?' She felt tears well in her eyes, but they were tears of anger. At least for now. 'And I told him I hope it goes well tonight. Gave him my blessing!' The words came out of her mouth forcefully. 'Grace, I'm Charles fucking Bovary!'

'What?' Grace was lost for a minute. 'Oh, now come on. Don't say that. You don't know for sure.'

'Don't I?' Leah said.

Her friend walked forward and wrapped her arms around Leah as she sank into her and sobbed. Grace's hands, wet with warm water and suds, soaked her T-shirt, but she didn't care. Because she felt suddenly, and without doubt, that she'd been an idiot. She'd been so desperate for things to be OK that she'd accepted Nathan's flimsy excuse. She hadn't questioned seeing him go into an apartment. She hadn't insisted on meeting Adeline. She'd tried instead to be supportive.

Somewhere, a door shut loudly. 'Shit. George,' Leah said, stepping back and wiping her nose. 'Do you think he heard?'

Grace shook her head. 'He won't have,' she said. 'And even if he did, you've nothing to be ashamed of. It's that husband of yours who has questions to answer.'

'Properly this time.'

* * *

'White, two sugars?' George said, handing a steaming mug to Grace. 'And strong, but sugar free,' he said, handing Leah hers.

The pair had decamped to the bench on the front porch and were soaking up the last few rays of the setting sun. George had kept himself scarce since Leah's outburst in the kitchen, and she still felt embarrassed that he'd probably heard her. But he's family, she thought, remembering Grace's words. At least, sort of.

'I'll just...' George said, indicating the door.

'I'm so sorry,' Leah said. 'You both probably need to get going.'

He shook his head. 'No rush,' he said. 'Happy to take the weight off, read the news. Take your time.'

Leah sipped her tea. It was hot and strong and hit the back of her throat in just the way she needed. She straightened up. 'He's a nice guy, isn't he,' she said.

'Yes, I really think he might be one of those rare creatures,' Grace told her.

'What he said about being "too nice". I really felt for him.'

Grace nodded. 'I know. Poor lamb.'

They were silent for a moment.

'So, what are you going to do?' Grace asked, looking at her pointedly.

'Well,' Leah took a huge sigh. 'I'm going to have to confront him. Properly this time.'

'Oh love. He still could be telling the truth...' Grace's voice wavered under Leah's gaze. 'Or something close to it.'

'But he's hiding something.'

'It does seem,' Grace said, 'as if you might not have the whole picture. But look, I'm no relationship expert. And certainly not the most optimistic of people when it comes to matters of the heart.'

'Oh, I don't know,' Leah said, smiling a watery smile. 'You're quite a fan of Darcy – and even had the hots for Heathcliff before Alfie shattered all our illusions.'

'Ha. Well, there is that,' Grace agreed. 'But look. Don't let what I think cloud your judgement. Keep an open mind.'

Leah shook her head. 'I'm not sure that I can.'

Grace's hand was on her arm. 'Try,' she said. 'Hear him out, at least.'

Leah looked at her, surprised.

'I know,' Grace said. 'But maybe I've been too judgemental in the past. Maybe I'm getting more romantic in my old age. Especially after all these books.'

'Wonders will never cease,' Leah quipped, and the friends smiled.

'See, old dogs... well, they can learn new tricks, after all,' Grace said.

'Less of the old.'

Grace leaned forward slightly and seemed to be about to speak. But instead raised her hand and took a sip of tea, sighing with pleasure. 'You know,' she said. 'I am a great lover of fine wines. But you can't actually beat a cup of tea, can you?'

'You really can't,' Leah agreed.

They sat in silence for a moment more, hearing the gentle clucking of the chickens in their coop, the chatter of birds from the nearby trees. Somewhere in a nearby garden, children up past their bedtime shouted and squealed. There was a splash of water as someone dived into a backyard pool. The vegetable plots looked almost bountiful bathed in the golden light, the shoots just protruding from the earth in places, promising the possibility of something new forming underneath, as yet unseen.

'It is gorgeous here, isn't it?' Leah said.

'It really is.'

'I hope I don't... I don't want to, break things,' she said, her voice small.

'You can't,' Grace said. 'We won't let you. And things don't always go as planned, but you can fix them yourself. Even if... well, if you find out the worst. It doesn't mean it all has to end. It doesn't mean this... this dream of living here has to be over. Not if you don't want it to. Build something new. You can still have this life, or any life you want. I really believe that.'

And as they finished their traditional English tea, looking over the unmistakable French countryside, Leah felt in that moment that it was true.

29

'Ready?' George said, turning the key and looking at Grace as she slipped into the passenger seat.

Grace clicked her seatbelt into place. 'Yes. All set!'

The car lights clicked on, illuminating the drive and the roadway beyond. It was eleven o'clock – an hour later than they'd planned to leave. But Grace hadn't wanted to go until she was sure Leah was OK. 'Thanks for waiting,' she said now.

'Not a problem. She OK?' George gave her a sideways glance. 'Obviously, I'm not sure what you two were talking about, but... you can tell when someone's upset.'

'I think she's OK. I think she is, now,' Grace said, as the car turned onto the road.

They were silent for the first couple of minutes before George said. 'Good meeting tonight, though. Other than that. And well, Alfie...'

'Yes. Poor kid.'

'What you said, though,' said George. 'About being family. It was kind of beautiful.'

'Thank you. And you too.'

'Me?'

'Yes. What you said about... well, love. Your life. It was... It touched me.' They were silent for a moment. Then Grace started slightly. 'Oh! We forgot to choose the next book!' she said. 'What with... everything. And it's your turn, isn't it!'

He smiled, his eyes still on the road. 'Yeah, don't worry. I figured there was plenty of time to sort all that out. Besides, I might need your help to choose.'

'My help?'

He shrugged slightly. 'Your expertise, then,' he said. 'I've got a couple of ideas, but... well, I never did that well at school and you are the books expert and that.'

Grace laughed. 'I wouldn't call myself an expert. Maybe just someone who's had too much time on her hands over the years, so spent it reading.'

'Sounds like an expert to me,' he said, with a grin. Then, more seriously, 'I couldn't help but notice your books... well, in your front room are a bit... I'm pretty good at making shelves if you...'

He trailed off, perhaps sensing the atmosphere shift.

'It's OK,' she said. 'I know they're messy but...'

'Oh, God, don't worry about that,' he said. 'I wasn't being, like, mean or anything. It's just because all your stuff is so... well, tidy and sort of finished. But the books are—'

'A bloody mess?' she ventured.

He felt himself grin. 'I'd have put it more delicately,' he said.

She sighed – almost as if she was releasing something held in for too long. 'I know...'

'You know I'm not... criticising?' he ventured.

'Of course,' she said.

'It's just... I'd like do something for you,' he said. 'After all you've done for us. With the club and that.'

'Thank you.'

The silence resumed, but it was companionable. George turned the car gently into the next road. They were still twenty minutes away from Grace's house – then he'd have to make his way back into the centre to go home. She felt guilty, but he had insisted after all.

'You're not going to be too tired for work?' she said.

He laughed. 'If you saw the blokes I work with, you wouldn't be too worried about that,' he said. 'They think midday is the crack of dawn!'

She smiled. 'Thank you,' she said.

'For what?'

'For making me feel better about it.'

'It's just a lift. Really. It's nothing.' He paused for a moment, as if considering something. 'You give a lot, Grace. You help people. Even tonight, you've really put yourself out there for Alfie, for Leah.'

'Well, I suppose.'

'There is no suppose about it,' he said. 'But I'm not sure you realise that it's OK to accept it too.'

'Accept what?'

'Help,' he said. 'Friendship. You know, support.'

'Oh.'

'Love,' he said finally, never taking his eyes from the road.

She didn't respond at first. The silence resumed, first slightly awkward – his words hanging in the air. Then companiable, comfortable again. And she hardly wanted to break it but suddenly, she knew this was the time.

'I'd like you to,' she said into the quiet car.

'To...?'

'The shelves,' she said, her mouth feeling slightly reluctant, stiff. 'If you don't mind. I'd like that.'

He nodded. 'Done,' he said.

'But maybe... there's a room you could use,' she said.

Whenever visitors commented on the house – how beautiful it was, how well-kept, how finished, Grace felt like a fraud. Because it wasn't true. Upstairs, beyond her bedroom – decked in floral prints – the guest room – a cool blue – and the main bathroom, was another door she'd barely opened in fifteen years.

Now, once she was sure George's car had disappeared and she was alone, she found herself walking towards it, past her bedroom door, turning the handle, her fingers shaking just slightly, her heart in her throat.

Barely disturbed in almost fifteen years, the room had retained its smell – a smell that had been present in the whole house when they'd first taken ownership, but had since been eroded by other paints, meals, coffees, perfumes, polishes and the scent of living. Except here. In this room where she never let herself go. It was the smell as much as anything that took her back.

The blind was closed, but she switched on the electric light and flooded the room with dull yellow. And she was back, all those years ago, assembling the cot from the barely legible instructions, screwdriver in hand, dungarees straining slightly where her stomach pushed at the fabric.

It had been two weeks after Stephen left that she'd discovered she was pregnant. At first, she'd been terrified, angry even that it had happened now. Then scared of a possible loss, at her age. But the embryo had seemed to stick, clinging on for the three-month scan. As her body had started to change, so had her attitude. She'd begun to allow herself to believe that she wouldn't be alone for much longer – begun to purchase linen for the smallest room in the house, to order a cot. To begin to wonder what it might be like to be a mother.

It had been in this room, standing triumphantly by a newly installed changing table, that she'd first felt that flutter of life inside. Had stopped and put her hand to her stomach, the feeling like a little bird beating its wings against her skin. She'd laughed with the strangeness, the thrill of it.

Two weeks later, it had been in this room that she'd felt something was wrong. They called it mother's instinct. Only she'd never had the chance to be a mother.

At the hospital, the sonographer's face had been unreadable as he moved the ultrasound wand over her belly and clicked on the tiny monitor. But when he'd turned to her, she'd already known.

The cot was still there. The changing table. The stack of linen. There was dust, too. Several spiders' webs. A feeling, as she walked in, of despair – as if the room had held on to her emotions, had absorbed the turmoil of her miscarriage.

And she realised she was Miss Havisham, in her own way. She'd allowed the room to freeze in time and while she'd appeared to move on, there was a part of her still trapped.

Although it was dark outside, she walked across the parquet floor, ignoring the churning in her stomach, and pulled the catch of the blind, opened the window and pushed the wooden shutters back against the walls. The bang of it reverberated in the night air. Blue moonlight filled the tiny space, giving it a ghostly feel. And she sighed, deeply, gutturally, feeling the emotion that she still hadn't released gather inside her, provoked by the setting, the smell, the weight of it all.

Then a slight breeze blew in, and she felt the newness of it. The fresh air. Felt how the room had been waiting. She moved to the light switch and turned off the bulb, then returned to the open window, leaning on the sill and gazing into the blackness.

As her eyes adjusted, she realised that the sky wasn't black at all, but a deep, navy blue. And the more she gazed upwards, the more stars seemed to appear. They'd been there all along, of course, only she hadn't focused; her vision had been deadened by the electric light inside.

Tomorrow, she would empty the room, clean it. Then choose paint for the walls. And soon George would come, to create shelves for her haphazard books, to create order out of chaos, and her own little library in this little room where once again, she might be able to dream of something beautiful in her future.

* * *

It was a relief for Leah to close the door on George and Grace and be able to sink into a chair. Grace had been an enormous help, and made her feel so much better. But now she was alone, Leah could stop pretending she felt positive and determined about it all. If anything, she was completely drained.

She checked her phone. Nathan surely should be back soon, and this simply couldn't wait until morning. She'd confront him the moment he walked in the door, have it out with him. Finally wring the truth from him. The idea of it was terrifying. But not as terrifying as doing nothing at all.

The light had disappeared, morphing from golden into some-thing darker, blacker. But the solar lights in the garden had come on, and beyond in the street, the lamps were glowing. Ordinarily, she loved this time of night, sometimes going out just to see the stars, loving the transition between day and night, between the fierce, hot brightness of the sun and the lower, glowing comfort that came in the evening. It made everything feel smaller, more enclosed. And somehow, it had always felt to Leah like an embrace.

Tonight, it simply marked how long Nathan had been out. Was he coming home at all? The thought of his staying out was horrifying, yet she'd practically given him permission to do whatever he wanted. She sent him another text:

Home soon?

She kept it simple, not wanting to let him know the interrogation to come. Five minutes later, she checked. It remained unread. Perhaps he was on his way home.

Perhaps he was never coming home.

* * *

Monica let herself into the flat and put her keys into the bowl on the hall table. 'Hello?' she said quietly.

The flat was silent; Bella was clearly asleep and her babysitter, Clemence, would probably be reading in the quiet of the living room. The girl – although she was a woman, Monica supposed, at twenty-two – still lived at home with her parents and two younger brothers while studying for her master's and appreciated the occasional hours spent at Monica's with a sleeping baby in the next room. 'It is wonderful in the silence,' she'd said to Monica earlier, and Monica had been struck by the way that the silence could be seen so differently. As an oppressor or a friend, depending on how you looked at it.

Monica still found the large apartment and its silent walls stifling at times – the noise from the street outside just serving to highlight her loneliness. But now she had the book group, and the mother and baby group were meeting again this week. Perhaps she could start to look at the silence in a different way too.

'Hello?' she called softly, not wanting to terrify Clemence, but even more determined not to wake the baby. She moved to the open door and looked in.

The shutters were still open and the light from the streetlamps and shop windows flooded in, making the whole room seem more yellow than white. As she stepped into the space, someone got to their feet. But it wasn't Clemence, it was someone altogether taller, broader and – although she really liked her babysitter – much, much more welcome.

'Peter!' she said, 'But you're... you're meant to be—'

He stepped forward and put his arms around her. 'What can I say?' he told her. 'I missed you.'

The sound of tyres on gravel sent an electric pulse of anxiety through Leah. She stood up, then sat down again, then stood up, not quite sure how to receive him. In the end, she moved to the hallway and stood, a little in from the door so as not to give him a heart attack. She wasn't going to let a medical emergency steal her opportunity tonight.

There was a click as he locked up, and the light dimmed outside as the car shut down. There were a couple of crunches, then the clink of a key in the lock. And the door opened.

Nathan stood, gave a sigh, and removed his coat, before turning and seeing her. He jumped a little, then laughed. 'Bloody hell!' he said, grinning. 'I didn't expect you to still be up. Good group? Was the wine OK?'

Then his smile faded as he saw her expression.

'We need to talk,' she said.

* * *

Alfie finished his drink and put the cup on the drainer to clean tomorrow. He sent Camille a quick goodnight text, then slipped the phone back into his jeans pocket as he walked around, clicking off lights and locking up for the evening.

He paused at the entrance to his mother's room and looked in, as he always did, to make sure she wasn't lying there awake and in pain. But she was sleeping. He'd left the shutters open a crack and the white light of the moon – almost a full one tonight, but not quite – made its way through the opening and gave the room a dull, yet almost ethereal, glow.

She looked thin, her body barely troubling the covers at all as they lay over her. He thought again about their time here in France – how he'd hated her for bringing him here, where he didn't know anyone and couldn't speak the language. But how he'd come to appreciate the sacrifices she'd made for him over the years. How she'd given him the upbringing she'd hoped to share with his father, and done it away from the estate whose gangs had stolen his dad away, changed him into someone she no longer recognised.

Now he was settled, studying, able to communicate. And grateful to her for stepping away from a life that could have dragged him under. He now saw what she'd meant years ago when she'd told him it was for the best.

As he watched, she turned onto her back, and the light fell fully on her face – the narrow strip bathing her in light. He didn't believe in God, or angels, or all the others things Camille was convinced existed. But in that moment, he felt something. Something somehow bigger than himself. Perhaps the sense that there was something out there, watching over them. Or perhaps it was just a rush of love for the woman who'd given him everything she had.

It was fleeting, but just for a second – and against the odds – he felt a flicker of hope that just maybe she would be OK.

30

'What is it?' Nathan said, his face furrowing in confusion. 'Has something happened?'

Leah gave him a look that she hoped told him everything he needed to know.

But apparently not.

'You're scaring me now!' he said, following her into the kitchen. 'What's happened?'

'Don't give me that,' she said, turning, her voice coming out loud and sharp in the kitchen. 'Come on, Nathan. I know what's going on. I'm not stupid!'

He at least had the grace to blush at this. 'What do you mean?' he asked.

'Nathan, where have you been?'

'But you know!' he said. 'I've been for a session with Adeline. We talked about...'

She laughed – a hollow, empty sound. 'For five, nearly six hours?'

He fell silent.

'That's the worst of it, isn't it? I've practically given you permission for this. I am such an idiot.'

He sank into a chair, as if exhausted. 'Sit down,' he said. 'Please.'

She felt the mood in the room shift and sank onto a stool, her knees suddenly weak. 'I've been so stupid,' she said. 'It's so obvious, isn't it? You're meeting up with this gorgeous woman. First behind my back – and now... well, in clear sight.'

'It's not like...'

'Nathan, I don't believe you're having counselling with this woman. I did... sort of. I think I wanted to believe it, so I kind of clutched onto it. Then tonight. It suddenly struck me when I was talking to Grace. It's not true, is it?'

He looked down at the kitchen surface as if hoping to find an answer there, then shook his head no. Just once. 'I'm sorry,' he said.

There's a huge difference between suspecting something and having it confirmed. Leah felt it now, like a punch to the stomach. 'Oh,' she said.

'But wait, it's not what you think,' he told her.

She looked at him then, anger surging through her. 'That,' she said, 'is an exact quote from the cheating bastard playbook.'

'No, I swear, I...'

'Whatever lies you want to tell me this time, Nathan, I'm too tired to hear them. I have a suspicion that it's *exactly* what I think.'

'You have to hear me out...' he began. He reached for her and she moved away. But before either of them could say anything, there was an enormous, thundering crash from upstairs. Their eyes met, united in parental fear. 'Scarlett?' he said.

They leapt up. 'Are you OK?' Leah called.

There was no answer from upstairs.

'Scarlett?' They both raced up the stairs towards their daughter's room.

Later, Leah would wonder what had made them run like that. They were used to the odd thud or crash from Scarlett as she went about her way with no consideration for the loudness of DMs on wooden floors, or decided randomly to tidy her bedroom at eleven o'clock at night, after being nagged about it all day.

Nathan was first, pushing the bedroom door open. 'Scarlett?' he said. 'Ouch!'

'What?' Leah pushed in behind him. 'Oh.'

An enormous glass dish, usually kept on Scarlett's windowsill, had crashed to the floor. The window, left slightly open, had clearly nudged it and it had fallen, smashing and spilling its contents – a collection of marble eggs, each heavy enough to practically break through a floorboard. No wonder it had made such a noise.

Nathan reached down and lifted a shard of glass that had pricked his foot. 'Bloody hell,' he said. 'I could have lost a limb there.'

'At least the crash wasn't anything worse,' Leah said. Then remembered they were mid-argument and stopped. Nathan had been about to confess something. This was no time for shared parental relief.

Only Nathan's face didn't look relieved. 'But Leah,' he said. 'Where is Scarlett?'

'Bathroom?' Leah suggested. But there it was again, the feeling of dread that had only just left her, creeping back with a new, determined certainty. 'Scarlett?' she called. 'Scarlett!'

Then they saw the note on the bed.

31

The note was written on pink paper, decorated with horses. Something Leah had bought for Scarlett a few years ago but that she'd rarely used. Nathan unfolded it and quickly scanned the content. 'Silly girl,' he said under his breath.

'What is it?'

'Apparently, she's gone to Mathilde's house for a few days. She's sick of us and needs a break.'

Leah was flooded with relief. 'Oh,' she said. Then, 'But how...?'

'Exactly,' Nathan looked at her. 'How did she get there?' He quickly dialled Scarlett's phone and put his mobile to his ear. 'No answer,' he said, frustrated.

Mathilde, one of Scarlett's best friends, lived a twenty-minute drive away. Not far at all. If you had a car. But it would take an hour or two at least to walk the same distance.

'Perhaps Mathilde's mum picked her up?' Leah said, hopefully.

'Wouldn't you have heard something? Seen something?'

'I don't know,' Leah said, pulling her phone from her pocket and dialling. Mathilde's mother, Manon, answered almost immediately. 'I'm sorry. I know it's late. It's Leah. Is Scarlett with you?' Leah asked, not bothering to try French as she would ordinarily. Manon spoke fluent English, but was very tolerant of Leah's French – patient and encouraging. But this wasn't the time.

Her eyes met Nathan's as she spoke, saying yes and OK and waiting for Manon to wake Mathilde up. She leaned against the wall, too weak to stand.

'What is it?' Nathan asked as soon as she ended the call.

'Scarlett's not there,' she said, simply. 'Manon just woke Mathilde to ask about it. Apparently, Scarlett had said she was coming over when they spoke earlier. She just assumed that we were going to be bringing her.'

'And she didn't say anything when Scarlett didn't arrive?' Nathan said, incredulous.

'I think she just called Scarlett, but didn't get an answer, and assumed she'd changed her mind or couldn't get a lift or whatever,' Leah said.

'Why didn't she...'

'Nathan, she's fourteen. It probably wouldn't have occurred to her to do anything else. How was she to know that Scarlett would walk over?'

Scarlett, too, was just a kid. Why had she begun to see her as such a monster?

'When was this?' Nathan said.

'About two hours ago.'

'But it's...'

Leah looked at her watch. 'Nathan, it's almost midnight. And she'd have had to... I mean, it's right across the city. It's not safe!'

She thought then, suddenly, of the bang of the door that had happened when she and Grace were talking in the kitchen. She'd assumed it had been George, going into the garden. She hadn't even considered it might have been Scarlett. But she'd not been thinking at all really. She'd been too upset talking about... It was when she'd realised that Nathan might be...

'Oh, God,' she said.

'What?'

'It's probably nothing,' she said, 'I don't know. It's just... I was talking to Grace in the kitchen earlier about... well, about us. You.' She looked at him, anger put aside for now. 'About you and Adeline. How I'm starting to get worried about... well, all of it, if I'm honest. That you're not being truthful with me. With us.'

'You think Scarlett heard?'

Leah shrugged. 'I don't know!'

'For God's sake,' Nathan said, looking at her briefly with a flash of anger. 'Couldn't you have talked about it some other time?'

She felt anger bubble up. 'So it's my fault?' she wanted to say. But it wasn't the time. It could wait. 'Ring her again,' she said.

But Scarlett still didn't answer.

'Come on,' Nathan said, turning towards the stairs.

'Where? The police?'

'The police won't be interested. Not yet,' he said. The 'yet' hung between them like a threat. 'We'll drive the route to Manon's – all of the possible routes if we have to. And we'll find her.' He looked at Leah. 'She'll be OK, won't she?' he said, his eyes filled with need.

'Of course she will,' Leah said, determinedly. Because she had to be. She just had to.

32

Feeling exhausted, Grace emptied the contents of the pouch into Hector's bowl and watched as the cat began to greedily devour the expensive cat food. 'Now can I go to bed, your highness?' she asked.

It was 12.15 a.m., and the air had finally cooled. While she enjoyed the summer sun, her body always protested. Now she was approaching sixty, her body seemed to complain about everything – the cold, the heat, too little sleep, too much. It ached and sweated and clicked and refused to budge in ways that were entirely new and made her feel completely ancient.

But she'd refused to be beaten. She'd managed to find a yoga class to squeeze into her hectic schedule and was determined to – as she'd said to Leah – recover her youthful bendiness.

She thought of the other new entry in her diary. A drink with George. A date, of sorts. It had felt odd, the idea of dating someone. She wasn't completely averse to the idea of having a partner, having a love life. It was just she'd spent a decade establishing her independence – making sure her life was full and rewarding. That she was strong enough not to need anyone. People called it brave, living alone, being alone, making a life of self-reliance. 'I could never do it,' friends told her. 'You're just so confident, so amazing.'

But was she brave? she thought, pulling the shutters together and blocking out the moonlight. Was it really brave to shut yourself down? Or was Leah right? Had she been hiding?

She thought about Leah and Nathan – how her friend might be heading for a break-up. How devastating and life-shattering it could be. How, when you put your trust in someone, allowed yourself to love them, you exposed yourself to potential pain.

But George, sensitive soul that he'd turned out to be, was taking a risk too, wasn't he in getting closer to her? He'd clearly been hurt in the past, but it hadn't stopped him trying again. And there was something about him. His easy smile, his humour. The way he was naturally curious about things – about the literature they'd read, but also about the various clubs and organisations Grace ran. Stephen had turned his nose up at getting involved, even in his short time in the country, and the one time they'd visited a local gallery had loudly compared it, unfavourably, to the ones he frequented in London.

Anyway, it was only a few shelves, and a drink together in the pub she'd agreed to, she told herself firmly. Not a proposal. A drop in the ocean.

Still, she felt in that moment, as she gave Hector a final stroke and made her way to her bedroom, that somehow, saying yes to an evening with George was more than that. That the tiny stone dropped in water would have ripples that spread out further than she could imagine. That somehow, in saying yes, she'd opened herself up to the possibility of a different kind of future.

33

Perhaps they should have split up – each taken a car. But in the moment, it had seemed sensible to leap into the same vehicle and drive the streets as quickly as they could. 'Any idea what she was wearing?' Nathan asked.

Leah shook her head. 'I don't think I've even seen her today,' she admitted. 'Have you?'

He shook his head once.

'I mean, it's normal for teenagers to spend a lot of time in their rooms, isn't it?' she said. 'I... I think it's OK that we've been giving her a bit of space, isn't it?' She thought of the times in recent weeks when she'd considered calling Scarlett down, asking her to give her a hand, then decided against it. She hadn't wanted to face Scarlett's distain or complaints or obvious annoyance at being asked.

When Scarlett had first started to pull away from them, Leah had tried hard to involve her. Encouraging her to still help in the garden, to come shopping. Calling her down to the kitchen so they could peel carrots (if there were any available) and chat. And Scarlett had been reluctant, foot-dragging, almost impossible to engage in proper conversation. She'd made Leah feel rejected, annoying, and made her attempts at conversation feel pathetic.

Leah thought back to herself at fourteen. She remembered clashing with her own mother at times. But she didn't remember being as prickly, as resentful as Scarlett seemed. And all she remembered about the time her Mum still referred to as 'that horrible year,' wasn't the rebellious exterior her mum had had to face, but how she'd felt on the inside. Not hating people around her as much as hating herself, the new body that she didn't know what to do with or how to dress, the spots that kept coming and making her feel ugly and disgusting. She remembered how nobody had seemed to understand, that everyone simply judged her and shouted at her.

Had Scarlett been feeling that way on the inside?

She wasn't sure. And she hadn't asked. Had stopped asking.

Leah knew in that moment that she'd made a mistake. Because she'd focused too much on how Scarlett made *her* feel – how bereft *she* was without the little girl who'd loved her unequivocally, and how dismayed *she* was at the older version of her daughter who seemed to sneer at everything she did.

She'd thought about her own feelings when she should have been thinking about Scarlett's.

Had she actually been neglecting her daughter?

She blinked away her threatened tears. This wasn't the time for self-pity or recriminations. They had to find Scarlett. Then, well, they could worry about the rest after that.

An idea came to her and she pulled up a blank message on her phone.

'Who're you texting?' Nathan said, signalling and turning out of the driveway.

'The group,' she said.

'Your book group?' he seemed incredulous.

'Yes. They're my friends. And we need all the help we can get.'

34

Monica lay propped up on pillows as Bella – full and satisfied – slept curled on her chest. Peter, lying at her side, smiled at the two of them. She knew what he was thinking – what everyone thought: how idyllic, how timeless. The image of mother and child. He hadn't seen her on other nights practically tearing her hair out, or bursting into tears over the smallest thing.

'So, you're home for...?' she asked him.

'Just a couple of days. Got someone to cover,' he said. 'Maybe longer, though.'

'Longer?'

He shrugged, rolling onto his back, hands behind his head. 'I was thinking about what you said,' he told her. 'About being lonely.'

She felt herself flush slightly. 'Oh,' she said. 'I didn't mean to make you feel... I'm OK, you know?' she said. 'It's OK.'

He smiled. 'I'm glad,' he said. They were silent for a minute. 'But I wanted to say: I feel that way too sometimes. Lonely, I mean. And too far away. More now that Bella's here.'

'You do?'

'Yeah. I wish I could be here more. Be with you both.'

'Oh, hon.' She said, brushing his hair with a free hand. 'Well, we do too. You know that.'

Monica shifted herself gently and swung her legs over the side of the bed. She stood up slowly and placed Bella into her cot. The baby murmured slightly and Monica stiffened, willing her not to cry, not to shatter the peace in the bedroom, not to break the moment.

Luckily, Bella acquiesced, settling into sleep once more.

Monica climbed back into the bed and snuggled into her husband.

'I've asked if I can have a bit more time off,' he said, stroking her hair. 'For me as much as you.'

'That's brilliant,' she said.

'It's nothing,' he said. 'It's selfish, if anything. I need you guys.'

She smiled a little. 'It would be nice to have you around more. I *am* trying. I think I'm getting there. With the book club. And that new mums' group thing. But it hasn't been easy. I've been...' She paused, fixing her eyes on him.

'What?' he asked, brushing a strand of hair from her face.

'I wanted to wait until you were home. Until you were here in person. But I went to the doctor's and, well, he reckons I've got a bit of PND.'

'Postnatal depression? You should have told me!'

'I *am* telling you,' she said, smiling gently, feeling her lip wobble slightly. 'I've only just found out. Just realised that maybe not everything I was feeling was quite... well, normal. Some of it – tiredness, hating my body... well, that's par for the course sadly. But other things. Everything feeling too much, overwhelming. Feeling as if I'm failing.'

'Oh, Monica,' he shook his head. 'You're such a great mum. You are.'

'I'm not,' she said. 'People say that a lot, don't they? I'm not sure anyone's "great" at this. But I'm starting to realise that maybe I'm enough. That I can do this. I started counselling. Last week.'

He raised himself up on his elbows. 'God, Monica. I just didn't realise. I'm so... And there was me thinking you just needed some friends. Recommending that book club – and you're going through all that? I'm such an idiot. I should have seen—'

She shook her head. 'But you were right. The book club's been amazing,' she said. 'And I do need friends. I think just getting out there and being with people... it was what helped me to see that I needed that extra support.'

He reached out and gathered her into his arms, kissing her cheek and squeezing her tightly. 'You must tell me,' he said. 'I want to know these things. I guess I knew you weren't... quite yourself. But...'

'I know.'

'And I should have asked.'

'Maybe. But you know – we're both new to this,' she said.

They lay together, quietly, listening to the noise of people walking home, the odd voice talking too loudly. The sound of vehicles delivering for the day ahead. People winding up and going home, or stepping up and going out. Bordeaux was a quiet city compared to London, but still had that element of perpetual motion – it was quieter at night, but never completely still. Things moved and changed and evolved all the time.

The noises had once made Monica feel isolated – showing her a life she wasn't part of. But now she was trying to see them as representing the possibilities outside her window – the people and projects and activities and life that were hers to join. And although she knew she had a long way to go, when she finally drifted off to sleep, she was smiling.

35

'Come on, come *on*,' Nathan tapped at the steering wheel impatiently as he waited for the woman to cross the road. She seemed in no hurry. The moment the lights turned amber, he pressed his foot to the accelerator and they shot off.

The combination of dark streets and occasional unexpected pedestrians, who seemed more intent on their conversation than looking to see if cars were coming, made Leah feel nervous.

'Careful,' she said. 'You don't want to end up having an accident.' She dialled Scarlett's number for the tenth or eleventh time and waited again for the phone to ring out. 'Scarlett!' she said on the answerphone. 'You're not in trouble, but please can you call me? Or at least text to let us know you're alright.'

There was no real reason to believe anything had happened to their daughter, she told herself. She'd gone for a walk, late at night. She might have got lost, perhaps, or waylaid. Or turned back. She might not be answering her phone because she was embarrassed, or angry. She was fourteen – she wouldn't realise what all the fuss was about, probably.

Nathan turned the corner, 'Do you think she'd definitely have gone this way?' he asked. He was following the usual route they drove to Mathilde's house. But in reality, there were several different streets Scarlett might have chosen.

'I don't know, Nathan!' she snapped. Then, trying to calm herself. 'We'll just do them all,' she said. 'We'll drive them all.'

Her mobile beeped with a message from Grace.

Grace's text message had read:

In my car, keep me up to date.

It was like looking for a needle in a haystack, Leah realised. But it was a very precious, albeit prickly, needle that she simply needed to locate. Grace had offered to drive around some of the back streets close to the old town – the chances of her stumbling across their child were minuscule. Yet what was the alternative? They couldn't give up. And more people looking had to be a good thing.

Thank you

Leah replied, seeing Nathan glance at her, slightly irritated.

'Grace is helping,' she said, shortly. 'And George answered too. He says he'll have a walk around – he's quite close to Notre Dame, but we just don't know. It might help.'

'Does he know what she looks like?'

'I've sent a picture,' Leah said. It had been taken just a few months before, yet Scarlett looked entirely different now. In it, her daughter's face wore an open expression. Even a smile. She'd known that Scarlett had changed, was struggling. Why hadn't she done more to support her?

There'd been no response from Monica, but Alfie had offered to go to the local gendarmerie and hand in a picture – his fluent French would help him to explain their predicament, and although Scarlett would barely qualify as a missing person yet, she hoped they'd help.

Images raced across Leah's mind. The sort of things you see on the news every now and then. The picture of a child smiling innocently into a camera. Footage from CCTV, or of local locations. The parents sitting behind a table pleading with their child to come home. But she shook her head and focused her eyes on the buildings passing her window – this wasn't the time to spiral. Scarlett had only been missing a couple of hours and they were already doing everything they could to find her. It would be OK.

It would be OK because it had to be OK.

She'd driven the route to Mathilde's house so many times over the years. Often begrudgingly, picking Scarlett up later than she'd wanted, or taking over forgotten items for a sleepover. It had always seemed fairly close, fairly easy to navigate. Tonight, it seemed like a dangerous and perilous journey into the unknown. Her daughter. Out here. On the dark streets somewhere. She dialled the phone again. It continued to ring out.

'Turn left,' Leah said, pointing to a small road almost hidden off the main route. 'I usually go this way.'

'I know the way to Mathilde's!' Nathan snapped, signalling and slowing to make the turn.

'OK, sorry!' she said. 'It's just I'm usually the one to take...'

'Oh, so it's my fault, is it?' he said.

'What?'

'You're saying I don't spend enough time at home. There's no need to stick the knife in.'

'What are you talking about?' She looked at Nathan's face and saw that beneath the anger, he was close to tears. She felt her own eyes well up again. 'It's nobody's fault, Nathan. Let's just find her, OK?'

The small side-road was empty, the shops scattered along its length closed. A few lights in upper flats threw light onto the pavement. A cat shot from a doorway and scooted up a set of steps, making them both jump.

Nathan reached the end of the cut-through and signalled right.

Leah didn't say anything, simply hit redial yet again on her mobile. She thought about Scarlett's face and how it might look when she saw the eighty-seven missed calls from her mum. She imagined the eyeroll of disbelief and horror. But it didn't matter. It never really had, she realised. Scarlett was entitled to be a teenager – and Leah was entitled to be a mum. She shouldn't have altered her behaviour to suit what she thought Scarlett wanted. She'd made herself distant. But although they might call it annoying, children – even teens like Scarlett – needed to know their parents were there.

'Do you think…' she began, then stopped, froze and lifted the phone. 'Scarlett?' she said hearing a click as her daughter answered.

Next to her, she saw Nathan glance across. He flicked the signal on the car and pulled up sharply against the kerb.

'What?' her daughter said, sharply.

'What do you mean "what"?' she said. 'Scarlett, where are you?'

'What do you care?'

There was a silence after her daughter's words and for a heartrending moment, Leah thought Scarlett might have hung up.

Whatever recriminations might be coming, this was not the way to play it right now.

'Of course I care, Scarlett,' she said, keeping her voice level. 'Dad and I are just worried about you, that's all. We spoke to Manon and...'

'You called Manon? Mum!'

'We had to, Scarlett. We were worried. We still are.'

Nathan made a move to grab the phone. 'Let me speak to her,' he said.

Leah held up a warning hand. 'Look, sweetheart,' she said. 'You aren't in any trouble. We just want to come and get you. Bring you home. We can talk properly then.'

Another silence.

'Scarlett?' she prompted. 'Please.'

'I don't know.'

'You don't know whether you want us to come?' Leah said, working hard to retain her even tone.

'No,' said Scarlett, more quietly now. 'It's just, I don't know where I am.'

'You don't know...'

'Yeah, I'm stupid, I suppose.' The surly tone was back.

'No, that's not stupid at all. Things look very different when it's late...' Leah's eye drifted to the clock on the dashboard. It was almost one. Her daughter was fourteen years old and lost in a city – probably only a few minutes' drive away. But it might as well be a hundred miles. Anything could happen. Anyone might notice her. 'Listen, can you see anything...'

Nathan gently took the phone from her hand. 'Scarlett,' he said, 'turn on location on your phone – I can find you on the app.'

Leah looked at him gratefully; she hadn't thought of that. She was flooded with relief. They would soon know exactly where Scarlett was. They could have her with them, here in this car. The rest they could worry about later. She sent Grace a quick text with the words:

Think we've found her!

and her location.

It had been a long time since she'd last been out in Bordeaux in the evening. On other nights, she'd have taken the time to admire the buildings, the view over the river, the various patisseries and delicatessens, fashion boutiques and restaurants that peppered the streets as they drove. She'd have noticed the architecture, the enormous windows, stone carvings, fountains and statues.

But tonight, while she knew her daughter was alone, all she could see were the few solitary figures, the group of men walking to a taxi, the cars making their way to who-knew-where. Tonight, there was no beauty in Bordeaux, only potential danger.

They travelled in silence along a couple of streets, the electronic voice on Nathan's phone calmly telling them which way to turn. He took a right, a left, turned down a smaller street lit only by shop windows, then out to a wider road, with more traffic and a few people walking the pavements.

And then they both saw her. Dressed in a hoodie, the top pulled up, and with her backpack hanging off one shoulder, Scarlett was standing by a bus stop, her phone glowing just enough to illuminate her face. Nathan pulled over, earning a gesture from the driver behind, and bumping the kerb. But it didn't matter. They simultaneously flung open their doors and raced towards her, as if – even now – she could be spirited away.

Leah reached for her daughter's arm, wanting to grab her and hold on to her tight and tell her it was all alright. But as she did so, a hand slapped hers away. And she was confronted by the familiar scowl, the prickly tension, the warning to keep her distance. 'Scarlett!' she said.

'What did you think...' Nathan began, but Leah gave him a little nudge with her foot.

'Let's get you in the car,' she said, looking at her husband meaningfully. The last thing they wanted was to scare her off – for all they knew, she might decide to run or walk off, or disappear again in some way. Get her in the car, Leah thought, lock the doors and then we'll talk.

Scarlett looked at them both. 'God, you're pathetic,' she said.

'Scarlett! How dare you!' Nathan said, unable to keep up the pretence that as well as being relieved and euphoric, he was almost bubbling over with a heady mix of anger and anxiety.

'What?' she said, as if incredulous at his reaction. 'You are. You just want me to come back so you can put me in my room and ignore me. And make decisions about my life without ever wondering how I feel about it.'

'What do you mean?' Leah said. 'We'd never... I mean, you do spend a lot of time in your room...'

'Right, so it's my fault?'

'That's not what I meant. We want you back home so you're safe. We're not going to... What decisions about your life are you talking about?' She racked her brain, trying to think of anything they'd suggested or objected to in the last few months. She came up blank.

Scarlett shook her head slowly, infuriatingly.

'Scarlett, just get in the car... please,' said Nathan, gesturing at it as if this might help her to do the right thing. 'We can talk about it – all of it, at home.'

'Which *home* would that be?' she said, looking pointedly at Nathan.

Leah looked up, expecting Nathan to register confusion, only to see her husband's head drop, his eyes suddenly on the ground.

'Yeah, go on, Dad. Tell Mum how you've been looking at houses. Finding somewhere new to live in town.'

'Nathan?' said Leah.

'Mum, tell him that you know about his affair. How you realised that he was a liar.'

'But Scarlett...' Leah began.

'I heard you in the kitchen with your stupid friend, didn't I?' she said. 'And I saw Dad in town with that woman.'

'Yes, but that was...'

Scarlett turned, not yet done. 'And I heard you on the phone, Dad, in your office. You're always complaining that I'm too noisy in my room with my music or whatever. Well maybe you ought to think about keeping your voice down if you don't want people to know everything...'

'Scarlett,' said Leah, levelly, feeling the world swim just a little in her vision. 'What are you trying to say?'

'He,' she said, pointing a trembling finger at Nathan, 'is leaving us. And you're so blind, you've hardly noticed!'

'Scarlett!' Nathan said. 'It's not...'

'Didn't you think, didn't either of you think about me in all this?' she said. 'What am I meant to be doing. Staying with Mum? Trying to manage a garden that both of you hate? Oh, yeah,' she turned to Nathan, 'Mum hates having to do all the digging, I heard her say so. And she hates your stupid carrots. She doesn't want to do the stupid copywriting job. And... and... she wants to wring Gollum's neck!' The last words came out loudly and a passer-by looked over with a small frown.

Scarlett, unperturbed, turned to Leah.

'And Mum, Dad hates it too. He feels like a failure. He wants to have a fresh start, isn't that what you said, Dad? Find somewhere new to start again?'

Nathan was still looking at the floor. 'I think we should go home,' he said, but looking up to see the two women in his life staring at him, he let his words fade to nothing.

'Nathan,' Leah said, her voice trembling, 'is this true?'

'Oh, it's true,' Scarlett said. 'But you can't decide, can you, Dad? "Town house or something with a little more space",' she spat out the words, clearly repeated verbatim from a conversation she'd heard. 'Why couldn't you just talk to Mum about it? And Mum, why couldn't you talk to Dad?' She stopped and took an enormous, shuddering breath. 'And why can't either of you talk to *me*?' she said, her voice breaking. 'Because I'm having a hard enough time deciding where I belong as it is, let alone having to choose between my parents. That's if either of you want me at all!'

This time, when Leah reached for her daughter, the prickliness was gone. Her daughter sank into her softly and let herself be held. 'What's going to happen to us, Mum?' she said. 'What are we going to do?'

37

'Alfie?'

The voice was so quiet, he wasn't quite sure whether he'd dreamt or heard it.

'Alfie?'

He put his phone down and got up, his legs aching slightly from being curled under him in bed and walked to her room. 'Mum?' he said. 'Everything alright?'

The room was filled with dull light, the shutters still open as she'd requested. It was a hot night and the breeze buffeted slightly between the half-open windowpanes, giving a little relief. Her eyes were closed.

'Alfie?'

'I'm here, Mum,' he said, going to her side. He sat on the small chair at the side of the bed and reached for her hand. 'Is it the pain?' he asked. 'Are you thirsty?'

She shook her head, a small smile on her lips. 'You're a good boy,' she told him. 'The best boy.'

'Only because of you,' he told her. 'Only because of everything you did.'

She shook her head again. 'No, Alfie. Because of *you*.'

He squeezed her hand gently. 'Can I get you anything?'

Another shake of the head. The small smile playing on her lips. 'Just you,' she said.

'OK.' He leaned back slightly in the chair to make himself more comfortable. He'd stay until she was sleeping.

'You know, when I found out I was pregnant with you, I said the f-word,' she said, quietly.

'You did?' he grinned. It was impossible to think of his Mum swearing. Had he ever heard her?

'Yeah. I mean I was only eighteen, not much different from you now. And you know, I didn't think I was ready.'

'Oh, Mum,' he said.

'I was wrong,' she said. 'Your dad wasn't ready. He soon scarpered. And my mum let me know exactly what she thought of it all. You know that. But I was ready. Or, you made me ready. When you were born, it was like everything else fell away. This little baby I had to take care of. And I swore to you then that I'd do everything in my power to keep you safe. To keep you from the life that I'd had. That your grandparents had.'

'I know, Mum. And you did,' he said.

'They're not good people, Alfie.'

'I know, Mum.'

'And we've been happy here, haven't we?' she said, one eyelid flickering. 'All those summers by the river, that trip to Paris. It's been good.'

'It's been—' he said, feeling suddenly as if he couldn't catch his breath. 'Mum, it's been wonderful. I'm... it's still wonderful.'

'I'm sorry,' she said.

'About?'

'Having to look after me. At your age. It isn't right.'

He smiled. 'Mum, you looked after me at the same age. And I'm willing to guess that was a lot harder.'

The smile on her lips broadened slightly. 'You're not wrong,' she said. A little laugh or cough escaped her.

They fell into silence again. For a moment, he thought she'd fallen asleep. Then she opened her eyes slightly and looked at him. 'Alfie?' she said, and her voice was hesitant. A little like a child's. Confessional, somehow.

'Yes, Mum?'

'I don't think I'm going to make it, Alfie.'

He sat up. 'You are, Mum,' he said. 'We've got the trial next month. And you know there's been promising results from immunotherapy. And the doctor said—'

But she was shaking her head.

And suddenly, he realised what she was saying. Realised it viscerally, in every cell of his body.

'Oh,' he said.

'I'm so sorry, love,' she said.

He wanted to say that she *should* be sorry. That she shouldn't be talking like this. That she should fight. Sit up in bed! Eat something. Call the doctor. That she couldn't possibly leave him, because what on earth would he do without her?

Instead, he said, 'It's OK, Mum. It really is. I'll be OK.'

'My good boy,' she said.

'I love you, Mum.'

'I know, Alfie. I know.' Her hand moved towards him and he took it in his. Her skin was soft, cold. Her hand small and fragile.

Please, he wanted to say. But he managed to hold it back. Because he knew that if there was a way for her to stay, then there was no way she would leave him. She'd suffered so much pain, fought so hard for so long. Instead, he found himself saying a gentle 'shhh' the way she had to him as a small child, when she'd sat by his bed on the nights he couldn't sleep. 'Shh, it's OK.'

Her breathing gradually slowed, her fingers relaxed slightly in his. She gave a breathy sigh – the air escaping from deep inside her tiny frame – and he sensed her relief. That she'd given herself permission to escape from the body that had let her down, that hadn't been as strong as her spirit.

He'd known, minutes later and without checking, that she was no longer with him.

38

Nathan approached his wife and daughter gently, as if he was worried they would both disappear. 'It's not what you think,' he said.

Leah looked up at him from over Scarlett's shoulder and shook her head gently. 'Enough, Nathan,' she said. 'I think it's pretty obvious exactly what it is.'

'No,' he said, his voice coming out more loudly. 'No! It's not.'

'Look, I think we should just go home,' Leah said, suddenly bone-weary. 'We can talk more in the morning.'

'No,' he said again. 'It has to be now. Please. Hear me out.' He gestured to a bench, as if saying they could all take the weight off and talk it out. His face was illuminated on and off in the flash from the car's hazard lights. He looked like a villain in a film, just about to be arrested, thought Leah. The game was up now, surely.

'We'll stand, thanks,' she said, feeling a heady mixture that came with having the bottom fall out of her world, yet have Scarlett in her arms – something she'd longed for.

He shook his head. 'OK,' he said, lifting his hands up and then letting them fall to his sides in a gesture of defeat. 'OK. Scarlett's right. I'm not happy. Haven't been happy for a while, actually.'

This was not quite how Leah had expected the conversation to start. She took in a little, startled breath.

'But not with us. Not with our family. Not with... anything.'

'I swear,' Leah said. 'If you say, "it's not you, it's me", we're out of here.'

'I'm not saying that!' he said. 'Although, actually it *isn't* you. It *is* me. Scarlett's right.'

At her side, Scarlett gave a little gasp.

'But it's not what you think,' Nathan continued. 'I... look, I hate the garden, alright? I hate the vegetables. I hate bloody radishes. Digging. Being covered in mud. I hate the chickens – I'd eat the lot of them, but the bastards would probably give me food poisoning. I hate the creaky old house, hate fucking soup for lunch every day—'

'Oh,' said Leah.

'And I miss working,' he said. 'Miss being good at what I do, instead of feeling like a failure all the time. I miss putting on nice clothes and bringing home... well, the bacon rather than twelve pathetic, unusable potatoes!'

Aha! Leah's mind – which had a tendency to wander a little when stressed – cried. *So he didn't think it was a good crop of potatoes after all? Gotcha!* She said nothing.

'But I know you love it here. And I do too. I love France. I love the culture, the way of life,' he said, rubbing his face with his hand. 'I think Scarlett... I think you're doing brilliantly, Scarlett. When I hear you speaking French... that accent! It takes my breath away, I'm so proud.'

'Shut up, Dad,' Scarlett retorted. But her voice was softer than usual.

'Sorry. But it's true,' he said. 'And I wanted to tell you, of course

I did. I wanted to say that I thought I'd made this enormous bloody mistake thinking I could be bloody Tom – Richard Briers – whatever. With my fork and my bountiful harvests. And being happy all the time. Even when things don't go as you planned.'

'What are you talking about?' asked Scarlett.

'It was a sitcom,' Leah said softly, 'from the seventies. Called *The Good Life.*'

'Has he lost it, Mum?' Scarlett asked, her question seemingly genuine.

'Leah,' he said, stepping forward and taking both her hands. 'I'm not a Tom. I'm not a cheery chap who can make do and mend. I'm... if anything, I'm a Jerry!'

'Don't say that!' she told him. 'You're not... a Jerry. With his stupid suits and his quips – he didn't understand what they were trying to do by living self-sufficiently at all!'

'Hang on,' Scarlett said, too incredulous, clearly, to inject the normal amount of venom into her tone. 'Jerry? Are we talking about a cartoon now?'

'Well, then I'm not sure who I am,' Nathan said. 'All I knew is that I had to make a change. I had to find a way to make our life work in a different way. Over here.'

'Why didn't you just talk to me?'

'Because I'd persuaded you that this would be good for us. I'd made you buy into this ridiculous dream. And I wanted to find a good alternative to it before I ripped it away. I wanted to be able to present you with the possibility of another kind of life – with me, with Scarlett – rather than let you down.'

'You wouldn't have,' Leah said, softly, allowing him to hold her hands still. Somewhere, a church clock chimed two.

'Wouldn't have what?' he said.

'Let me down,' she said. 'It would have been a relief if you'd said something,' she told him, shaking her head. 'I mean, I liked the idea of it. When we were working too much and always stressed and feeling ill. The idea of having land and making our own stuff. And living that kind of self-sufficient life. Yes. But the reality of it? The getting up early, sowing seeds, digging in seedlings, bloody home-made fertiliser and vegetable soup? Nathan, couldn't you see I was desperate to do something different?'

'What?! Why didn't you tell me?'

'Because,' she said, 'I thought it was *your* dream.'

They smiled uncertainly at one another. And she almost felt OK. Then she pulled her hands from his. 'But none of that explains Adeline,' she said. 'Unless she was just a way for you to... keep yourself happy?' The last part came out in a sort of cry. For a moment, she'd forgotten about his trips out – she was so relieved that things seemed to be coming together.

'Adeline *is* a counsellor,' he said, softly. 'I didn't lie. And a life coach too. But she's also a hand-holder – you know, helps people manage the bureaucracy over here? And she's been helping me find a direction, set things up.'

'Set what up, exactly?'

'Well, to find a potential new property. A job. I wanted to present it all to you – like a gift. Make you happy.'

Leah snorted. 'If she's such a great life coach, why didn't she suggest you talked to me?'

Nathan coloured. 'She... well, she did. I guess, I'm just too stubborn.'

'Well, I won't argue with you there.'

'And, Leah, I've managed to get a new job. Tonight. She coached me. I had an interview. We waited in a bar for the call afterwards. That's why it took so long. And look, I haven't accepted it yet. I wanted to tell you. Now I could show you how it could all work.'

'So nothing's happened between you?'

He shook his head. 'Never,' he said. 'She's married in any case. To someone who looks like bloody Ryan Gosling. But it wouldn't matter if she wasn't because I'm just not interested.'

'Really?'

'What's the job?' came a voice. Scarlett.

'Sorry?' Nathan said.

'You said you've got a job. What is it?'

'An editor. There's a paper – an English-language one; bigger in Paris at the moment. But they want to start a Bordeaux edition. And they have asked me to head it up. See if there's a market for it.'

'Oh.'

'The good news is I can work from home, or in a shared space they're renting. So I can be around as much as you want...' His words faltered. 'If you want. If you still want, Leah.'

'But what will I do?' she asked quietly.

He tentatively reached for her. 'Well, once we've sold our place and found something more... suitable. Less garden, more house. More central maybe. Whatever suits you. Both of you,' he said, reaching an arm for Scarlett too. 'You can do whatever you want to do.'

'I'm not sure what that is,' Leah said.

'But you'll have the space to figure it out, once I'm earning,' he said. 'Quit the copywriting. Help me with the paper if you want. Or do something completely different.'

'I just don't know,' she said.

'Oh.'

'It's fine. It's good,' she said, the start of a smile forming on her tired face. 'I might not know what I want to do. But I definitely know what I don't want.'

'No more radishes?'

'No more radishes.'

'No more carrots.'

'Enough with the bloody carrots.'

'And no more Gollum?'

'Definitely,' Leah said, this time with real passion. 'Definitely no more bloody Gollum!'

A passer-by on the street might have wondered what had made the family stop the car, put on the hazards, get out and stand as a trio on the pavement. What had prompted them to move together and disappear into a hug in the shadows on a road in Bordeaux at almost two in the morning.

But at that moment, in that random place, at a stupid time of the night, Leah felt that they were all exactly where they ought to be.

Moments later, with a slight screech, Grace pulled up next to them and got out of the car. 'Is everything alright?' she said, sounding breathless. Her hair was in disarray, her eyes looked slightly red. And she was wearing leggings. Leah had never seen Grace anything other than immaculately turned out. She must have rushed out of the house the minute she'd got the message.

'Yes,' she said, hearing a sob in her voice. 'Yes. She's... we're fine. I was about to call.'

'Don't worry about that,' Grace said. 'I'm just thankful you're all OK.'

'I'd better ring George.'

'Leave it with me,' Grace said, moving back towards her car.

'Thank you, Grace. I really am grateful...'

'It's nothing,' she said. 'Honestly.' She smiled. 'But I'll leave you to it now.' Moments later, her car passed, as she moved off into the darkness towards home.

'Was she looking for me too?' Scarlett said. 'That's a bit embar-rassing.'

'No, it's not,' Leah said. 'It's actually quite wonderful.'

39

Leah climbed the three concrete steps and pushed open the glass door. Inside, the building was quiet – the hush that comes before a funeral. Music played from a small speaker in the corner – light, classical, unobtrusive. Nathan wrapped his hand around her back and gave her a little squeeze. 'You alright?' he said.

Another glass door off the entrance opened into a bright, light room with wooden chairs set out in neat rows either side of a carpeted aisle. Her eyes rested for a moment on the light, wooden coffin with its small, white, floral garland, then moved to the front row where Alfie – his hair newly cut, ears sticking out like a small boy's – was standing, wearing an oversized black jacket, his shoulders hunched.

Camille was next to him, her hair shimmering down her back. She wore black jeans and a white shirt and, as the door sighed back into place behind Leah and Nathan, she looked around and gave them a small, tight smile.

On Alfie's other side was Grace, shoulders back, hands by her sides, wearing a black shift dress. To her right, George, who'd managed somehow to find a pair of jeans that weren't paint-splattered and had brushed some sort of gel through his hair.

Ten days ago, when Alfie's mum had died, it was Grace he'd rung to ask for help the following morning. 'I'm not sure what to do,' he said. 'Obviously, Camille's here and being amazing, but I need...'

'Of course,' she'd said. 'Of course.'

Leah and Nathan tucked themselves into seats in the third row – close enough to show concern, far enough not to impinge on anyone's grief. Part of Leah wanted to reach out and touch Alfie, but for now he looked lost – deep in thought or sadness or grief – and somehow, she felt it would be an intrusion. But as she watched, she saw Grace reach a hand and touch Alfie's fingers lightly and moments later, they were holding hands as naturally as if they'd known each other for years.

So many times over the years, Leah had rolled her eyes when talking about Grace. How her friend seemed to get involved in everything. How she seemed to know everyone's business.

Yet looking forward now at her friend, shoulder-to-shoulder with Alfie, she found herself thinking, *thank God. Thank God for Grace.* Because unlike others – herself included, she supposed – who hung back feeling awkward, not knowing what to do, Grace was there, in the thick of things, holding Alfie up.

* * *

Grace had never had the chance to be a mother – she didn't know what it felt like to have a son or daughter. But she sensed something motherly in the fierce protectiveness she felt over this young, slightly fragile man who had lost so much more than he should have for someone of his age.

She looked over her shoulder and saw Leah and Nathan,

noticed Monica in the far corner, clutching the order of service. Felt the slight touch of George at her side, smelling of soap and dependability.

It was odd, how close she felt to them all. They'd only spent five evenings together, really. Exchanged a handful of emails. But something about the things they'd spoken of, talking about characters in books written by long-dead authors, had bound them together in a way that she couldn't explain. Maybe it had just opened them all up without them realising. Over the months, she'd spoken a little about Stephen, Alfie about his mum. Even George had poured his heart out. Would that have happened over Canasta or karaoke? Probably not. She'd opened up more in those five evenings than she had in the three years beforehand, she realised. Because when, really, did you get to talk about love?

Books had been Grace's friends in childhood. When her father and mother had screamed at each other, she'd curled up in her room and escaped into a book. When they'd made up, noisily and in ways she couldn't understand, she'd turn a page and escape into fiction. Her teenage preoccupations had pushed books to the periphery of her life – but even then, she'd always read a chapter or two before bed. And when Stephen left, it had been books, at first, that had got her through.

Now it was books that had brought her a whole new group of friends, and opened all of them up to each other. Books that had opened her eyes to the possibility of something new with George. Books that had helped her to understand that Alfie – young as he was – needed an old bird like her to step in and help. It might be books that could help him move on and grieve. And even if not, the book group was there for him. All of them. They'd all help him.

'Are you OK?' George whispered now.

'Yes,' she said. 'Yes. I'm OK.'

The ceremony was small, but beautiful. The flowers perfect.

Alfie's words about his mum touching and from the heart. There had been twelve of them in all – Alfie, Camille, two of his mum's neighbours, Margaret, the nurse who'd visited each day. Alfie's friends Jean-Paul and Richard from college and the four of them: the rest of the book group.

Grace hadn't cried since the miscarriage, not really. Not that deep, visceral crying that comes when you empty yourself of everything and feel both bereft and cleansed. But she cried at the ceremony. It was strange, shedding tears for a woman she'd never met. But she felt Alfie's need for her, his love for her, and she'd found herself quietly grieving for the mum of a man who was still a boy, really. She wished she'd taken the time to come and meet her. To say, perhaps, *Don't worry. If you have to go. I'll look after him. We all will.*

40

Grace applied a layer of lipstick, looked in the mirror then wiped it off. Too much. Still, she looked pretty good for an old bird, she thought, admiring her newly straightened bob. She'd chosen a neat, fitted, black top and cream-coloured, cotton trousers, teamed with wedge shoes for the date. Smart, but not too much. Elegant, but not too eager.

Her bedroom was a jumble sale of discarded outfits. Jeans, a dress, a few different skirts. Tops that she'd put on and twirled in before ripping off. Nothing had seemed quite right. But when she'd pulled on the top and looked in the mirror, she'd seen herself as she'd want George to see her. Just Grace. Not an attempt to be someone she wasn't.

Her room, she thought, looked a little like it had when she was sixteen and first got into clothes and makeup. A muddle of indecisions. She thought about bundling everything up and shoving it into a wardrobe, but decided against it. It could all wait.

Instead, she exited into the hall and opened the front door. A wave of heat hit her; it was evening, but the day had been scorching. She'd spent much of it under her sunshade in the back garden, feet in a paddling pool she'd bought for the purpose, reading a copy of *I Capture the Castle* and trying not to think too much about the evening ahead.

It wasn't that she was nervous, exactly. She was always out and about, never ran out of conversation. She wasn't worried she wouldn't know what to say. She was just worried at how she might feel; whether she was opening a door that should have remained closed.

But it wasn't like before, she told herself. She didn't need someone to complete her, to make her whole, the way she'd felt she did when younger. But that didn't mean she couldn't make a little room for the right person. It was OK to let someone in.

She'd wanted to meet him there, at the restaurant. But he'd told her to stop being so stubborn. 'There's no point both of us driving there,' he'd said. 'The parking's horrendous, for starters. Plus, this way, you can have a glass of wine and not worry about it.'

It was a winning argument. Especially on a hot day like today. She'd go for a spritzer – something light, she thought.

Her heart skipped as she heard the familiar rumble of George's car coming to collect her.

She locked the door and walked down the front path, securing the gate behind her and meeting George on the pavement outside. He pulled up and doffed an imaginary cap. 'Taxi for Miss Grace?' he asked, jauntily.

She smiled and climbed into the passenger seat, feeling suddenly much younger than her fifty-something years. 'Thank you, Parker,' she said, picking up the baton. 'Drive on, please.'

He grinned and signalled before pulling out into the empty road. 'Right you are, ma'am.'

They fell into a silence as he made a left and turned towards central Bordeaux. But it was a comfortable silence. One Grace, to her surprise, didn't feel the need to fill.

She looked out of the window as the buildings became taller and more frequent. George signalled right and they turned towards the centre.

She wasn't sure where they were going. George had asked her to suggest a restaurant, but she'd surprised herself by leaving it up to him. Now she was on the way to an unknown destination, where she might or might not like the food, the ambiance, the décor. And it didn't matter. Because that wasn't why she was there.

George reversed into a space in one swift, fluid movement and, once he'd pulled the handbrake into position, they both got out.

'Italian OK?' he said, pointing at the stone building opposite a courtyard dotted with trees. It glowed with a soft light from the inside, and bore the words *La Vento* on its black sunshade.

'Well, when in France,' she joked, and he laughed.

'Afraid you'll find I've got terrible taste,' he said.

'Don't worry,' she smiled. 'So have I.' And she looked at him with pointed humour. 'After all, I was a big fan of Heathcliff until recently.'

As they walked towards the restaurant, he linked his arm in hers. And it felt nice.

41

JULY

To: Bordeaux Book Club
From: Grace
Subject: Meeting

Hi all,

Thought it might be time to book a date for a meet-up, if that suits? George has got a couple of books up his sleeve to suggest, but can't decide. And I thought – why not just have a get-together, catch-up and decide together? It's been far too long.

It's George's turn to host, officially, but I've offered him my place if that works for everyone? Shall we say 7 p.m.?

Look forward to seeing you all!

Grace

This time, Grace had set everything up in the garden. Chairs had been arranged under the cherry tree, with an enormous sunshade to give them extra cover. It had been a hot week and although the temperatures often dipped around 8 p.m., the heat was set to remain above twenty-five until at least midnight.

Grace had set a table with wine glasses, home-made vegetable crisps and a dip; George had brought along some beer and bags of ice which he'd emptied into a bucket along with Grace's four bottles of sparkling.

Nobody had said anything outright when George and Grace had answered the door together, but it was clear to everyone from the interactions between the pair that something had shifted. Grace's hand left momentarily on George's arm; George going to the fridge without asking, to find the orange juice for Monica's Buck's Fizz. Leah caught Monica's eye when George had his back turned, filling up Grace's glass, and made a face that said everything. They both grinned. It was surprising. But brilliant.

Alfie looked a little pale, but was soon installed in a rather low deckchair with a beer in his hand. Monica leaned over and gave his arm a little squeeze and he shot her a grateful look. Nobody needed to say anything more. Camille was busy in the kitchen, laying tiny pastries and olives on a platter for them to enjoy.

'So, you're signing the *compromis* tomorrow?' Grace said to Leah, once they'd all settled down.

'Yes,' she said. 'It's quite exciting really.' They'd accepted the offer the previous week, and once this document was signed the transaction would be binding.

She'd met Grace for coffee the day after that terrible, wonderful night with Leah.

'Thank you,' she'd said. 'For coming. For helping.'

'Where else would I be?'

They'd smiled at each other, both tired but relieved after the night's events. Leah told her about Nathan, how he'd explained everything. How everything now seemed to make sense.

'And you feel OK about it?' Grace had asked.

'I will,' she'd said. 'I think.'

They'd spoken about Scarlett. How upset her daughter had been. How she, too, had sensed something was wrong. 'I'm going to try harder with her, to talk to her,' Leah had said. 'Even if she... well, if she dismisses me. I've got to grow a backbone, I suppose. Be the adult.'

Two weeks later, she and Nathan had put the house on the market and shortly after had found a couple who wanted to buy. 'They're so excited about the allotment,' Leah had said quietly to Nathan. 'I hope they know what they're getting themselves into.'

They'd decided to rent an apartment closer to the centre, but still near enough that Scarlett could attend the same school. 'We're not going to leap into buying something brand new and regret that too,' Leah had told Grace on the phone once they'd made their decision. 'We're taking it more slowly this time.'

'Sounds like a very good idea.'

'And this time, we've only got a balcony to worry about. And a shared garden, but there's a gardener for that.'

'So no chickens.'

'Definitely no chickens.'

After their viewing, Nathan had introduced Leah to Adeline; he was still having the odd session, but he seemed so much happier. And Leah had warmed to the woman she'd thought was stealing her life. It was clear she was nothing but professional.

'Well, I think it sounds brilliant,' George said now, topping up Leah's glass yet again. 'A brand-new start for the three of you.'

* * *

'So, what's this with you and George?' Leah asked Grace later, when they were in the kitchen filling bowls up with olives.

Grace – usually resolutely even-shaded – developed pink spots of colour on her cheeks. 'Well, I'm not sure yet,' she said. 'I'm not sure it's ready to have a name. But, well. Let's say it's definitely something.' She smiled. 'You were right. It's nice to have lowered a few of my boundaries.'

'Well, I'm glad.'

'Did I mention the bookshelves?'

'Just once or twice.'

They returned to find Alfie, Monica, George and Camille talking animatedly.

'Have you heard?' George said, turning around. 'These two are getting a place together. Selling, well, his old place and having a fresh start.'

Camille reached over and took Alfie's hand. 'It will be wonderful,' she said.

Grace smiled at him fondly. 'It sounds like a great idea,' she said.

'More wine?' George said, topping up Monica's glass again.

'Why not?' she said. 'I'm not driving.'

'I can give you a lift if you want,' Leah said. 'I can take a detour.'

'It's fine,' Monica said. 'Peter's collecting me.'

'Oh, so we'll finally get to meet the mysterious Peter!' Grace said.

'Yes,' Monica said. 'And he's... actually he's going to be around much more than before.' After their chat, Peter had spoken to his work, who'd changed his schedule. 'I'm two weeks on, three weeks off now' he'd told her. 'It's more regular, more manageable.'

It had been just the right compromise.

'So,' George said. 'Now it's time for the sixty-four-billion-dollar question.'

For a moment, Grace thought he might propose. Oh, please don't, she thought. Not now. Not yet.

But he was smiling. 'Help me decide between these two.' He

held up a couple of dog-eared paperbacks, one a famous old book they'd all heard of, the other that had been a hit the year before. 'Time to choose the next one. Old classic or something brand new?'

'Well,' said Grace, 'you can't go wrong with an old classic. Tried and tested and dependable.'

They all nodded.

'But you know what,' she said. 'Actually, maybe it's time we all tried something completely new!'

ACKNOWLEDGEMENTS

Thank you to everyone who helped bring this book into being: to my brilliant editor Isobel Akenhead and all the Boldwood team – especially Nia, Jenna, and Amanda. I always feel so supported and valued by them all.

Thanks to Ger, my agent, and her unfailing faith in me – despite my wobbles.

To the D20 authors, especially Nicola Gill, the 'Savvy Authors' group and for all those who've offered me advice and support along the way – both online and off.

Thanks to authors including Heidi Swain, Sue Moorcroft, Isabelle Broom, Ritu Kaur, Beth Morray, Nancy Peach, Natalie Jenner, Alex Brown for cheerleading, reading, retweeting, quoting or supporting. I really hope I haven't missed anyone!

Thank you to my children for not minding when I disappear to my office to scribble, and for being excited when my author copies arrive.

To Ray, who has put up with more than a husband should at times. Thanks for the tea. And the biscuits – and for bringing me chocolate even when I tell you not to. I always secretly want it. But you know that.

Thank you to the communities online – The Book Load, Chick Lit and Prosecco, Global Authors, The Fiction Café Book Club – where I've enjoyed getting to know other readers and received some fabulous recommendations!

Finally, thank you to my readers. It goes without saying that none of this would mean anything without you.

ABOUT THE AUTHOR

Gillian Harvey is a freelance journalist. She has lived in Limousin, France for the past twelve years, from where she derives the inspiration and settings for her books.

Sign up to Gillian Harvey's mailing list for news, competitions and updates on future books.

Visit Gillian's website: https://www.gillianharvey.com/

Follow Gillian on social media:

facebook.com/gharveyauthor

x.com/GillPlusFive

instagram.com/gillplusfive

bookbub.com/profile/gillian-harvey

tiktok.com/@gillianharveyauthor

ALSO BY GILLIAN HARVEY

A Year at the French Farmhouse

One French Summer

A Month in Provence

The French Chateau Escape

The Bordeaux Book Club

LOVE NOTES

LOVE IN EVERY CHAPTER

WHERE ALL YOUR ROMANCE
DREAMS COME TRUE!

THE HOME OF BESTSELLING
ROMANCE AND WOMEN'S
FICTION

 WARNING:
MAY CONTAIN SPICE

SIGN UP TO OUR
NEWSLETTER

https://bit.ly/Lovenotesnews

Boldwood

Boldwood Books is an award-winning fiction publishing company seeking out the best stories from around the world.

Find out more at www.boldwoodbooks.com

Join our reader community for brilliant books, competitions and offers!

Follow us
@BoldwoodBooks
@TheBoldBookClub

Sign up to our weekly deals newsletter

https://bit.ly/BoldwoodBNewsletter

Printed in Great Britain
by Amazon

49131086R00175